Robert Williams Buchanan

The Drama of Kings

Robert Williams Buchanan

The Drama of Kings

ISBN/EAN: 9783337376956

Printed in Europe, USA, Canada, Australia, Japan

Cover: Foto ©Andreas Hilbeck / pixelio.de

More available books at **www.hansebooks.com**

By ROBERT BUCHANAN

STRAHAN & CO., PUBLISHERS

56 LUDGATE HILL, LONDON

1871

CONTENTS.

TO THE

SPIRIT OF AUGUSTE COMTE

I INSCRIBE

THIS DRAMA OF EVOLUTION.

O THOU of the great brow!
Fire hath thy City now:
Her wild scream shakes the earth and troubles Man.
O spirit who loved best
This City of the West,
See where she shatter'd lies—great centre of thy plan.

Spirit of the great brow!
Look back, and whisper *now*:
Dost thou despair? Was thy vast scheme a cheat?
Doth it move sad strange mirth
To think thou dreamedst Earth
A God to its own soul, a Light to its own feet?

Out of the sphere of pain
All gods have warn'd in vain,
Brahm, Buddha, Balder, and the Man Divine—
Still blend in bloody strife,
Throat to throat, life for life,
Struggles the Human still, struggles this God of thine.

Say, is there hope up there,
Or doth thy heart despair?
Out of the deep once more shall Man arise?—
Here on the dark earth see
Stricken Humanity,—
Is there no lamp indeed beyond his own sad eyes?

While thy poor clay sleeps sound
All hush'd beneath the ground,
Dost thou the quest thy soul denied pursue?
And on some heavenly height,
With pale front to the light,
Art dreaming still—what dream?—since thy first
dream fell thro'.

Lo, 'tis the old sad chance!
Comte, look this day on France—
Behold her struck with swords and given to shame,
She who on bended knee
First to Humanity
Knelt, and with blood of Man heap'd Man's new
Altar-flame.

She who first rose and dared;
She who hath never spared
Blood of hers, drop by drop, from her great breast;
She who, to free mankind,
Left herself bound and blind;
She whose brave voice let loose the Conscience of
the West.

Lo, as she passes by
To the earth's scornful cry,
What are those shapes who walk behind so wan?—
Martyrs and prophets born
Out of her night and morn:
Have we forgot them yet?—these, the great friends of
Man.

We name them as they go,
Dark, solemn-faced, and slow—
Voltaire, with sadden'd mouth but eyes still bright;
Turgot, Malesherbes, Rousseau,
Lafayette, Mirabeau—
These pass, and many more, heirs of large realms of
Light.

Greatest and last pass thou,
Strong heart and mighty brow,
Thine eyes surcharged with love of all things fair;
Facing with those grand eyes
The light in the sweet skies,
While thy shade earthward falls, dark'ning my soul to
prayer.

And I discern again
The perfect sphere of pain ;
And there lies France, great heart of thy great plan—
In her dark hours of gloom,
In her worst sin and doom,
Hath she not ev'n by fire tested the soul of Man?

Sure as the great sun rolls,
The crown of mighty souls
Is martyrdom, and lo ! she hath her crown.
On thy pale brow there weigh'd
Another such proud shade—
O, but we know ye both, risen or stricken down.

Sinful, mad, fever-fraught,
At war with her own thought,
Great-soul'd, sublime, the heir of constant pain,
France hath the dreadful part
To keep alive Man's heart,
To shake the sleepy blood into the sluggard's brain ;

Ever in act to spring,
Ever in suffering,
To point the lesson and to bear the load,
Least happy and least free
Of all the lands that be,
Dying that all may live, first of the slaves of God.

Hers is the martyr's part,—
To bear a hungry heart,
A bursting brain, brave eyes, an empty hand ;
Such is the lot in store
For great souls evermore,
For her, for thee, great soul, for all God's chosen
band.

Shall the cold lands stand by,
Each with proud pitying eye,
While by her own heart's fever she is torn ?—
Shall the dull nations draw
Light from her woes—and law ?
Yea ! but her hour shall come ; she too shall rest,
some morn.

To try each crude desire
By her own soul's fierce fire,
To wait and watch with restless brain and heart,
To quench the fierce thirst never,
To feel supremely ever,
To rush where cowards crawl—this is her awful part.

Ever to cross and rack,
Along the same red track,
Genius is led, and speaks its soul out plain ;
Blessed are those that give—
They die that man may live,
Their crown is martyrdom, their privilege is pain.

Spirit of the great brow !
I need no whisper now—
Last of the flock who die for man each day.
Ah, but I should despair
Did I not see up there
A Shepherd heavenly-eyed on the heights far away.

No cheat was thy vast scheme,
Tho' in thy gentle dream
Thou saw'st no Shepherd watching the wild throng—
Thou walking the sad road
Of all who seek for God,
Blinded became at last, looking at Light so long.

Yet God is multiform,
Human of heart and warm,
Content to take what shape the Soul loves best,
Before our footsteps still
He changeth as we will—
Only,—with blood alone we gain Him and are blest.

O, latest son of her
Freedom's pale harbinger,
I see the Shepherd whom thou could'st not find ;
But on thy great fair brow,
As thou did'st pass but now,
Bright burnt the patient Cross of those who bless
mankind.

And on her brow, who lies
Bleeding beneath the skies,
The mark was set that will not let her rest—
Sinner in all men's sight,
Mocker of very Light,
Yet is she chosen thus, martyr'd,—and shall be blest.

Go by, O mighty dead !
My soul is comforted—
The Shepherd on the summit needs no prayers—
Best worshipper is he
Who suffers and is free—
That Soul alone blasphemes which trembles and
despairs.

ROBERT BUCHANAN.

May, 1871.

PROEM.

STILL blowing and growing,
With sound like torrents flowing,
The Storm of God in thunder
    Hath raged the whole night long :
Now in the grey of morning,
With never a note of warning,
O wonder ! just under
    Mine eaves there sounds a song !

There springing and singing,
To the bare branches clinging,
Just as the clouds are raising,
    A Bird sings fresh and loud—
Sings tho' the rain is falling,   .
Sings while the winds are calling,
Sings praising, and gazing
    Up to the breaking cloud.

O ditty of pity,
Sung just without the City,
Sung in the dark to heighten
    The waking hope of light,

Sung, lest the heart should harden,
By a white bird in my garden,
To lighten and brighten
    After a woeful night!

And higher, with fire
Of passionate desire,
While heaven's eye of azure
    Is opening far away,
The white bird sings full cheerly
Of all that man loves dearly,
A measure for pleasure
    Of the bright birth of day.

Deriding the tiding,
The soul within me biding
Smiles at the song to cheer it,
    But drinks the sound like wine.
Hark! louder yet of summer
Sings out the sweet newcomer—
The spirit, to hear it,
    Trembles to tears divine.

Bright ranger! white stranger!
Singing most loud in danger,
Whom storm nor wrath can frighten,
    Who hast no note for care,
Teach me to turn thy ditty
Into brave words of pity,
To brighten and lighten
    Man's passionate despair!

When, flying and dying,
The Storm of God is crying,
Now when they least desire me
　Who wake and look around,
Lest from ill-dreams they harden,
O white bird in my garden,
Inspire me and fire me
　With thy prophetic sound!

                              ROBERT BUCHANAN.

May, 1871.

PRELUDE

BEFORE THE CURTAIN.

B

THE HEAVENLY THEATRE.

The LORD. *The* ARCHANGELS. *The*
CELESTIAL SPECTATORS.

CHORUS.

RING within ring,
  Seventy times seven,
Ring within ring
Is blossoming
  The Rose of Heaven :
From the darkness under
  To the radiance o'er,
Bursting asunder
  Threefold at the core ;
Threefold is glowing
  The Eternal Light,
Close round it snowing
  Are the Seraphs white,

And next more dim
The Cherubim;
And from rings to rings,
Circles of wings
  Seventy times seven,
Inward close
The leaves of the Rose
  Of Heaven!

The Heart of the Rose,
  Like the flame on an altar,
    Burns dim and sweet,
And the leaves of the Rose
Are folded close,
  That they tremble and falter,
    To feel it beat:
From ring to ring,
Ever widening,
  Seventy times seven,
The glory flows
From the Heart of the Rose
  Of Heaven!
And dimmer growing
  From the burning Heart,

Still fainter flowing
  Thro' every part,
The sweet life sighs
  To the outermost leaves
    Most frail and wan ;
And there it lies,
Trembles and dies,
  For the outermost leaves
    Are the soul of Man.

Ring within ring
  Seventy times seven,
Ring within ring
Is blossoming
  The Rose of Heaven !
And for evermore
The flame at the core
Burns on, consuming
The circlet blooming,
Suffused and bright,
Next to the Light :—
Yea, as oil feedeth flame,
  The innermost part
    Of the seventy times seven

Melts ;—and the same
  Becomes one with the Heart
    Of the Rose of Heaven.

And evermore
Burning on to the core
The rings of the Rose
  Narrow inward, and turn
    More white and bright,
Yea, the rings of the Rose
  Contract and burn
    Till they reach the Light ;
And ever-renewed
  From root and seed,
With the fire for food
  Whose flame they feed,
First dim and wan
As the soul of Man,
They lessen, brightening
  From fold to fold
    Seventy times seven,
Whitening and lightening
  Till they die in gold
On the Heart of the Rose of Heaven.

Burn and close,

O leaves of the Rose!

Spread and shine,

O Flower divine!

Ring within ring

   Seventy times seven,

Ring within ring,

Grow blossoming,

   O beautiful Rose of Heaven!

Clouds rise. LUCIFER *appears upon the Stage.*

LUCIFER.

Hail, ye Spectators! whose immortal eyes
Within the Theatre Divine have seen
So many moving plays and interludes
To while away the tedious perfect time!
To-night, once more upon this stage of Earth
[Behold it! fair as ever, green and bright,
Carpeted still with flowers as beautiful
As any gems that blossom in the hair
Of you great Angels, and still canopied
With the ethereal azure star-enwrought]

To-night, upon this well-worn stage of Earth,
I come Choragus to your highnesses,
Announcing now a sort of tragedy,
A Choric trilogy of tragedies
In the Greek fashion ; and I have selected
The fairest cherubs and the sweetest-voiced
To play the part of Chorus.   What we play
Is called for briefness Δρᾶμα Κυριῶν,
The actors mortal, Earth the scene, the Time
The Present—if I dare use an abstract term
Fashion'd by purblind world-philosophers,
To ears that measure out eternity.

A Spirit.

Is it not then forbidden for the poet
To dramatise contemporary woes ?
Have ye forgot the sin of Phrynichos ?

Lucifer.

Is that Euripides or Æschylos ?
Or some poor poet blest to nothingness
Whose name has perish'd from the Attic
    scroll ?

Excuse me, then, the Author forms his theme
In his own fashion, and I must confess
He ever aims at planning novelty.
The Author is a most distinguished person,
Perhaps there is no mightier honour'd here,
But for the present chooses to remain
Unknown, unseen.   What we present to
    night
Is but a fragment of a series
Beginning with the first Man and the Snake.

Orchestra, now begin the overture !
And all ye sleepy Seraphs who delight
In lolling under rosy-coloured clouds
And blowing silvern trumpets, all ye Angels
Who only turn your slothful eyes on Art
When like a naked Phryne she awakes
Celestial appetite and dainty dream,
All triflers in the blue ethereal courts,
All idle gentlemen in singing robes,
Close eyes, shut ears !—for we prepare a
    show
Most tragic and most solemn; we design
To treat of mighty matters movingly,

Nor shall our actors in their skill disdain
The higher pathos—ye shall look on scenes
To make the very angels moan, and draw
Tears from the eyelids of the Son of God!

THE DRAMA OF KINGS.

PROLOGUE.

PROLOGUE.

Enter TIME, *cloaked and hooded, leaning on a*
Staff.

I AM that ancient shadow men call Time,
Silent, infirm, frail-footed, snow'd upon
By many winters, faring westward still,
And ever looking backward to the east.
How far these feeble feet must wander yet
I know not. All is dark before my steps ;
And oft it seems to my bewilder'd sense,
That I alone of all things do not move,
But like the pale moon plunging on thro'
    mist
Make but a fancied motion for the eye,
And stationary with enchanted eyes
Seem still to pass all shapes that swift as
    clouds
Slide by for ever. Behind me like the sea
Seen amid tempest from a mountain top,

Innumerable years break awfully

To foam of living faces and to moan

Of living voices ; and upon that waste,

Looming afar off ghost-like in my track,

ONE still moves luminous-footed, stretching

    hands

To bless the angry waves whereon He walks.

To night I come as Prologue, to prepare

Your ears for subtle matter.   Do ye hear

That wind of human voices anguishing

Afar off, like the wind Euroclydon

Moaning around Mount Ida ?   Hark again !

" Liberty ! Liberty !" the wild voice cries,

" Liberty !" now,—and ever " Liberty !"

But whom they call by that mysterious

    name

I say not, nor can any angel say,

Nor one thing under God.   God knows and

    hears.

That one word and none other hath been

    cried

By men from the beginning.   I have heard

The sound so long, I smile ; but at the same

Kingdoms have fallen like o'er-ripen'd fruit,

Realms wither'd, heaven rain'd blood and
  earth yawn'd graves,

The seasons sicken'd changing their due
  course,

The stars burnt blue for many awful nights

The corpse-lights of a world that lay as dead.

And now to-night we show on this same stage

How, uttering each that one mysterious word,

Two mighty Nations gather'd up their crests

Against each other, struck and struck
  again,

Met, mingled, roar'd, fell, rose, fought throat
  to throat,

Until their hate became the wide world's
  scorn ;

How dimly, darkly, for the great Idea,

Each smote, and stagger'd on from blow to
  blow,

While one by one came Leaders veil'd to
  each,

Phantoms, each cloak'd and hooded and led
  by me,

Each saying " In the name of Liberty !"

And drew them as the white moon draws the
　　sea;
How one by one these threw their cloaks
　　aside
And stood in a red sunset, bloody men
Who juggled with the mystic word of God;—
Yet how from sorrow came mysterious good,
Seeing Man's wrong'd Soul hoarded its deep
　　strength
In silence, making ready for that day
When God Himself, who knows the secret
　　only,
May bless it with that single truth it seeks.

　　　　　　　　　　　[A confused noise.

It is begun.　Germania overthrown,
Mad, stricken, lies upon her back and glares
At heaven from a bloody battle-field,
And dimly sees in the dark void above her
A dark Shape, a dim-footed Phantasy,
And deemeth 'tis the mighty truth men seek.
Hark, the drums beat! the cannons thunder
　　deep!
Earth shakes! . . Now all is silent, and I go

To walk at dark across the battle-field,

And, stooping o'er each stricken bleeding man,

Point with a skeleton finger to the stars,

And whispering my other awful name,

Draw back my hood a moment—thus !

[*Unhoods—shows the mask of a Caput Mortuum.*

My name

Is also Death ; and I am deathless. I

Am Time and most eternal. I am he,

God's Usher, and my duty it is to lead

The actors one by one upon the scene,

And afterwards to guide them quietly

Through that dark postern when their parts

     are played.

They come and go, alas ! but I abide,

And I am weary of the garish stage.

THE DRAMA OF KINGS.

Part I

BUONAPARTE;

OR, FRANCE AGAINST THE TEUTON.

SPEAKERS.

Kings, &c.

NAPOLEON BUONAPARTE.

ALEXANDER I., CZAR OF RUSSIA.

JEROME BUONAPARTE, KING OF WESTPHALIA.

LOUISA, QUEEN OF PRUSSIA.

THE KING OF SAXONY.

THE PRINCE PRIMATE, VON DALBERG.

Kings, Princes, and Dukes of the Rhenish Confederation.

Members of the Tugendbund ·

THE BARON VON STEIN.

THE PROFESSOR JAHN.

THE POET ARNDT.

CHORUS.

SCENE—*Erfurt, in the Duchy of Saxe Coburg Gotha.*

TIME—*October,* 1808, *during the great Congress of Powers.*

SCENE.—THE TOWN OF ERFURT, IN THE
DUCHY OF SAXE COBURG GOTHA.

STEIN. *An* OFFICER.

OFFICER.

HARK how they shout, thronging the busy
    streets,
While the imperial butcher passes by
To course the hare on Jena's fatal plain!

STEIN.

Ill-omen'd place and hour! ill-omen'd day!
Friend, I beheld them coming forth! I
    looked
On Cæsar's sallow face—I saw it, I—
And found no sunlight there to dazzle me :
Only the insolent frost-bitten cheek

Bloodless and hard like iron, only eyes
Snake-like, the snake's eyes of the Corsican.
On a white charger rolling like a wave,
He rode sunk deep into his saddle thus,
His shoulders rounded, while his bridle hand
    hand
Hung at his side as heavily as lead
Tho' the steed champ'd against the pitiless
    rein ;
And all the while with low soft speech he
    smiled
To Russia, who, on a black Barbary mare
Riding with stirrups long and easy rein,
Fixing his evil eyes in one fond stare
Of fascination on his royal comrade,
Show'd like a cheated wolf. Behind these
    twain,
Who riding hung together amorously,
Follow'd the lacqueys,—Prussia's prince and
    chief,
Würtemberg, Saxony, Bavaria,
Westphalia leering at the burghers' wives,
Hesse, Baden, all the princedoms and the
    powers,

So mingled up with equerries, knights-at-
    arms,

Blackcoats and redcoats, horsemen, footmen,
    huntsmen,

That all became a shameful garden-show

Wherein no eye could pick the several parts;

Only those two proud Emperors rode
    supreme,

In their proud sunshine dwarfing all the rest

That follow'd them to less than nothingness;

And yet I swear,—I saw it with mine eyes,—

Not one of those but drew his lacquey's air

In gaily, not one face but was content

So to be shone upon by those that led,

Not one, not one, but like a very dog

Follow'd behind his masters tame and proud,

Fawning upon their footprints step by step.

OFFICER.

My heart aches, and my tongue fails. All
    thy words

Are wormwood. Yet the people of the earth

Are helpless, seeing those that lead are blind.

STEIN.

O God, God, God! that these things should
    be known
In the same land, beneath the self-same sky,
That saw the giant Karl arise his height
The head of all the earth at Paderborn,
When dwarf'd beside him great Pope Leo
    stood,
And the great Caliph of the heathen East
Rain'd gold and gems at the imperial feet!
O God! are the ghosts laid for evermore
That walk'd about the Teuton vales at night
And awed the souls of men, and kept them
    free?
Is Karl forgotten? Is great Fritz's spirit
Spell-laid within the shade of Sans Souci?
Is Germany, is every German soul,
Dumb, fetter'd, broken, miserable, dead?
Are this man's functions supernatural,
Divine above all life, all love, all law,
That he should walk upon the waves of
    earth

Casting his bloody shade as on a sea,

And they should hush themselves around his
    feet

Lightly as ripples on a summer pond ?

Earth, water, air—the clouds, the waves, the
    winds,—

The stars in their pale courses,—day and
    night

Forgetful of their natural equipoise,

Shape their mysterious functions to his will;

Kings lick his feet like dogs; he lifts his
    finger

And epileptic in his chair the Pope

Foams speechless at the mouth ;—body and
    soul

Obey him as an impulse and a law ;—

The eyes, the ears, the tongues, of all the
    world

Are blown one way like all a forest's leaves

To see, hear, and entreat him ;—by his smile

The earth is brighten'd,—and 'tis straight fine
    weather !

Let him but frown, all darkens and the sun

Uprises bloody as a vulture's crest !

Like hawks obedient to the falconer
The Kings of Europe wait, and at a sign
Soar, while he sits and smiles, in fierce pursuit
Of any wretched quarry he would slay;
But let him whistle, and with bloody beaks
They turn, and preen their plumage, and are
    fed.
Cry? I will cry to God with all my soul!
Can God keep calm, and look upon these
    things?

CHORUS.

O Spirits dreaming,
  With blue eyes beaming,
  With bright locks flowing
    And folded wings,
  Your lips are parted,
  While happy-hearted,
  To rapture glowing,
    Sweet things each sings—
And the bright song quivers
Like the wash of rivers,
Like west winds blowing,
    Like bubbling springs;—

In quiet places

Shine your soft faces,

While we are throwing

    Our curse at Kings.

Sweet music never,

But something ever

To curse and cry for,

    Till death appear ;

No dreamy singing,

But scorn and stinging,

Deep shame to sigh for,

    Doom drear to fear ;

Hunger and sorrow

Both night and morrow,

While all we try for

    Grows harsh and sere :—

O'er barren meadows

We drift like shadows,

We dream, we die for

    The Golden Year.

O year! O summer!

O promised comer—

Promised to us
        Since time began—
As in the beginning,
Deep craft and sinning
Swiftly pursue us
        And ban each plan ;
A thousand rulers
And soul-befoolers
Have perish'd through us
        After a span ;
But fresh fierce faces
Still take their places,
New Kings subdue us
        And trouble Man.

Slay them ?—we slay them :—
Our souls gainsay them—
Comes Até bringing
        Her fatal boon ;
But still fresh creatures,
With the old false features,
Rise up, all singing
        The moon-mad tune ;—

What comfort to us
When these undo us ;
To know their stinging
    Must cease so soon—
When with fierce laughter
New Kings come after,
As quickly springing
    As grass in June ?

O Spirits dreaming,
With blue eyes beaming,
Your song, like ours,
    Is still the same—
Ye hear in glory
A familiar story,
But it sings of flowers,
    Not shame and blame—
And your lips are parted,
Ye smile sweet-hearted,
And ye join in your bowers
    With eyes aflame.
To a note as weary,
But dark and dreary,

Our souls, our powers,
    Lie sick and tame.

O, wherefore ever
Kill Kings, and never
Find earth outlast her
    Exceeding pain?
All man o'erthroweth
Again regroweth,
O'er each disaster
    We gain, in vain.
Slain Kings each morrow
Bring seed of sorrow.
Doth grass grow faster,
    Or golden grain?
After each reaping
We see upcreeping
Another Master!
    Another chain!

Like waves of ocean
Is our wild motion,
In sad storm blended,
    With winds opprest,

Ever perceiving
New cause for grieving :—
From storm defended,
    O blest were rest!
Tho' in its season
We know each treason
Must sink wave-rended
    In our great breast ;
Tho' all that win us
Are tomb'd within us,—
Would all were ended !
    Yea, rest were best.

O Spirits dreaming
With blue eyes gleaming,
With nought to sigh for
    As we sigh here,
Beyond disaster,
With one fix'd Master,
With nought to vie for,
    With fear, nor tear—
The soul speeds thither,
Our dreams go with her,

D

We yearn to fly, for
All life seems sere.
By waters dreary,
Moon-wan and weary,
We dream, we die for
The Golden Year !

STEIN. ARNDT. JAHN.

STEIN.

Good morrow, friends.   Have ye been feast-
ing sight
On Cæsar's triumph, that ye walk the earth
With eyes so fevered and with mien so
wild ?

JAHN.

Why, yes, we did our turn of gape and
stare.
'Twas hot, hell-hot—and the heat turned my
brain,
So that methought (laugh with me, lest ye
weep !)
'Twas very Cæsar whom I look'd upon,

And I as soothsayer was stepping forth
To croak my warning threat into his ear,
When Arndt here clutched me fast and held
    me back,
And I awoke again to the wild day;
So open-mouthed as he went by we stared
All in the sunshine and the festal light,
Like two black ravens on a bridal path
Hopping in omen of a funeral.

STEIN.

O blessed omen for the weary world!

JAHN.

How many hours, and days, and months, and
    years,
Shall this go on? Deeper and deeper yet
We wallow. Is there any living hope?

STEIN.

Hope lasts with life. Life lasts; so hope
    thou on.

JAHN.

Life lasts? I know not. Oft it seems that
    all
Is dead, dead—dead and rotten—Liberty
No more a living shape supremely fair,
But a mere ghost unpleasant to the thoughts
Of foolish Kings at bedtime. Every wind
Is tainted by this pestilence from France.
No man may sitting at his private board
Discuss in quietness his own affairs,
Debt, his last illness, private history,
But straight the Skeleton of Law appears,
Pressing its bony finger on the lips. ·
In every corner twinkle weasels' ears,
Long noses snuffing treason, sharp white
    teeth
Hungry for blood; the unclean things of
    scent
Swarm numerous as locusts, eating up
Our grain, our very substance; ay, and
    mark!
If thou and I—poor devils that we are—

Would fly from Malebolge, from this Hell,

And speed to some far land and colonise,

Straightway upon the frontier rises up

The Skeleton, waving us back again,

In this new Cæsar's name, to beggary.

Meantime the once blest frame of Germany

Sickens : disease and famine gnaw her
   breasts,

Sorrow and shame destroy her.   All appeal

To law is fatal, since this tyrant France

Is law, fate, death ; and each man's flesh and
   soul

Are fruit his myrmidons may pluck at will.

All men of noble birth must flock perforce

To spend three months of every year at
   court,

There to be taught to play this mad French
   tune

Upon the one-string'd fiddle of despair.

All the fresh streams of trade are choked and
   stuff'd

With antique carrion and new garbage.
   Nought

Goes out or in our poor Germania's mouth.

But the great thief clutches his lion's share;

And even the poor peasants,— Hans who
    chops

Wood in the cold, Fritz who grows rheu-
    matic

Leech-hunting in the marshes,—even these,

Are robb'd, poor slaves, of their mere mite of
    salt,—

While every pipe they smoke beside the
    fire

To warm their agued limbs in wretched
    age,

And every pinch of snuff they feebly take

To clear their purblind eyes of rheum and
    mist,

Is interdicted till they first have given

Due pinch and pipeful to the Emperor!

Stein.

Still courage!   Evil days have been ere
    this,

Social disease as deep, civic disease

As dreadful.   It shall end.   Have we not
    sworn

By Christ that it shall end ?   Sow thy fierce
    words

Abroad, my Jahn,—they shall be wingëd
    seed—

Prepare, my Arndt, thy passionate sweet
    songs,

Sing them at night by the Babylonian river,

They shall create a new and Teuton soul.

ARNDT.

And yet I scarce can speak for bitterness.

O Stein, while I prepare an eager cry

To move the stagnant hearts of simple men,

Voices more strong and more intense than
    mine,

Souls gifted and accredited from God,

Cry to the monster, "Hail," sing in his ear

Pindaric hymn and pæan, fan his glory

Like light winds full of scent from beds of
    flowers.

STEIN.

Voices of parasites and summer bards—

For such have ever sung to conquerors.

ARNDT.

But yestermorn the old man Wieland stood
Enlarging his weak vision for an hour
Upon the demigod, who of Greece and Rome
Talk'd like a petulant schoolboy; and this day
I beheld Goethe with a doubtful face,
Part dubious and part eager, proof of thoughts
Half running on ahead, half lingering,
Enter the quarters of the Emperor;—
But when he issued forth his features wore
Their pitiless smile of perfect self-delight,
His lips already quiver'd with a pæan,
His stately march was quicken'd eagerly,
And all his face and all his gait alive
With glory that the sun of Corsica
Had shone upon him to his heart's content.
Which of our singers is not garrulous
In praise of Europe's curse and Prussia's
        shame?

JAHN.

I trust no poets.   They are moonshine men,
And like the folk in Persia fall abash'd

At sunlight. There is mightier matter *here*,—

Short, sharp, and like himself,—a word of
  hope

From Marshal Vorwärts, our old fire-eater,

The old one with the bright heart of a boy,

Who jingles his sharp spurs and curses
  France

Morn, noon, and night in Pomerania—

Reads, "Thieves!" "cowards!" "windbags!"

  "men of straw!" "geese!" "swine!"

The strength of Blücher lies in expletives

And sword-thrusts) with such words hurl'd
  out like blows,

He cries, concluding with a trooper's curse,

A round "God-damn-his-soul-to-hell-fire"
  oath

On the French Satan. As for your singing-
  men,

Your lute-players, your festal Matthissons,

They buzz in their own fashion, in the
  old

Blue-bottle fashion. While the blue-flies
  hum,

The curs yelp gladly. I have heard they eat

Dog-pie in China as a delicacy :—
O to be cook to Cæsar for a day !
To mince John Müller and dish Zschokke
    up,
As dainties set before the Emperor!

STEIN.

The life of every man is as a wave,
And having risen its appointed height
It must descend ; and I believe this day
Our eyes have look'd upon Napoleon
Crested to his full glory, and in act
Of over-fall.   The power of tyranny
Can go no higher; henceforth its fierce
    strength
Shall be expended downwards, be assured.

JAHN.

I could have roar'd for joy like any bull
To see him fondling Russia.   To be tamed,
Bears must be taken in their infancy ;
But I beheld the old bloodthirsty look
Deep in the eyes of this one, tho' they blink'd

So tamely. Why, his paws are scarcely
   clean
From Austerlitz! Have patience! this last
   pet
Was caught too old, and it will hug him yet!

STEIN.

Honour to Austria, that he holds aloof—

JAHN.

O there is life and soul in Austria still:
The poor old Bird hath struck and struck and
    struck,
Till he is shredded to a scarecrow, worn
To a thin shadow. In the undaunted one
I honour what I hated, and yet fear!
Were I a poet (I am none, thank God)
Why I would sing a pæan in his praise.

STEIN.

For something fairer far and more divine
Poets shall sing and prophets cry full soon.

O friends, we shall become a people yet—

Tho' the first bond was like a wisp of straw

Torn by this Ape asunder, tho' no more

Under the banner left by Karl the Great

We fight against oppression, still, thank God,

We are a people yet, and I believe

Not wholly blind and helpless, tho' we reach

Our hands out darkly, waiting on for light.

Austria is torn from her imperial seat,

Prussia lies healing of her last wide wound,

The lesser Kingdoms walk in flowery chains;

Germania, the name, the word, the race,

Still lives, and by Germania soon or late

Shall Buonaparté die.   At Austerlitz

Fell Austria, here the Prussian eagle fell.

On both those memorable battlefields,

Rose like a Spirit from a murder'd man

The white truth, hovering for a moment there

An Iris on the Death-cloud.   Out of the
     proud

Imperial Austrian ruin shall emerge

The TEUTON : not a temple such as that

Napoleon overthrew—not a mere name

Descending thro' a line of shadowy Kings—

Not a delusion and patrician lie,

A pasteboard Crown and an unholy Sword—

Not these, but more than these, a life, a soul,

A living man, the Teuton, lord of all

He from his fathers first inherited,—

The heart of Europe water'd by the Rhine.

For ours too long hath been a mighty house

Divided in itself against itself,

Too eager to be dragged by peevish Kings

Out of itself to wander in the world :

And we indeed are stricken at this day

Because we follow'd in an evil hour

Blind rulers who affrighted for their crowns

Led us against the house republican

Built by our brethren in the fields of France.

For, mark me, they who follow and fight for

    crowns

Fight for a figment merely and a sign,

And should the dwellers in a nation say

Within our chambers there shall sit no Kings,

They err who blindly for the sake of Kings

Would carry thither sword and flaming fire.

A people is a law unto itself,

The law of God will shape that lesser law,

And if there come a time when Kings are
    doom'd,
Why let them like a feast-day pageant pass
And be forgotten, or like some old tale
Become a goodly theme for the fireside.
O if the Teuton soul we all inherit
Would rise supreme, and for the one white
  . truth
Strike blow on blow half as persistently
As Austria hath, because she fear'd to lose
The jewels in her crown, the world were free
Of this accredited and crownëd Shape,
That walketh at his will, and when he will,
Into the porches of the great Abodes
Of nations: knocks like Death at every
    door,
And enters every kingly bed-chamber
As sleep doth, bringing there instead of sleep
Sleepless Despair and haunting shapes of
    Fear!
What, shall this Robber sit with folded
    arms
Upon the hearth of our fair dwelling-place,
And shall the foolish people of the house

Do courtesies and kill the fatted calf?

Nay, rather let him reckon up his days,

For he was doom'd (and so all Kings are
doom'd)

Whene'er he ceased to wield the righteous
sword

Upon the threshold of his threaten'd land,

And wander'd out into the open world

To plunder in the name of Liberty.

CHORUS.

'Twas the height of the world's night, there
was neither warmth nor light,

And the heart of Earth was heavy as a
stone;

Yet the nations sick with loss saw the surge
of heaven toss

Round the meteor of the Cross; and with a
moan

All the people desolate gazed thereon and
question'd fate,

And the wind went by and bit them to the
bone.

Hope was fled and Faith was dead, and the
    black pall overhead
  Hung like Death's, for doom was heavy
    everywhere,—
When there rose a sudden gleam, then a
    thunder, then a scream,
  Then a lightning, stream on stream upon
    the air!
And a dreadful ray was shed around the Cross,
    and it grew red,
  And the pallid people leapt to see the
    glare.

Fire on the heights of France! Fire on the
    heights of France!
  Fire flaming up to heaven, streak on
    streak!
How on France Kings look't askance! how
    the nations join'd in dance!
  To see the glory glance from peak to peak!
How the chain'd lands curst their chance, as
    they bent their eyes on France!
  Earth answer'd, and her tongues began to
    speak.

Now hark!—who lit the spark in the miserable
    dark?
O Washington, men miss thee and forget.
Where did the light arise, in answer to man's
    cries?
    In the West; in those far skies it rose and
        set.
Who brought it in his breast from the
    liberated West?
    Speak his name, and kneel and bless him:
        Lafayette.

O Sire, that madest Fire! How with pas-
    sionate desire
    Leapt the nations while it gather'd and
        up-streamed;
Then they fed it, to earth's groans, with
    Man's flesh and blood and bones,
    And with Altars and with Thrones; and
        still it screamed.
Then they cast a King thereon—but a flash,
    and he was gone.
    Then they brought a Queen to feed it:—
        how it gleam'd!

E

Then it came to pass, Earth's frame seem'd
    dissolving in the flame,
  Then it seem'd the Soul was shaken on its
    seat,
And the pale Kings with thin cries look'd in
    one another's eyes,
  Saying, "Hither now it flies, and O how
    fleet!
Sound loud the battle-cry, we must trample
    France or die,
  Strike the Altar, cast it down beneath our
    feet."

Forth they fared.   The red fire flared on the
    heights of France, and glared
  On the faces of the free who kept it fed;
Came the Kings with blinded eyes, but with
    baffled prayers and cries
  They beheld it grow and rise, still bloody-
    red;
When lo! the Fire's great heart, like a red
    rose cloven apart,
  Open'd swiftly, to deep thunder overhead.

And lo, amid the glow, while the pale Kings
watched in woe,
Rose a single Shape, and stood upon the
pyre.
Its eyes were deeply bright, and its face, in
their sad sight,
Was pallid in a white-heat of desire,
And the cheek was ashen hued ; and with
folded arms it stood
And smiled bareheaded, fawn'd on by the
Fire.

Forehead bare, the Shape stood there, in the
centre of the glare,
And cried, "Away ye Kings, or ye shall
die."
And it drove them back with flame, o'er the
paths by which they came,
And they wrung their hands in shame as
they did fly.
As they fled it came behind fleeter-footed than
the wind,
And it scatter'd them, and smote them hip
and thigh.

All amazed, they stood and gazed, while their
  crying kingdoms blazed,
  With their fascinated eyes upon the
    Thing ;—
When lo, as clouds dilate, it grew greater and
  more great,
  And beneath it waited Fate with triple
    sting ;
All colossus-like and grand, it bestrode the
  sea and land,
  And behold,—the crownëd likeness of a
    KING !

Then the light upon the height that had
  burned in all men's sight
  Was absorb'd into the creature where he
    smiled.
O his face was wild and wan—but the burning
  current ran
  In the red veins of the Man who was its
    child :—
To the sob of the world's heart did the meteor-
  light depart,
  Earth darken, and the Altar fall defiled.

Then aloud the Phantom vow'd, "Look upon
  me, O ye proud!
 Kiss my footprints! I am reaper, ye are
  wheat!
Ye shall tremble at my name, ye shall eat my
  bread in shame,
 I will make ye gather tame beneath my
  seat."
And the gold that had been bright on the
  hair of Kings at night,
Ere dawn was shining dust about his feet.

At this hour behold him tower, in the dark-
  ness of his power,
 Look upon him, search his features, O ye
  free!
Is there hope for living things in this fiery
  King of Kings,
 Doth the song that Freedom sings fit such
  as he?
Is it night or is it day, while ye bleed beneath
  his sway?
 It is night, deep night on earth and air and
  sea.

Still the height of the world's night. There is
  neither warmth nor light,
  And the heart of Earth is heavy as a stone;
And within the night's dark core where the sad
  Cross gleam'd before
  Sits the Shape that Kings adore, upon a
  Throne;
And the nations desolate crawl beneath and
  curse their fate,
  And the wind goes by and bites them to
  the bone.

O Sire that mad'st the Fire, and the Shape
  that dread and dire
  Came from thence, the first and last born of
  the same,
To Thee we praying throng, for Thou alone
  art strong,
  To right our daily wrong and bitter shame:
From the aching breast of earth, lift the red
  Fire and its birth!
  Consume them—let them vanish in one
  flame!

BUONAPARTE. *The* CZAR. JEROME
BUONAPARTE. LOUIS BUONAPARTE.
The KINGS *of* SAXONY, BAVARIA,
WURTEMBERG. *The* PRINCE PRIMATE
VON DALBERG. *The* HEREDITARY
PRINCES *and* DUKES OF THE RHENISH
CONFEDERATION.

BUONAPARTE.

Thank God Almighty for a peaceful day.
Would we had never nobler game to chase
Than that just slain on Jena. What say'st
    thou,
Von Dalberg? Is there any living thing
Runs faster from the hunter than a hare?

PRINCE PRIMATE.

A man, Sire, when the hunter is a God.

BUONAPARTE.

Sayst thou? Well, be of courage, tho' we
    saw
Men's backs at Jena. Here indeed we stand
In pomp of peace and perfect amity,

The constellated rulers of the earth,

Forming (God willing) for the years un-
    born

A prosperous and golden horoscope.

We miss our cousin Austria.   Were he
    here

Our pageantry were perfect, and we grieve

To see him sitting sullen far away,

Like some poor cudgel-player with crack'd
    crown

Scowling upon the victor in the game;

But since he holds aloof persistently,

And will not be entreated, we will try

Without his help to mend the tatter'd
    realm,

And tonic the sick stomach of the time.

Long centuries of social night indeed

Have lent to our belovëd cousin's eyes

A certain owl-like hatred of the light,

And, taking little note how time slips by,

He in the nineteenth century would pre-
    serve

The worm-worn charters left by mighty
    Charles.

The Holy Roman Empire did its work,

Flourish'd, decay'd, grew rotten, till at last

We threw the wither'd fragments 'for in
    truth

They were as stumbling-blocks to all earth's
    Kings)

To the limbo of all logs—Oblivion.

O there is much to say, and more to do,

Ere we can heal earth's wounds, and right
    man's wrong,

And open up the last long reign of peace.

Meantime thank God for one most peaceful
    day.

Enter LOUISA *of* PRUSSIA.

BUONAPARTE.

Why, how now, lady? On thy knees—in
    tears—

Rise—rise,—this is not well.

QUEEN.

              Tho' I should rest

My forehead in the dust beneath thy feet,

Tho' thou shouldst trample this sad face to
    clay,
I could not fall more low in misery;
Yet not for mere self-sorrow do I weep,
No, not for sorrow, but for pity, Sire,
Rending my heart with pain unutterable;
And not in self-abasement do I kneel,
No, for I am thy peer, a crownëd Queen,
But pleading, praying, as a mother doth
For her lost children, interceding now
For my poor people, who like scatter'd
    sheep
Cry homeless up and down the blood-stain'd
    land.

BUONAPARTE.

Rise, lady! Well? In sooth there is no
    rest
For Princes, and by these hysteric tears
Our peaceful day is broken. Calm thyself!
Drops that become a lovely woman's face
Suit ill the proud-fringed eyelids of a
    Queen.
How can we serve thee?

O Sire, first and last,
By being honest with us in our woe,
By publishing our perfect sum of doom,
Nor suffering our tortured eyes and ears
To watch and listen, hoping on in vain,
While in the secret chambers of thy soul
New treasons hatch themselves to policy.

BUONAPARTE.

Dost thou accuse us of dishonesty?

QUEEN.

It bodes no good to any in the world,
When France and Russia from the self-same
    cup
Together drink "swift death to Germany!"

BUONAPARTE.

Hearest thou, brother?

CZAR.

Ay, I hear, and smile.
Our gentle sister speaks her heart in ire,
Forgetful of our love and fellowship
Proved under Heaven on many a bloody
    field.

QUEEN.

I forget nought.   Would that 'twere possible
To drink forgetfulness of thine and thee.
What dost thou here at Erfurt by the side
Of thy sworn foe smiling in amity?
What dost thou here on alien German soil
Sunning thyself beneath the Emperor's eyes,
When scarce a summer moon hath come and
    gone
Since thou wert standing at our palace-gate
Calling all Europe's curse upon his head?

CZAR.

Doubtless we called, for those were troublous
    times—
Forget not also, that we called in vain,

That Prussia slept when we would have her
    rise,

And then too late, when all the world was
    changed,

Awaken'd up on Jena!

BUONAPARTE.

                         Add, moreover :

Our brother Russia, sick of fretful broils,

And most peace-loving, takes in honesty

Our hand and on our loving friendship
    leans ;—

Unto his eyes we bare the heart of France

In council; to none other France shall stoop.

QUEEN.

And ye—ye Princes, idly standing by,

What is it that ye think, and say, and do ?

JEROME.

They bless the hand that made and keeps
    them Kings.

SAXONY.

Duty and perfect love we owe to France,
Whereby indeed we live, and thrive, and
    grow.

QUEEN.

Hear them, ye blessed Spirits of the Dead !
Dread Kings of Hapsburg, hear! Thou
    kingly Soul
Who walkest in the shades of Sans Souci,—
Hear them! By France these lacqueys live
    and grow!
On France's prop these sweet-pea-Princes
    bloom!

BUONAPARTE.

Peace, lady—or, if thou must play the shrew,
Go back to him who sent thee here, to him
Whom 'tis thy wifely privilege to scold.

QUEEN.

He speaks of peace. Hear him again, ye
    dead!
The firebrand of the earth doth speak of
    peace.

By Heaven, these women, whose big eyes can
    rain
So easily, know how to thunder too.
Lady, get hence, get hence,—call as thou
    wilt,
The dead are deaf and will not answer
    thee.—
Old Fritz is snug asleep among his dogs ;
And even though he heard thee, he would
    groan
And sleep again—so little did he love
Life, men and women, the mad world,—and
    wives ;
And for the rest 'twas only yesterday
We took away the same old heathen's sword,
And now it hangs above our hearth in
    France,
In memory of one who was a King,
In token Prussia once begat a man,
And of a land that was a people once,
But now hath pined away into a voice.
Come, brother.

QUEEN.

Stay.

BUONAPARTE.

How?

QUEEN.

     Stay. I appeal
To Man against thee! I cry out to God
To shame thee!—if on this unhappy day,
Taking the hand of thy sworn enemy,
Thou addest one wrong to the million wrongs
Heap'd upon Prussia's head by thee and thine.

CZAR.

O peace;—thou tearest thy patch'd cause the
  more,
With so intemperate and fierce a tongue
Crying against anointed majesty!—

QUEEN.

I am anointed who cry out to thee—
I whose fair royalty, though it bleeds so deep,

Is worth a thousand empires such as rise
Based on the bloody tumult of a day !

JEROME.

A kingdom founded by a hunchback ape,
The puppet of a harlot of the town !

QUEEN.

Who prates of apes and harlots ? and for-
  sooth
Of puppets ? What, the King of marionettes,
Who holds our stolen fiefs upon the Elbe !
Emperor of Punchinello ! mighty Lord
Of Pierrots, fiddlestrings, and dancing-girls !

CZAR (*to* BUONAPARTE).

Why dost thou smile upon the woman so,
Folding thine arms and nodding to beat time
Like one that listens to a merry play ?

BUONAPARTE.

Tho' I have brought the pick and pride of
  France
As players hither in my retinue,

F

The best of them is dull and wearisome

To her whose speech we have just hearken'd
    to.

Fair Queen, adieu! We honour thee the more

For rating us so roundly and so well,

And love thy luckless Kingdom none the
    less:

Indeed it shall not perish,—thou shalt learn

That the Earth's masters can be generous.

> [*Exeunt all but the* QUEEN.

QUEEN.

Pitiless! pitiless! pitiless! pitiless!

"Earth's masters?"—O thrice miserable Earth

If these are masters of thy continents!

Bodies without a heart! tyrants whose thrones

Are based upon unutterable pain,

One on the frozen ice of the East's despair,

One on the bloody lava hard and black

Scatter'd by the volcano of the West!

What hope for the poor world if these join
    hands,

Murder with Avarice, Poison with the Sword,

Cunning with Hatred, Pride with Cruelty,

The heir of Despots with the Parvenu,

Moloch, whose cold and leaden eyeballs gloat

On old familiar woes deep as the grave,

With the quick soul of subtler Lucifer

Ever devising novel agonies !

O Spirit of God, who with mysterious breath

Dost fashion e'en the will of men-like fiends

And fiend-like men to obey thee and to work

Thy strange dim ends, thy doom, thy deep

  revenge,

Penetrate this day into very Hell,—

Into the heart of Earth that is as Hell,—

Work in the council-chamber, in the ears

Of these arch-tyrants whisper doubts and

  fears,

Disturb their privy-councils, let them mark

The viper on each other's smiling lips,

And while they seek to cheat humanity

And portion Europe's bleeding body in twain,

Let each outwit the other,—like two thieves

Fall at each other's throats,—fiery with greed

Strike in new hatred at each other's hearts,—

And struggle, to the laughter of the world,

Till one or both fall impotent and dead !

[*Enter* STEIN.

STEIN.

All happy greetings to your Majesty !

QUEEN.

Ah, faithful friend, such greetings ill befit
A poor weak woman lost in misery.
Look, I am weeping—ah, what bitter tears :
A beggar's, Stein, a beggar's, even such
As weary women, starving, ragged, sick,
Shed when they ask (as I have asked) for
    alms.

STEIN.

Of whom ? of France ? Alms ! of the Em-
    peror ?

QUEEN.

Emperor, Cæsar, Satan, what ye will.
To him, Napoleon, to this Corsican,
I, I, Louisa, in whose veins there runs
The royal blood of honest Kings and Queens.

Have knelt, cried, pleaded, interceded,
    prayed,
Conjured like any starving beggar-girl,
Craving one crust of comfort all in vain.
He stood here ; he, this man, this parvenu,
Compound of Scapin and Olympian Jove,
This monster of the earthquake, this foul
    thing
Bred of the world's corruption ; here he stood,
While at his back the trembling puppets
    waited
Whom with one string he works upon their
    thrones ;
And as I pleaded for the plunder'd land,
He, with compassion such as one might cast
Upon the dead corse of an enemy,
Mingled with flashes of sheer mockery,
Did ever and anon, with haughty smile
Raising his eyebrows, motion to the Czar.
O friend, we are trampled on in our despair,
Mocked in our miserable overthrow,
Robbed, plunder'd, butcher'd, spat upon,
    despised !
And now indeed would yonder heartless men,

Yonder two fatal powers of frost and fire,
Portion our fair dominions in two halves,
Deeming us worse than the intestate dead.

Stein.

Madam, be calm : this is the one dark hour
Ere daybreak.   Look to the east ; for there is
    hope.

Queen.

What   hope ?   what   hope ?   Impoverish'd,
    wounded, sick,
Penniless, swordless, we are lost past hope ;
Our last hope died on Jena ; there, indeed,
Dead Prussia lies, cold, gazing up at God !

Stein.

On Jena Prussia died,—if the strange swoon
Of Lazarus was dying.   Christ went by,
And Lazarus smiling in his grave-clothes rose,
Wiser—ah, how much wiser !—out of death.

Queen.

Christ died.   The age of miracles is past.

STEIN.

Called by new names, Hope, Faith, or
    Liberty,
Called by a thousand names, by each man's
    mouth,
Called by the name that man deems loveliest,
A Spirit walketh still about the Earth
Compassing resurrection. At this hour
Strange stirs disturb the darkness of the
    grave,
Deep aspirations of the cold dark lands
Ready to burst their swathing clothes and live.
The Figure comes, I see its shadow loom
Gigantic in the east—it comes this way,—
A ghostly liberator comes this way ;
And when it sayeth " Rise," dead Germany
Shall spring erect, one life, one heart, one
    soul !

QUEEN.

O Stein! are these not words to an old song,
A tune with little meaning which men sing
To keep their hearts from breaking utterly ?

STEIN.

Sure as the earthquake shook the frame of
    France
And swallow'd up the pallid King and Court,
Tempest is gathering here. The Tyrol
    trembles,
Austria is sharpening her sword anew,
Bavaria groans under the yoke of France :
All ripens, 'tis the darkness of the cloud
Full charged with thunder: at the one word
    "Rise!"
The cloud shall burst, graves open, lightning
    flash,
Prussia rise smiling, and the Despot fall.
O lady! learn to hear and utter forth
The word men love, the strange word
    "Liberty!"
Stand up above thy people (all men's hearts
Answer the flash of a fair woman's face),
And in the chosen moment point them on
With passionate invocation and appeal.
Not once again let slow suspicion part
Teuton from Teuton, but may all the powers

Heat their slow thunders to a thunderbolt,

Such as shall shake the fabric of the world.

England is with us, by us fights the Swede,

The Turk new-threaten'd ranges on our side:

These one by one shall spring erect to strike

Like sleepers waken'd by the shriek of " fire."

On Jena Prussia's feeble body died,

The peevish frame worn out with long
    disease

Struck, fell, and ended. There shall rise
    instead

A MAN, touch'd and miraculously strengthen'd,

Calm with exceeding knowledge and strange
    truth

Gain'd only in such utterness of doom,

And with a light in his inspired eyes

Before which Buonaparté's soul shall quail.

QUEEN.

Thy voice awakens echoes in my heart

Like something strange and supernatural.

Stein, I believe thee ; and thy lips have lent

New light and inspiration. Yes, yes, yes,

No more divided councils, but one heart,
One soul, one hope, one mighty Germany!

Stein.

So runs the song indeed, your Majesty,
An old tune and a true one, long forgot
For new French chansonettes and lute-
    playing.
Let every Teuton throat but utter it,
And lo ! the very wind of the strong cry
Will storm the wondering world. This man,
    this arm
And head of France, has never yet beheld
A foeman worthy of a great man's steel ;
His enemies have been divided nations,
Kings purblind, selfish, trembling for their
    crowns,
Statesmen that chose their brief wild hour of
    power
To strip the shrine and rob the treasury,
Half-hearted leaders guiding with shut eyes
Brute-mercenaries clamouring for gold.
To these the light of the man's lurid Star

Hath been a blinding portent and deep awe,
A superstition paralysing will
And numbing the strong arm in act to strike.

QUEEN.

Strong words, Stein, yet God knows, so true,
   so true!

STEIN.

The legions of the conqueror are weak
Against the strength of the free Thought of
   Man,
Which, fluid like the water or the air,
More subtle than the glistening mercury,
Inseparable by the sword, coheres
In mystical divine affinity;
And, spite of all that tyranny can plan
To separate the wondrous elements,
Gathers its drops and particles anew,
Imperishable by the laws of God.
Why see how England, floating on the sea,
Winding her arm around the Continent,
Seizes the proud foot of the conqueror,

And holds him, while with impotent fierce
　　hate

He striketh at her helmëd head in vain.

See how a few poor peasants with one will,

Led by a few mad monks with shaven
　　crowns,

Have rent the vulnerable ranks of France

And scattered them like wind-blown chaff,—
　　in Spain.

The Spirit of Man begins to know its
　　strength;

That strength once known, it is invincible.

CHORUS.

Our eyes are troubled with strange tears,
　　Our souls are startled to strange light,
We stand snow-pale like one that fears
　　Loud sounds of earthquake in the night;
A mystic voice is in our ears,—
Afar the River of the years
　　Pauses and flashes white—
And o'er it in the East appears
　　Dim gleams of rose-red light.

Semi-Chorus II.

The dark clouds where the set sun lies
   Are parted back like raven hair
From off a maiden's gentle eyes;
   Beyond, most lily-like and fair,
White, shaded soft with azure dyes,
Heaven opens; and from out the skies
   Comes one with pensive care—
Before whose path a white dove flies
   Thro' the rich amber air.

Semi-Chorus I.

She hasteneth not, but her cheeks glow,
   Her feet scarce stir, her glances stray
Oft backward; while her soft feet sow
   Brightness beneath them as of day,
And whiteness as of softest snow;
And she, thro' locks bright breezes blow,
   Smiles as no mortal may—
Her feet come hither, but how slow!
   Her eyes look not this way.

A Voice.

Sing ye a song, right loud and strong,
　　To speed her on her way.

Chorus.

O thou whose shape at last breaks the dark-
　　ness of the Vast,
　　　　Come, O come,
Dream no longer there afar; like a swiftly
　　shooting star,
　　　　Hasten home!

Like waves that murmur white round the re-
　　flex of a light
　　　　In the sea,
Like buds that feel all blind for the warm
　　light and the wind,
　　　　Murmur we.

We see and know thee now by the white im-
　　mortal brow;
　　　　By the eyes

Dim from death's divine eclipse; by the me-
    lancholy lips
        Sweetly wise.

We have named thee by a name sweeter far
    than Love or Fame,
        Or all breath,
Thy name is Liberty, and another name of
    thee
        Hath been Death.

By the blood that we have shed, by the lost
    and by the dead,
        By our wrong,
By our anguish, by our tears, by the leaden
    load of years,
        Come along.

SEMI-CHORUS I.

She hears, she hears, with glistening tears,
    She turneth sad and sweet,
With quick glad breath she hasteneth—
    O God, she cometh fleet.

SEMI-CHORUS II.

Sing we a song most wild and strong,
     To hasten her blest feet.

CHORUS.

See the lightning and the rain, see the bloody
     fields of slain,
          See the sword
That we draw with fierce desire to wreak the
     dreadful ire
          Of the Lord;

Hear that other name Revenge, that shall
     wither up and change
          Nature's worst;
Hear the judgment God hath written, by
     whose lightning shall be smitten
          Kings accurst;

See the wreck of crowns and thrones, watch
     the earthquake, hear the groans
          Of the great,

See the prince's golden porch dash'd to ashes,
mark the Church
Desolate ;

Picture wrongs as yet undone, and the red
fields to be won
Ere we die ;
Then O leader of the van, O thrice holy hope
of man,
Hear our cry !

SEMI-CHORUS I.

O wherefore shrinks that Spirit frail,
Like one that shrinks from something
dire ?
Her lips are parted, her feet fail
And falter, and with sudden fire
She looketh hither while we hail
Her advent, and quick sighs assail
Her gentle breast and tire
Her glad heart : there she lingers pale—
Half terror, half desire.

G

SEMI-CHORUS II.

O dim and faint, with cheeks snow-white,
　She pauses hearkening to our hymn :
Against the gentle heavenly light,
　With rose-shades on each rounded limb,
She stands in sudden act of flight
Bent forward, with her tear-stain'd sight
　Piercing the distance dim ;—
Below stands One on the world's height,
　And lo ! she looks on him.

SEMI-CHORUS I.

Ah woe, ah woe, who stands below,
　Still, tall, a shape of clay,
Before whose breath slow lingereth
　That fair shape far away ?

SEMI-CHORUS II.

Be our song deep and strong,
　A thunder-song this day.

CHORUS.

O shape that towerest there in the black and
    dreadful air,
        Napoleon !
O Man, O crowned King, heark unto us while
    we sing,
        And beware.

Underneath thy feet this day lie the nations
    cold as clay,
        Cold and dead ;
But, behold, to bid them " Rise " waiteth one
    with blessëd eyes
        Overhead.

With light shadow in the sea, lo, she pausing
    looks on thee,
        Napoleon !
And ye pause there eye to eye, while the
    world rings with the cry
        Of the free.

She cometh from the Lord ; with no fire, with
    no sword
        See her rise !
She cometh fair and mild, but all things tame
    or wild
        Love her eyes.

More than all men that are, she perceives thee
    from afar,
        Napoleon !
And the reason she doth weep is because she
    pities deep
        Thy sad star.

For she loveth all that be, even Kings, yea,
    even thee
        And thy seed,
She would have thee like the rest very beauti-
    ful and blest,
        Being freed.

And by Man's own hand alone, not by hers
    which smiteth none,
        Napoleon !

By the might of Man's own plan must the
    traitor against Man
        Be o'erthrown.

For by her no blood doth flow, and she
    worketh no man woe,
        No man fear;
But when all the blood is done, she the
    gentle-hearted one
        Cometh here.

Yet not till thou art slain will she walk
    upon the plain,
        Napoleon!
We must slay and smite thee down, thou
    must perish, she must crown
        What we gain.

But since thy soul is flame, and o'er fiery
    fierce to tame
        Thy desire,
Lie thee down and try to cease, while she
    cometh white as peace,
        Bright as fire.

Lie thee down and die, and rest, with that
fierce flame in thy breast,
Napoleon !
And by her whose day is nigh, the grave
where thou dost lie
Shall be blest.

For the dead lands as they rise shall but
bless thy closëd eyes,
Lying there,
And thy sleep shall broken be by no voices of
the sea
Or the air.

But when wild winds blow this way, we shall
think of thy wild day,
Napoleon !
And when hurricane and rain shake the sea
and sky and plain,
We shall say :

" Ev'n as these that rend and rave, was this
Man upon whose grave
Poets sing :

A wild wind that in wrath clear'd the mists
   before the path
      Of the Spring."

BUONAPARTE, *reading a dispatch.* *A*
CARDINAL.

BUONAPARTE.

Why, how now? Hath Pope Pius lost his
   wits?
Or hath he drunk too deep of that proud
   wine
Which ever and anon hath made your Popes
Reel drunken off their seats? Is the man
   mad,
That he should howl in our imperial ear
The flat old thunders that so long have
   turned
The small-beer kingdoms sour with jeopardy?
And thou—thou whose dry lineaments look
   white
With secret brimstone, art thou also mad,
With front so insolent and tread so proud
To step into the presence of thy lord?

CARDINAL.

I have no lord but Christ, and under Him
Christ's Vicar and thy Master. While thy
    soul
Trusted and honour'd these, we render'd
    thee
Like trust and honour: but, on this dark
    day,
When thou dost raise thyself into the seat
Of God's anointed Priest, I hold thee less
Than the least man who underneath the
    skies
Falls on his knee and sues to the Lord
    God.

BUONAPARTE.

So free! So loud! Runneth the new song
    thus,
Lord Cardinal?

CARDINAL.

        E'en thus, and at thy choice
Love or defiance come, by me, from Rome.

BUONAPARTE.

Have ye thought well of what ye do, who
    name
Defiance to the great imperial power
Which made and can unmake ye in a day?

CARDINAL.

We have weighed all.   We know thy boasted
    strength.
We who defy the Devil and all his works
Are not to quail at any lesser hand,
However evil and however strong.

BUONAPARTE.

Pause there.   Now, not to question in the
    dark,
Open thy mouth and give thy wrongs a
    name.

CARDINAL.

Read them, Sire! By his Holiness' own hand
Writ on the scroll thou holdest.   I am come
If thou wouldst question any issue there.

BUONAPARTE.

I question every scratch, Lord Cardinal!
Theme, title, every word and character,
First scrawl to last, down to the last round
      oath
Whereby thy moon-struck master styles him-
      self
Christ's Vicar and my peer.   He lectures me
As tho' I were a schoolboy and high dunce
Of all earth's dunces!   Let him look to it,
Or by St. Peter and his rusty Key,
That turns so slowly in the lock of Heaven,
This hand shall set the foolscap on his head
And fix a scarecrow on the heights of Rome
For all the world to point at passing by!

CARDINAL.

Blaspheme not, lest God's Angels strike thee
      down.

BUÒNAPARTE.

God's Angels never came to the thin squeak
Of trebly dotard and degenerate Rome.

Return to him who sent thee; tell him so.

Tell him, moreover, as thou lovest him,

Some further truths his tipsy soul forgets.

Who set him on his semi-regal seat?

Who propt up his stale scarecrow of a creed

Again within the hollow Vatican?

Who by a lifted finger can and will

Consign both Pope and Rome to sudden
doom,

Early oblivion, and the parting curse

Of all the Rome-sick lands of Christendom?

Ask him these questions, and be answer'd
straight,

By bloodless cheek, wild eye, and quivering
lips

That flutter with the name they fear to
speak.

CARDINAL.

One Name alone hath power to shake him
so;

And 'tis a Name which, spoken audibly,

Shall yet shake *thee* too, even were thy
throne

Rooted as deep as the slow fires of Hell,

And towering high as the proud arch of
Heaven.

Napoleon, beware the wrath of God!

Farewell!

BUONAPARTE.

Stay!—Stay, old man; thou shalt not stir,

Till thou hast heard our message to the end.

Now, mark me, for I swear by Peter's pence

I am resolved. Your Pope, in this same
scroll,

Strings grievance upon grievance garru-
lously,

Thus ending, "What Rome was of old, Rome
is,

The mistress of the conscience of the world,

Spiritual sovereign of all human Kings,

And temporally subject unto none."

Further, this Pope, this apostolic echo,

Yielding no jot of any boon we crave,

Forgetful of his predecessor's doom,

Vows excommunication and God's wrath,

Curse by bell, book, and candle, all the old
Stale stuff of necromancy, if our foot
Encroaches further on the Papal soil,
If with our impious and heedless sword
We still imperil Holy Church's power,
Her fame, her name, her aim in Christendom.
Is this so? Have I phrased your thunder
    right?

CARDINAL.

All these things have we written down for
    truth.

BUONAPARTE.

Good.   Listen now to me.   Your Pope
    and I
Need waste no specious lying terms to
    mince
The matter of this creed whereby he swears:
First, friend, 'tis a bald theologic lie,
And next, a moral falsehood long detected,
And last, a practical impediment
To every step the blind old world would
    take

To Freedom.   Well, what then ?   I knew that
 well,
I knew by heart the nature of King Log,
When, that wild day in France, I thrust my
 hand
And pluckt him from the Fire, and set him up
There where he stands, my ninepin of a
 Pope
To trundle over with a cannon-ball !
I did not think the world of human souls
Was ready yet for the keen mountain air
Of Freedom ; I believed they must be bent
And driven ; and I saw in Graybeard
 Church
The rusty fetters fitted for my purpose,
St. Peter's, fasten'd as an ankle-chain
About the stumbling Soul ages ago
To keep its stray feet from the mountain tops.
Wherefore I said, " King Log shall serve my
 turn,
Shall sit and scatter unction as he lists,
And I will sprinkle o'er the continents
Cardinals, bishops, priests, all lesser logs,
To fool the people with their feast-day shows,

And hold the wild geese back from anarchy."
So said, so done. Pope Pius ruled at Rome,
By grace of God and Buonaparté; France
Took back her dolls and idols ; the old door
Of knowledge creak'd and closed again on
    Man ;
And, used as scarecrows on earth's harvest
    fields,
Your vestments frighten'd off the last black
    birds
Of Revolution. In the lull I throve,
Giving men greater gifts than liberty,—
Food, power, and glory,—till, behold, my
    rule
Took form and consecration, shot its
    branches
O'er the green western world, slew one by
    one
Its enemies half hearted, and this day,
Here in Germania, yonder over France,
North, south, east, west, a mighty sword-
    sweep round,
The Empire shines, great heart of Christen-
    dom ;

Shines, still expanding by the law of growth,

Larger and richer, taking and giving forth

Light, like the sun at mid-day.   Even now,

At our full noon of glory, rises up

King Log, my creature, casting as he stands

The shadow six-foot long of his own grave,

And crying, " I am greater—I by grace

Of God supremer—I by sun and star,

The light, the soul, the head of Christendom ! "

Therefore I answer, "To thy puddle, Log !

The frogs will worship thee with their old
    croak ;

But, meantime, lest thou perish quite, be-
    gone—

Out of my sunshine ! "

CARDINAL.

              O proud man, beware !

Innumerable evil stars like thine

Have shot across the welkin and been lost,

Empire on empire hath been heap'd to dust,

Century hath been crusht on century,—

But Rome abides imperishably fair,

Based on the crystal Rock of holy thought.

The Figure thronëd on the blessed Seat

Hath changed as the swift generations
  change ;

But still the Seat stands, and the Rock en-
  dures,

And ever cometh God's Hierophant

To reign there, flashing thence mysterious
  light

Into the consciences of all earth's Kings.

Against thy sword the Figure sitting there

Doth interpose the incorporeal Soul,

A thing thou canst not slay by any steel,

A shape which has abided from the first

And shall abide when thou art back to dust.

When thou wouldst trench on the divine
  domain,

And be a second conscience to the world,

God's Vicar, perishable form and sign

Of the imperishable faith of man,

Doth in the very Soul's name bid thee pause.

BUONAPARTE.

Thou comest a few centuries too late

To interpose against the might of Kings

II

A shadow, such a shadow, the mere ghost
Seen by a shivering coward in the dark.
Old man, the world and I have wholly lost
Our faith in spectres, and philosophers
Aver this thing ye christen Soul, to awe
The world by, is but lustre given out
By bodies, like the phosphorescent light
Shed forth by certain jellies in the sea.
Be that pure fiction or a dim-seen truth
We fear no terror incorporeal,
Which, like your own in Rome, abides
    unseen,
Silent and physically impotent.

CARDINAL.

Is this thine answer to the Pope of Rome?

BUONAPARTE.

No!—Tell God's Vicar, as he styles himself,
That when in guise of priestly sanctity
And in humility he seeks the ear
Of Buonaparte, when he comes in love

Grateful for service and for very life,

We will incline our will unto his wish,

And as our equal meet and cherish him ;

But coming with toy-thunderbolt in hand,

With haughty looks and spiritual pride,

He shall be cast again into the fire

From which we snatch'd his body long ago.

In brief, another word such as these words

That we have read and thou hast echoëd,

And we will seize him in the heart of Rome,

And hale him screaming up and down the
    earth

A captive fastened to the fiery heels

Of conquest, and of all his Cardinals

Will make a bonfire that shall gladden Man

Where'er the false and juggling creed of
    Rome

Hath cast its shadow on the human heart !

CARDINAL.

These mad words will I straightway bear to
    Rome,

And be thou sure that there shall come full
    soon

A direr, darker, and less drunken hour,
When thou, no longer mad with fancied
    height
And stolen glory, shalt bewail the day
When thou did'st raise thy impious eyes so
    high,
And cast aside in recklessness of power
Thy deepest strength—Rome's prayers and
    silent aid.

BUONAPARTE.

Go!

CARDINAL.

I obey, leaving God's curse behind,
To trouble thee in thy supremest hour.

CHORUS.

SEMI-CHORUS I.

Echo the curse!

SEMI-CHORUS II.

Ah nay, ah nay!
Curse not, but rather wait and pray.

SEMI-CHORUS I.

Echo the curse!

SEMI-CHORUS II.

O echo not
That which shameth human thought—
'Tis so easy and so vain
To curse, and all may curse again!

SEMI-CHORUS I.

Echo the curse!

SEMI-CHORUS II.

Away, away!
Curse not, but turn to God and pray.
What would ye curse? The wintry snow,
The rain that falls, the winds that blow,
All mighty things that come and go;—
Your curses cannot cast them low.

SEMI-CHORUS I.

What shall avail, if this be so?

SEMI-CHORUS II.

It hath been written from the first
He who deals curses shall be curst;
Strike, but blaspheme not; overcast
King, Pope, and Idol, first and last;
Strike more, curse less; for ah, man's curse
Wearies the soul-sick universe.

SEMI-CHORUS I.

Echo the curse!   Lo, where he stands,
Casting o'er many weary lands
Darkness like blood; before his frown
And the fierce brightness of his crown
All withers!—curse him!   Drag him down!

VOICES.

Shall not man's curses drag him down?

SEMI-CHORUS II.

Never—O hush and cease!
Wait, pray, and be at peace.

A Voice.

Peace?

Semi-Chorus II.

Is God a tempest that ye call so loud?
Is God a whirlwind or a thunder-cloud?—
Is God an avalance that a mere cry
May loosen from the cold heights of the
    sky,
To fall at your wild will and crush the
    proud?

Nay, He is none of these. But soon or late,
Being the dark strength of inadequate
And seeming-vanquish'd things, He works his
    will:
Mad words avail not. He is deep and still,
Subtle as Love and sure of foot as Fate.

He is the gentle force destroying wrong
As water weareth stone; secret, yet strong;

Mighty, yet merciful; He is the dew
Round the King's feet, suck'd up into the
    blue,
Grown to the thunderbolt whose flash ere long

Strikes the King dead. But pray ye loud or
    low,
He will not hasten help or lessen woe—
He slayeth all things by the secret law
Through which He made them and from which
    they draw
Light, strength, and life; all these being gone,
    they go.

If it will cheer your hearts while ye wait here,
Pray, but of cursing comes no sort of cheer.
God works within all wrongs, and wastes in-
    deed
The secret force on which they live and feed;
This being withdrawn, they die and disappear.

SEMI-CHORUS I.

Shall we then wait with folded hands
Impotent, while the tyrant stands

Lord of the earth and air and brine—
Shall we then wait and make no sign?

A VOICE.

Echo Rome's curse!

SEMI-CHORUS I.

Yea,—at his frown
And at the brightness of his crown
All withers; curse him, drag him down—

A VOICE.

Shall not our curses drag him down?

SEMI-CHORUS II.

Nay, but arise, if so your hearts aspire,
Arise and strike him down with sword and
fire.
God gave ye hands for that, God made ye
strong,
Body and soul, to rise and right your wrong;
But on the burning flame of your desire

Fear falls like salt.   What shall avail your
    sighs
And imprecations if ye will not rise,
Lords of your living wills and hands of might?
Man knows no wrong but man himself may
    right,
Being a Titan who sits down and cries

Like a sick weary child upon the ground,
And knoweth not his strength, and gazeth
    round
On water, earth, and heaven, with blind sick
    stare:
Though of a glorious kingdom he is heir,
And all things free await to see him crown'd.

Echo Rome's curse?   O weary sons of man,
Echo no more as any cavern can—
For have ye not been echoing day by day
Whatever idle sound hath blown your way,
Gentle or awful, since the world began?

God gave ye living wills for other aim,
Voices for other sounds than moans of blame,

Hands for more use than folding on the
    breast;
Daily the sun goes down into the west—
How long shall it go down upon your shame?

For if on any day ye would be free,
If any day with one voice like the sea
Ye do demand your freedom every one,—
Utter the word, 'tis given, all is done,
And ye share freedom with all things that be.

But now ye yield to wild divided cries—
Broken abroad and echoing any lies;—
A thousand feeble voices go and come,
But to your own souls' utterance ye are
    dumb,—
For that all wait,—earth, ocean, air, and
    skies:

All lesser things that flit 'tween pole and pole,
All liberated things that leap and roll
Unfetter'd under yonder heaven, await
The one free voice triumphant over Fate,
The one free voice of Man, the Life, the Soul.

Semi-Chorus I.

Are we not bound?

Semi-Chorus II.

                    Ye are not bound;
Ye cry, ye follow empty sound,
This way and that way, round and round.

Semi-Chorus I.

Have we not sought and never found?
Are we not chain'd and undertrod
By God and Man?

Semi-Chorus II.

                    By Man, not God—
By your own hands, by your own will,
Are your bonds fashion'd, and no skill
But yours can break them. Slaves! still griev-
        ing,

Impotent, trembling, self-deceiving,
Over the woes of your own weaving!
Gull'd by false creeds and moral lies,
Changeful as are the April skies,
At all times weak and never wise!
Standing beside Time's running River,
Seeing your own shades there for ever,
Knowing them not for what they be,
And blaming them most bitterly!
O hush, blaspheme no more—your curse
Wearies the soul-sick universe:
Curses of every creed that Man
Hath built to God since time began,
From Israël's first curse of power
Down to the curse of Rome this hour.
Hush, let God be; the voice ye raise
Hinders His work in secret ways;
Strike ye at wrong with all your might,
And if ye fail to set it right,
Pray if ye list—no prayer is ill;
But curse not what ye cannot kill:—
Leave it to God, whose law alone
Wears it, as water weareth stone.

BUONAPARTE.

The cup is overflowing.   Pour, pour yet,
My Famulus—pour with free arm-sweep still,
And when the wine is running o'er the brim,
Sparkling with golden bubbles in the sun,
I will stoop down and drink the full great
    draught
Of glory, and as did those heroes old
Drinking ambrosia in the happy isles,
Dilate at once to perfect demigod.
Meantime, I feast my eyes as the wine runs
And the cup fills.   Fill up, my Famulus !
Pour out the precious juice of all the earth,
Pour with great arm-sweep, that the world
    may see.

O Famulus—O Spirit—O good Soul,
Come close to me and listen—curl thyself
Up in my breast—let us drink ecstasy
Together ; for the charm thou taughtest me
Is working like slow poison in the veins

Of the great nations: each, a wild-beast
  tamed,
Looks mildly in mine eyes and from my hand
Eats gently; and this day I speak the charm
To Russia, and, behold ! the crafty eyes
Blink sleepily, while on the fatal lips
Hovers the smile of appetite half-fed,
Half-hungry : he being won, all else is won,
And at our feet, our veritable slave,
Lies Europe. Whisper now, Soul of my Soul,
Since we have won this Europe with the sword,
How we shall portion it to men anew.

First, in the centre of the West, I set
My signet like a star, and on a rock
Base the imperial Throne: seated whereon,
The royal crown of France upon my head,
At hand the iron crown of Lombardy,
And in my sceptre blended as a sign
The hereditary gems of Italy,
Spain, Holland, I shall see beneath my feet
My puppets sit with strings that reach my
  hand :
Murat upon the throne of Italy,

Jerome upon new-born Westphalia,

Louis the lord of Holland, and perchance

A kinsman in the Prussian dotard's place ;

And, lower yet, still puppets to my hand,

Saxony, Würtemberg, Bavaria,

The petty principalities and powers,

All smiling up in our hot thunderous
air ;—

And all the thrones, the kingdoms, and the
powers

That break to life beneath them, murmuring

"Hail, King of Europe—Emperor of the
West."

Thus far.   Still farther?   Driven to the
East,

First by fond cunning, afterwards by blows,

The Russian's eyes bloodshot with greed will
watch,

While still our flood-tide inexhaustible

Of Empire washes to the Danube, rolls

Into the Baltic, and with one huge wave

Covers the plains of Poland.   Then at last

The mighty Empires of the East and West

Shall clash together in the final blow,

And that which loses shall be driven on

To lead the heathen on in Asia,

And that which hurls the other to such doom

Shall be the chosen Regent of the World.

Shall this be so, O Spirit? Pour, O pour—

Yea, let me feast mine eyes upon the wine,

Albeit I drink not. See!—Napoleon,

Waif from the island in the southern sea,

Sun to whom all the Kings of the earth are
  stars,

Sword before which all earthly swords are
  straws,

Child of the Revolution, crown and head,

Heart, soul, arm, King, of all Humanity.

O Famulus—in God's name keep my soul

From swooning to vain-glory. I believe

God, not the other, sends thee, that thy mouth

May fill me with a message for the race,

And purge the peevish and distemper'd world

Of her hereditary plague of Kings.

For Man, I say, shall in due season grow

Back to the likeness that he wore at first,

One mighty nation peopling the green earth,

One equal people with one King and head,

One Kingdom with one Temple, and therein

No priest, no idol, no dark sacrifice,

But spheric music and the dreamy light

Of heaven's azure and the changeless stars.

The curse of earth hath been the folly of
    peace

Under vain rulers, so dividing earth,

That twenty thousand kings of Lilliput

Strutted and fretted heaven and teased the
    time,

Kept nature's skin for ever on the sting

Like vermin, and perplex'd humanity

With petty pangs and peevish tyranny,

While the soul sickened of obscure disease,

And the innumerable limbs of state

Moved paralysed, and half earth's system
    dead.

Came Revolution like avenging fire;

And in the red flash miserable men

Beheld themselves and wondered—saw their
    Kings

Still strutting lilliputian in the glare,—

And laugh'd till heaven rung,—gave one
    fierce look

To heaven, and rose. Outraged Columbia

Breath'd o'er the sea, and scorch'd the in-
    solent cheek

Of Albion. Albion paled before the flame.

The darken'd embers faded in the West,

And all was still again; when one mad
    morn

Men wakening, saw the heights of France
    afire !

Earth shook to her foundation, and the light

Illumed the hemispheres from west to east,

And men that walk beneath and under us,

Holding their heads to other stars, beheld

The glory flaming from the underworld.

The little Kings of Europe, lily-pale,

Scream'd shrill to one another. Germany

In her deep currents of philosophy

Mirror'd the fiery horror. Russia groaned,

Sheeted in snows that took the hue of blood

Under the fierce reflection. Italy,

Spain and the Tyrol, wild Helvetia,

Caught havoc; and even on the white Eng-
    lish crags
A few strong spirits, in a race that binds
Its body in chains and calls them Liberty,
And calls each fresh link Progress, stood
    erect
With faces pale that hunger'd to the light.
Then, like a hero in his anguish, burnt
Poor gentle Louis, whom the stars destined
To be a barber and who was a King,
And as he flamed and went like very straw,
Earth shriek'd and fever'd France grew
    raving mad.

Pass o'er the wild space of delirium,
When France upon her stony bed of pain
Raved, screamed, blasphemed, was medicined
    with blood,
Forgot all issues and the course of time;
And come to that supremer, stiller hour
When, facing these fierce wasps of Kings
    who flocked
To sting the weary sufferer to death,
I rose and stood beside her, drove them back

So! with a sword-sweep.   Those were merry
    days,
My Spirit! These were spring days, winds of
    war
Sharp-blowing, but the swallow on the way
Already bringing summer from the south!
Then one by one I held these little Kings
Between my fingers and inspected them
Like curious insects, while with buzz and
    squeak
Their tiny stings were shooting in and out;
And how I laugh'd
To think such wretched vermin had so long
Tortured unhappy Man, and to despair
Driven him and his through infinite ways of
    woe,
When with one sweep of his great arm, one
    blow
Of his sharp palm, he might annihilate
Such creatures by the legion and in sooth
Exterminate the breed.   O Spirit of Man!
A foolish Titan! foolish now as then,   '
Guided about the earth like a blind man
By any hand that leads,

And then and now unconscious of a frame
Whose strength, into one mighty effort
    gathered,
Might shake the firmament of heaven itself!

Well, we have done this service. We have
    freed
Earth from its pest of kings, so that they crawl
Powerless and stingless; we have medicined
Desperate disease with awful remedies;
And lo, the mighty Spirit of mankind
Has stagger'd from the sick-bed to his feet,
And feebly totters, picking darken'd steps,
And while I lead him on scarce sees the sun,
But questions feebly " whither?"   Whither?
    Indeed
I am dumb, and all earth's voices are as dumb—
God is not dumber on his throne.   In vain
I would peer forward, but the path is black.
Ay,—whither?

        O what peevish fools are mortals,
Tormented by a raven on each shoulder,
" Whither?" and " wherefore?" Shall I stand
    and gape

At heaven, straining eyes into the tomb,

Like some purblind philosopher or bard

Asking stale questions of the Infinite

Dumb with God's secret? questioning the
    winds,

The waves, the stars, all things that live and
    move,

All signs, all augurs? Never yet hath one

Accorded   answer.   "Whither?"   Death
    replies

With dusky smile. "Wherefore?" the echoes
    laugh

Their "wherefore? wherefore?" Of the
    time unborn,

And of the inevitable law, no voice

Bears witness. The pale Man upon the
    Cross

Moan'd,— and beheld no further down the
    Void

Than those who gather'd round to see him
    die.

Ay,—but the Soul, being weather-wise, can
    guess

The morrow by the sunset, can it not?
And there are signs about the path whereon
I guide the foolish Titan, that imply
Darkness and hidden dangers.   All these last
I smile at; but, O Soul within my Soul,
'Tis he, the foolish Titan's self, I fear;
For, though I have a spell upon him now,
And say it, and he follows, any morn
(Awakening from his torpor as he woke
One bloody morn in Paris and went wild),
He may put out his frightful strength again,
And with one mighty shock of agony
Bring down the roof of Empire on my head.
He loves me now, and to my song of war
Murmurs deep undertone, and as he goes
Fondles the hand that leads; but day by day
　　day
Must I devise new songs and promises,
More bloody incantation, lest he rouse
And rend me.   Oftentimes it seems he leads,
I follow,—he the tyrant, I the slave,—
And it, perchance, were better had I paused
At Amiens, nor with terrible words and
　　ways

Led him thus far, still whispering in his ear
That he at last shall look on " Liberty."

Liberty? Have I lull'd him with a Lie?
Or shall the Titan Spirit of Man be led
To look again upon the face of her,
His first last love, a spirit woman-shaped,
Whom in the sweet beginning he beheld,
Adored, loved, lost, pursued, whom still in
    tears
He yearns for, in whose name alone all
    Kings
Have led and guided him a space and
    throve,
Denying whom all Kings have died in turn,
Whose memory is perfume, light and dream,
Whose hope is incense, music, bliss, and
    tears,
To him whose great heart with immortal
    beat
Measures the dark march of humanity.
I do believe this shape he saw and loved
Was but a phantasm, unsubstantial, strange,
A vision never to be held and had,

A spectral woman ne'er to be enjoyed ;
But such a thought whisper'd into his ear
Were rank as blasphemy cried up at God.
The name is yet a madness, a supreme
Ecstasy and delirium !   All things
That cry it move the tears into the eyes
Of the sad Titan.   Echoed from the heights
Of France, it made him mad, and in his rage
He tore at earth's foundations.   Evermore
He turns his suffering orbs upon the dark,
Uplifts his gentle hands to the chill stars,
Pauses upon the path, and in the ear
Of him who leadeth cries with broken voice,
" How long, how long, how long ? "

                            And unto him,
This Titan, I, supreme of all the earth,
Am but a pigmy (let me whisper it!) ;
And I have won upon him with strange lies,
And he has suffer'd all indignities,
Bonds, chains, a band to blindfold both his
     eyes,
Patient and meek, since I have sworn at last
To lead him to the trysting-place where waits

His constant love and most immortal bride.
Still in mine ears he murmureth her name,
And follows.   I have led him on through fire,
Blood, darkness, tears, and still he hath been
    tame,
Tho' ofttimes shrinking from things horrible,
And on and on he follows even now,
Blindfold, with slower and less willing feet—
I fear with slower and less willing feet—
And still I lead, thro' lurid light from
    heaven,
Whither I know not. "Whither!" Oftentimes
My great heart fails, lest on some morn we
    reach
That portal o'er which flaming Arch is writ,
" All hope abandon ye who enter here ! "
And he, perceiving he hath been befool'd,
Will cast me from him with his last fierce
    breath
Down thro' the gate into the pit of doom.

Meantime he follows smiling.   O Famulus!
Could I but dream that she, the shape he
    seeks,

Whom he names Liberty, and gods name
   Peace,
Were human, could inhale this dense dark
   air,
Could live and dwell on earth and rear the
   race,
'Twere well,—for by Almighty God I swear
I would find out a means to join their
   hands
And bless them, and abide their grateful
   doom.
But she he seeks I know to be a dream,
A vision of the rosy morning mist,
A creature foreign to the earth and sea,
Ne'er to be look'd upon by mortal soul
Out of the mortal vision.   Wherefore still
I fear the Titan.   I can never appease
His hungry yearning wholly.   He will bear
No future chains, no closer blindfolding,
And if a fatal whisper reach his ear,
I and all mine are wholly wreck'd and lost.

Yet is this Titan old so weak of wit,
So senile-minded though so huge of frame,

So deaf to warning voices when they cry,

That, should no angel light from heaven and
   speak

The mad truth in his ear, he will proceed

Patiently as a lamb.   He counteth not

The weary years; his eyes are shut indeed

With a half smile, to see the mystic face

Pictured upon his brain; only at times

He lifteth lids and gazeth wildly round,

Clutching at the cold hand of him that
   guides,—

But with a whisper he is calm'd again,

Relapsing back into his gentle dream.

O he is patient, and he will await

Century after century in peace,

So that he hears sweet songs of her he seeks,

So that his guides do speak to him of her,

So that he thinks to clasp her in the end.

The end? Sweet sprite, the end is what I
   fear—

If I might live for ever, Famulus!—

Why am I not immortal and a god?

I have caused tears enough, as bitter tears

As ever by the rod divine were struck
Out of this rock of earth.   O for a spell
Wherewith to cheat old Death, whose feet I
    hear
Afar off, for I hate the bony touch
Of hands that change the purple for the
    shroud !
Yet I could go in peace (since all must go)
So that my seed were risen and in its eyes
I saw assurance of imperial thoughts,
Strength, and a will to grasp the thunderbolt
I leave unhurl'd beside the Olympian throne.
Ah God, to die, and into the dark gloom
Drag that throne with me, to the hollow laugh
Of the awakening Titan !   All my peers
Are   ciphers,   all   my   brethren   are   mere
    Kings
Of the old fashion, only strengthen'd now
By my strong sunshine; reft of that, they
    die,
Like sunflowers in the darkness. Death, old
    Death,
Touch me this day, or any dark day soon,
And I and mine are like the miser's hoard,

A glorious and a glittering pile of gold

Changed to a fluttering heap of wither'd
    leaves.

This must not be. No, I must have a child.

I must be firm and from my bed divorce

The barren woman. Furthermore, to link

My Throne with all the lesser thrones of earth,

I must wed the seed of Kings. Which seed,
    which child?

Which round ripe armful of new destiny?

Which regal mould for my imperial issue?

Thine, fruitful house of Hapsburg? Russia,
    thine?

The greater, not the lesser. I must wed

Seed of the Czar, and so with nuptial rites

Unite the empires of the East and West.

Fill, fill, my Famulus, the golden cup

I thirst for; all the peril as I gaze

Hath faded. I no more with fluttering lips

Cry "Whither?" but with hands outstretch'd
    I watch

Rubily glistening glory. It shall thrive!

King of the West, sowing the seed of Kings!
First of the Empire of the Golden Age,
The sleeping Titan, and the quiet Sea;
Light of the Lotus and all mortal eyes,
Whose orbit nations like to heliotropes
Shall follow with lesser circle and sweet sound!

CHORUS.

SEMI-CHORUS I.

Form of her the Titan full of patience
Sees amid the darkness of the nations;
Voice of her whose sound in the beginning
Came upon him desolate and sinning;
Face of her and grace of her whose gleaming
Soothes his gentle spirit into dreaming;
Spirit whom the Titan sees above him!

SEMI-CHORUS II.

Gentle eyes that shine and seem to love him!
Tender touch, the touch of her quick fingers,
Touch that reach'd his soul and burns and
        lingers;
Breath of her, and scent of her, and bliss of
        her;

Dream of her, and smile of her, and kiss of
  her!
Come again, and speak, and bend above him,
Spirit that came once and seemed to love him.

A Voice.

How long, how long?

Semi-Chorus I.

Courage, great heart and strong,
Break not, but beat low chime
To the dark flow of Time;
Follow the path foot-worn,
Sad night and dewy morn,
Under the weary sun
Follow, O mighty one;
Under dim moon and star!

.

A Voice.

Whither? How far, how far?

Semi-Chorus I.

Spirit of the fathomless abysses,
Spirit that he looked upon and misses,

K

Free and fair and perfect, more than human,

Bringing love and peace-gifts like a woman ;

Come unto him, listen to his pleading.

Semi-Chorus II.

Mark his patience, hear his gentle interceding ;

O'er mountain upon mountain left behind
thee,

He hath cheerly climb'd in vain to find
thee :

Wild waters he hath cross'd, wild sea and
river,

All countries he hath traversed, faithful ever,

Ever hoping, ever waiting, never seeing.

Chorus.

Spirit seen in some long-darken'd being,

Spirit that he saw at the world's portal,

Saw, and knew, and loved, and felt immortal,

Spirit that he wearies for and misses,

Answer from the fathomless abysses !

A Voice.

How long, how long?

Semi-Chorus I.

Courage, O Titan strong!
Courage, from place to place
Still follow the voice and the face!

A Voice.

Whither?

Second Voice.

O hither!

First Voice.

Whither?

Semi-Chorus I.

Voice of her he follows in dumb pleasure,
Camest thou from the earth or from the azure;
Camest thou from the pastures on the moun-
tains,
From the ocean, from the rivers, from the
fountains,

From the vapours blowing o'er him while he
    hearkens,
From the ocean hoar that beats his feet and
    darkens,
From the star that on the sea-fringe melts
    and glistens?

SEMI-CHORUS II.

O homeless voice, he maddens as he listens,
O voice divine, his wild lips part asunder;
He speaketh, and his words are a low
    thunder.

A VOICE.

Whither, O whither?

SECOND VOICE.

        Hither!

FIRST VOICE.

Whither? Wherefore, while I wait in patience,
Mock her voice, O voices of the nations;
    Wherefore by night and day,
    Where'er my slow feet stray,
Trouble all hours with wild reverberations.

Mountain winds, ye name her name unto me
Flowing rivers glance and thrill it thro' me !

Earth, water, air, and sky,

Name her as I go by !
With her dim ghost the floating clouds pursue me !

All of these have seen her face and love her,
Earth beneath and heaven that bends above
her ;

The rain-wreck and the storm

Mimic the one fair form,
The whirlwind knows her name and cries it
over.

Flowers are sown by her bright foot wherever
They are flashing past by mere and river ;

Birds in the forest stir,

Singing mad praise of her;
All green paths know her, tho' she flies for
ever.

CHORUS.

Joy of wind and wave and cloud and blossom,
Pause at last and fall upon his bosom !

First Voice.

None behold her twice, but having conn'd her,
While she flashes past with feet that wander,
    Remember the blest gleam,
    And grow by it and dream,
And fondle the sweet memory and ponder.

All have known her, and yet none possess
    her;
None behold her, yet all things caress her;
    The warmth of her white feet,
    Where it doth fall so sweet,
Abides for ever there, and all things bless her.

Faster than the prophesying swallow,
Fast by wood and sea and hill and hollow,
    Sought by all things that be,
    But most of all by me,
She flieth none know whither, and I follow.

Semi-Chorus I.

    O wherefore, radiant one,
    Under the moon and sun,
    Glimmer away?

SECOND VOICE.

Here on the heights I stay ;
Come hither.

FIRST VOICE.

Whither ?

SECOND VOICE.

O hither !

CHORUS.

Form of her the Titan full of patience
Sees amid the darkness of the nations ;
Voice of her whose song in the beginning
Came upon him desolate and sinning ;
Face of her and grace of her whose gleaming
Soothes his gentle spirit into dreaming ;
Touch of her, the touch of her quick fingers,
Touch that reach'd his soul and burns and
    lingers ;
Breath of her, and scent of her, and bliss of
    her,
Dream of her, and gleam of her, and kiss of
    her !

Soul beyond his soul, yet ever near it,
His heart's home, and haven of his spirit;
Joy of wind and wave and cloud and blossom,
Pause at last, and fall upon his bosom!

END OF THE FIRST PART.

CHORIC INTERLUDE:

THE TITAN.

CHORIC INTERLUDE.

CHORUS.

STRANGE hands are passed across our eyes,
Before our souls strange visions rise
   And dim shapes come and flee.
The mists of dream are backward roll'd—
As from a mountain we behold
   What is, and yet shall be.

A VOICE.

Speak! while the depths of dreams unfold,
   What is it that ye see?

SEMI-CHORUS I.

'Tis vision. Lo, before us stands,
Casting his shade on many lands,

The mighty Titan, by the sea
Of tempest-tost humanity ;
And to the earth, and sea, and sky,
He uttereth a thunder-cry
   Out of his breaking heart,
And the fierce elements reply,
   And earth is cloven apart.

SEMI-CHORUS II.

Like sparks blown from a forge, the spheres
Drift o'er us ;—all our eyes and ears
   Are full of fire and sound.
With blood about him blown like rain,
We see upon a darken'd plain
   Another Shape, but crown'd.
Silent he waits, and white as death,
   Looks in the Titan's eyes.
They stand—the black sky holds its breath—
   The deep sea stills its cries,
The mad storm hushes driving past,
The sick stars pause and gaze—the blast,
The wind-rent rain, the vapours dark,
Like dead things crouch, and wait, and hark ;

And lo! those twain alone and dumb
  Loom desolate and strange.

SEMI-CHORUS I.

Is the time come ?

SEMI-CHORUS II.

    The time is come.

CHORUS.

Titan, to thy revenge!

SEMI-CHORUS I.

O look and listen !
His great eyes glisten,
Like an oak the storm rendeth
He swayeth and bendeth,
With lips torn asunder
He shakes, but no thunder
Comes thence.

SEMI-CHORUS II.

    While still nigh him,
With smiles that defy him,

The crown'd one is standing,—
His pale look commanding
A tigress that crouching
Beneath him and touching
   His feet with low cries,
Waits, fiercely betraying
Blood's thirst yet obeying
   His eyes.

CHORUS.

Is he doom'd?

A VOICE.

He is doom'd.

CHORUS.
Oh, by whom?

VOICE.

By the child yet unborn in the womb,
By the dead laid to sleep in the tomb,
He is doom'd, he is doom'd.

CHORUS.

Speak his doom!

First Voice.

Napoleon ! Napoleon !

Second Voice.

Who cries ?

First Voice.

I, child of the earth and the skies,
I, Titan, the mystical birth,
Whose voice since the morning of earth
Hath doom'd such as thou in the end,
Speak thy doom !

Second Voice.

Speak !   I smile and attend.

First Voice.

Because thou hast with lies and incantations,
With broken vows and false asseverations,
    For thine own ends accurst,
    Betrayed me from the first,
I speak and doom thee, in the name of
    nations.

Because I have wander'd like a great stream
    flowing
From its own channel and thro' strange
    gulfs going,
  So that for years and years
  I must retrace in tears
The black and barren pathway of thy show-
    ing.

Because one further step after thy leading
Had hurl'd me down to doom past interced-
    ing,
  So that I never again,
  In passion or in pain,
Might look upon the face I follow pleading.

Because thou hast led me blind knee-deep
    thro' slaughter,
Thro' fields of blood that wash'd our way like
    water,
  Because in that divine
  Name I adore, and mine,
Thou hast bruised Earth, and to desolation
    brought her.

Because thou hast been a liar and blas-
    phemer,
Deeming me trebly dotard and a dreamer.
  Because thy hand at length
  Would strike me in my strength,
Me, deathless! me, diviner and supremer!

Because all voices of the earth and azure,
All things that breathe, all things curst for
    thy pleasure,
  All poor dead men who died
  To feed thy bitter pride,
All living, all dead, cry—mete to him our
    measure.

Because thou hast slain Kings, and as a
    token
Stolen their crowns and worn them, having
    spoken
  My curse against the same;
  Because all things proclaim
That thou didst swear a troth, and that 'tis
    broken.

L

By her whom thou didst swear under God's
    heaven
To find; by her who being found was driven
  O'er earth, air, sky, and sea,
  Thro' desolate ways by thee,
With voice appealing and with raiment
    riven!

Because thou hast turned upon and violated
Her soul to whom thou first wert conse-
    crated,
  Because thro' thy soul's lie
  And life's delusion, I
Must wait more ages who have wept and
    waited

Since the beginning. By the soul of Patience
Sick of thy face and its abominations,
  I speak on thine and thee
  The doom of destiny,
Hear it, and die, hear in the name of na-
    tions.

SEMI-CHORUS I.

Is he doom'd?

SEMI-CHORUS II.

He is doom'd. 'Tis the end.

FIRST VOICE.

Napoleon!

SECOND VOICE.

Speak! I attend.

FIRST VOICE.

Utter the doom thou dost crave.

SECOND VOICE.

'Tis spoken. A shroud and a grave.

FIRST VOICE.

O voices of earth, air, and sky,
Hear ye his doom, and reply.

VOICES.

Death is sleep. Let him wake and not die.

FIRST VOICE.

Because by thee all comfort hath been taken,
So that the Earth rocks still forlorn and
    shaken,
  Staring at the sad skies
  With sleepless aching eyes,
Thou shalt not die, but wait and watch and
    waken.

This is thy doom.   Lone as a star thy being
Shall see the waves break and the drift-cloud
    fleeing,
  Hear the wind cry and grow,
  Watch the great waters flow,
And seeing all, shine hid from all men's
    seeing.

Here on this Isle amid a sea of sorrow
I cast thee down.   Black night and weary
    morrow,
  Lie there alone, forgot,
  So doom'd and pitied not;
Let all things watch thy face and thy face
    borrow

The look of these mad elements that ever
Strike, scream, and mingle, sever and dis-
      sever;
  Gather from air and sea
  The thirst of all things free,
The up-looking want, the hunger ceasing
      never.

All shall forget thee. Thou shalt hear the
      nations
Flocking with music light and acclamations
  To kiss his royal feet
  Who sitteth in thy Seat,
Surrounded by the slaves of lofty stations.

A rock in the lone sea shall be thy pillow.
In the wide waste of gray wave and green
      billow,
  The days shall rise and set
  In silence, and forget
To sun thee,—a black shape beneath a
      willow

Watching the weary waters with heart
    bleeding;
Or dreaming cheek upon thy hand; or
    reading
  The book upon thy knee;
  And ever as the sea
Moans, raising eyes to the still heaven, and
    pleading;

.

Till like a wave worn out with silent
    breaking;
Or like a wind blown weary; thou, forsaking
  Thy tenement of clay,
  Shalt wear and waste away,
And grow a portion of the ever-waking

Tumult of cloud and sea. Feature by feature
Losing the likeness of the living creature,
  Returning back thy form
  To its elements of storm,
Thou shalt dissolve in the great wreck of
    Nature.

SEMI-CHORUS I.

Is it done?

SEMI-CHORUS II.

It is done.

SEMI-CHORUS I.

Look again.

SEMI-CHORUS II.

I see on the rock in the main
The Shape sitting dark by the sea,
And his shade, and the shade of the tree
Where he sitteth, are pencil'd jet-black
On the bright purple sky at his back;
But lo! while I gaze, from the sky
Like phantoms they vanish and die :—
All is dark.

SEMI-CHORUS I.
Look again.

SEMI-CHORUS II.

Hark, O hark!

SEMI-CHORUS I.

A shrill cry is piercing the dark—
Like the multitudinous moan
Of the waves as they clash, comes a groan
From afar—

FIRST VOICE.

What is this, O ye free?

SEMI-CHORUS II.

He has gone like a wave of the sea—
Day dieth, the light falleth red,—
O Titan, behold he is dead! . . .

CHORUS.

Strange hands are passed across our eyes,
Before our souls strange visions rise,
  And dim shapes come and flee;
The mists of dream are backward rolled—
As from a mountain we behold
  That island in the sea.

SEMI-CHORUS I.

Now bow thy face upon thy breast,
O Titan, and bemoan thy quest!
O look not thither with thine eyes,
But lift them to the constant skies!

A VOICE.

What do ye see that thus to me
Ye turn and smile so bitterly?

SEMI-CHORUS I.

'Tis vision.   On that island bare
Sits one with face divinely fair,
   And pensive smiling lips;
And on her lap the proud head lies,
Pale with the seal on its proud eyes
   Of Death's divine eclipse;
All round is darkness of the sea,
And sorrow of the cloud.

SEMI-CHORUS II.

                              Yet she
Is making with her heavenly face
Sweetness like sunlight; and the place

Grows luminous; and the world afar
Looks thither as to some new star,
All wondering; and with lips of death
Men name one name beneath their breath,
Not cursing as of yore, for now
All the inexorable brow
Is mouldering marble.

SEMI-CHORUS I.

Hark, O hark,
A silver voice divides the dark!

A VOICE.

Hither, O hither!

ANOTHER VOICE.

Whither?

FIRST VOICE.

O sweet is sleep if sleep be deep,
And sweetest far to eyes that weep;
He who upon my breast doth creep
Shall close his weary eyes and sleep.

Yet he who seeks me shall not find,
And he who chains me shall not bind ;
For fleeter-footed than the wind
I still elude all human kind.

Yet when, soul-weary of the chase,
Falleth some man of mortal race,
I pause—I find him in his place,
I pause—I bless his dying face.

Whatsoever man he be,
I take his head upon my knee,
I give him words and kisses three,
Kissing I whisper, "Thou art free."

O free is sleep if sleep be deep !—
I soothe them sleeping, and I heap
Greenness above them, and they weep
No longer, but are free, and sleep.

O royal face and royal head !
O lips that thunder'd ! O eyes red
With nights of watch ! O great soul dead,
Thy blood is water, thy heart lead !

They doom'd thee in my name, but see
I doom thee not, but set thee free ;
Balm for all hearts is shed by me,
And for all spirits liberty.

He finds me least who loves me best,
His Soul in an eternal quest
Wails still, while one by one are prest
Tyrants, that hate me, to my breast.

The sad days fly—the slow years creep,
And he alone doth never sleep.
Would he might slumber and not weep.
O free is sleep, if sleep be deep.

SECOND VOICE.

Irene!

THE DRAMA OF KINGS.

PART II.

NAPOLEON FALLEN.

SPEAKERS.

————

NAPOLEON III.

AN OFFICER OF THE IMPERIAL STAFF.

A ROMAN CATHOLIC BISHOP.

A PHYSICIAN.

MESSENGERS.

CHORUS OF SPIRITS.

————

SCENE—*The Château of Wilhelmshöhe, in Cassel.*

TIME—1870, *shortly after the surrender of Sedan.*

CHORUS.

STRANGE are the bitter things
God wreaks on cruel Kings;
Sad is the cup drunk up
   By Kings accurst.
In secret ways and strong
God doth avenge man's wrong.
The least, God saith, is Death,
   And Life the worst.

Sit under the sweet skies ;
Think how Kings set and rise,
Think, wouldst thou know the woe
   In each proud breast?

M

Sit on the hearth and see
Children look up to thee—
Think, wouldst thou own a throne,
    Or lowly rest?

Ah, to grow old, grow old,
Upon a throne of gold—
Ah, on a throne, so lone,
    To wear a crown;
To watch the clouds, the air,
Lest storm be breeding there—
Pale, lest some blast may cast
    Thy glory down.

He who with miser's ken
Hides his red gold from men,
And wakes and grieves, lest thieves
    Be creeping nigh;
He who hath murder done,
And fears each rising sun,
Lest it say plain, "O Cain,
    Rise up and die!"

These and all underlings
Are blesseder than Kings,
For ah! by weight of fate
　　King's hearts are riven;
With blood and gold they too
Reckon their sad days thro'—
They fear the plan of man,
　　The wrath of heaven.

In the great lonely bed,
Hung round with gold and red,
While the dim light each night
　　Burns in the room,
They lie alone and see
The rustling tapestry,
Lest Murther's eyes may rise
　　Out of the gloom.

Dost thou trust any man?
Thou dost what no King can.
Friend hast thou near and dear?
　　A King hath none.

Hast thou true love to kiss?
A King hath no such bliss,
On no true breast may rest
   Under the sun.

Ah, to sit cold, sit cold,
Upon a throne of gold,
Forcing the while a smile
   To hide thy care;
To taste no cup, to eat
No food, however sweet,
But with a drear dumb fear,
   Lest Death be there!

Ah, to rule men, and know
How many wish thee low—
That, 'neath the sun, scarce one
   Would keep thee high:
To watch in agony
The strife of all things free,
To dread the mirth of Earth
   When thou shalt die!

Hast thou a hard straw bed ?
Hast thou thy crust of bread ?
And hast thou quaff'd thy draught
   Of water clear ?
And canst thou dance and sing ?—
O blesseder than a King !
O happy one whom none
   Doth hate or fear !

Wherefore, though from the strong
Thou sufferest deep wrong,
Tho' Kings, with ire and fire,
   Have wrought thee woe :
Pray for them ! for I swear
Deeply they need thy prayer—
Most in their hour of power,
   Least when cast low.

And when thou castest down
King, sceptre, throne, and crown,
Pause that same day, and pray
   For the accurst.

Ah, in strange ways and strong
God doth avenge man's wrong—
The least, God saith, is Death,
And Life the worst.

NAPOLEON. *A* PHYSICIAN.

PHYSICIAN.

The sickness is no sickness of the flesh,
No ailment such as common mortals feel,
But spiritual : 'tis thy fiery thought
Drying the wholesome humour of the veins,
Consuming the brain's substance, and from
    thence,
As flame spreads, thro' each muscle, vein,
    and nerve,
Reaching the vital members. If your High-
    ness
Could stoop from the tense strain of great
    affairs
To books and music, or such idle things
As wing the weary hours for lesser men !
Turn not thine eyes to France ; receive no
    news ;

Shut out the blinding gleam of battle; rest
From all fierce ache of thought; and for a
    time
Let the wild world go by.

NAPOLEON.

                    Enough, old friend :
Thine is most wholesome counsel.   I will
    seek
To make this feverish mass of nerve and
    thew,
This thing of fretful heart-beats,
Fulfil its functions more mechanically.
Farewell.

PHYSICIAN.

Farewell, Sire.   Brighter waking thoughts,
And sweeter dreams, attend thee !   [*Exit.*

NAPOLEON.

                    All things change
Their summer livery for the autumn tinge

Of wind-blown withering leaves. That man
    is faithful,—
I have been fed from his cold palm for
    years,
And I believe, so strongly use and wont
Fetter such natures, he would die to serve
    me ;
Yet do I see in his familiar eyes
The fatal pain of pity.   I have lain
At Death's door divers times, and he hath
    slowly,
With subtle cunning and most confident
    skill,
Woo'd back my breath, but never even
    then,
Tho' God's Hand held me down, did he regard
    me
With so intense a gaze as now, when
    smitten
By the mail'd hand of Man.   I am not
    dead !
Not dying ! only sick,—as all are sick
Who feel the mortal prison-house too weak
For the free play of Soul !   I eat and drink—

I laugh—I weep, perchance—I feel—I think—
I still preserve all functions of a man—
Yet doth the free wind of the fickle world
Blow on me with as chilly a respect
As on a nameless grave. Is there so sad
A sunset on my face, that all beholding
Think only of the morrow ?—other minds,
Other hearts, other hands ? Almighty God,
If I dare pray Thee by that name of God,
Strengthen me! blow upon me with Thy
    breath !
Let one last memorable flash of fire
Burst from the blackening brand !—

               Yes, sick—sick—sick ;
Sick of the world ; sick of the fitful fools
That I have played with ; sick, forsooth, of
    breath,
Of thought, of hope, of Time. I staked my
    Soul
Against a Crown, and won. I wore the
    Crown,
And 'twas of burning fire. I staked my
    Crown

Against a Continent, and lost. I am here;

Fallen, unking'd, the shadow of a power,

Yet not heart-broken—no, not heart-broken—

But surely with more equable a pulse

Than when I sat on yonder lonely Seat

Fishing for wretched souls, and for my
    sport,

Although the bait was dainty to the taste,

Hooking the basest only. I am nearer

To the world's heart than then; 'tis bitter
    bread,

Most bitter, yea, most bitter; yet I eat

More freely, and sleep safer. I could die
    now:

And yet I dare not die.

                    Maker of men!

Thou Wind before whose strange breath we
    are clouds

Driving and changing!—Thou who dost
    abide

While all the laurels on the brows of
    Kings

Wither as wreaths of snow!—Thou Voice that
    dwellest

In the high sleeping chambers of the great,

When council and the feverish pomp are
    hush'd,

And the dim lamp burns low, and at its side

The sleeping potion in a cup of gold :—

Hear me, O God, in this my travail hour!

From first to last, Thou knowest—yea, Thou
    knowest—

I have been a man of peace : a silent man,

Thought-loving, most ambitious to appease

Self-chiding fears of mental littleness,

A planner of delights for simple men—

In all, a man of peace. I struck one blow,

And saw my hands were bloody ; from that
    hour

I knew myself too delicately wrought

For crimson pageants ; yea, the sight of
    pain

Sicken'd me like a woman. Day and night

I felt that stain on my immortal soul,

And gloved it from the world, and dili-
    gently

Wrought the red sword of empire to a
    scythe

For the swart hands of husbandmen to reap
Abundant harvest.—Nay, but hear me swear,
I never dreamed such human harvests blest
As spring from that red rain which pours this
    day
On the fair fields I sowed. Never, O God,
Was I a butcher or a thing of blood ;
Always a man of peace :—in mine ambition
Peace-seeking, peace-engendering ;—till that
    day
I saw the half-unloosen'd hounds of War
Yelp on the chain and gnash their bloody
    teeth,
Ready to rend mine unoffending Child,
In whose weak hand the mimic toy of empire
Trembled to fall. Then feverishly I wrought
A weapon in the dark to smite those hounds
From mine imperial seat; and as I wrought
One of the fiends that came of old to Cain
Found me, and since I thirsted gave to me
A philtre, and in idiocy I drank :
When suddenly I heard as in a dream
Trumpets around me silver-tongued, and saw
The many-colour'd banners gleam in the sun

Above the crying legions, and I rode

Royal before them, drunk with light and
  power,

My boy beside me blooming like a rose

To see the glorious show. Yet God, my God,

Even then I swear the hideous lust of life

Was far from me and mine; nay, I rode
  forth,

As to a gay review at break of day,

A student dazzled with the golden glare,

Half conscious of the cries of those he ruled,

Half brooding o'er the book that he had left

Open within his chamber. "Blood may
  flow,"

I thought, " a little blood—a few poor drops,—

A few poor drops of blood: but they shall
  prove

Pearls of great price to buy my people peace;

The hounds of War shall turn from our fair
  fields,

And on my son a robe like this I wear

Shall fall, and make him royal for all
  time!"

O fool, fool, fool! What was I but a child,

Pleased beyond understanding with a toy,

Till in mine ears the scream of murther'd
    France

Rang like a knell. I had slain my best
    beloved!

The curse of blood was on mine hands again!

My gentle boy, with wild affrighted gaze,

Turn'd from his sire, and moaned; the hounds
    of War

Scream'd round me, glaring with their pitiless
    eyes

Innumerable as the eyes of heaven;

I felt the sob of the world's woe; I saw

The fiery rain fill all the innocent air;

And, feeble as a maid who hides her face

In terror at a sword-flash, conscience-struck,

Sick, stupefied, appalled, and all alone,

I totter'd, grasped the empty air,—and fell!

CHORUS.

Vast Sea of Life that 'neath the arc
    Of yonder glistening sky,
Rollest thy waters deep and dark,
    While windy years blow by:

On thy pale shore this night we stand,
And hear thy wash upon the sand.

Calm is thy sheet and wanly bright,
    Low is thy voice and deep ;
There is no child on earth this night
    Wrapt in a gentler sleep ;
Crouch'd like a hound thou liest now,
With eye upcast and dreadful brow.

O Sea, thy breast is deep and blest
    After a dreadful day ;
And yet thou listenest in thy rest
    For some sign far away ;
Watching with fascinated eyes
The uplifted Finger in the skies !

Who broods beside thee, with dark shade
    Upon the moonlit sands,
Who looks on thee with eyes afraid,
    And supplicating hands ?—
Creep closer, lap his feet, O Sea !
'Tis the sad Man of Destiny.

He says a word, he names a name,
    He cries to the Most High,
Half kneeling, torn with sudden shame,
    He utters his lone cry.
Thou watchest the blue heaven; but he,
Praying to heaven, watches thee.

He pleads to God, yet dares not lift
    His eyes to find the Face;
But rather, where the waters drift,
    Stands in a shadowy place,
And looking downward sees at last
Fragments of wreck thy waves upcast.

A hundred years thy still tides go
    And touch the self-same mark—
Thus far, no farther, may they flow
    And fall in light and dark;
The mystic water-line is drawn
By moonlit night and glimmering dawn.

Sure as a heart-beat year by year,
    Though winds and thunders call,
Be it storm or calm, the tides appear,
    Touch the long line and fall,

Liquid and luminously dim ;
And men build dwellings on their brim.

O well may this man wring his hands,
   And utter a wild prayer.
He built above thy lonely sands
   A Feast-house passing fair ;
It rose above thy sands, O Sea,
In a fair nook of greenery.

For he had watched thee many days,
   And mark'd thy weedy line,
And far above the same did raise
   His Temple undivine.
Throng'd with fair shapes of sin and guilt
It rose, most magically built.

Not to the one eternal Light,
   Lamp of both quick and dead,
Did he uprear it in thy sight,
   But with a smile he said :
" To the unvarying laws of Fate,
This Temple fair I dedicate.

N

"To that sure law by which the Sea
  Is driven to come and go
Within one mystic boundary,
  And can no further flow;
So that who knoweth destiny
May safely build, nor fear the Sea!"

O fool! O miserable clod!
  O creature made to die!
Who thought to mark the might of God
  And mete it with his eye;
Who measured God's mysterious ways
By laws of common nights and days.

O worm, that sought to pass God by,
  Nor feared that God's revenge:
The law within the law, whereby
  All things work on to change;
Who guessed not how the still law's course
Accumulates superfluous force;—

How for long intervals and vast
  Strange secrets hide from day,
Till Nature's womb upheaves to cast
  The gather'd load away;

How deep the very laws of life
Deposit elements of strife.

O many a year in sun and shower
　The quiet waters creep!—
But suddenly on some dark hour
　Strange trouble shakes the deep :
Silent and monstrous thro' the gloom
Rises the Tidal Wave for doom.

Then woe for all who, like this Man,
　Have built so near the Sea,
For what avails the human plan
　When the new force flows free ?
Over their bounds the waters stream,
And Empires crash and despots scream.

O, is it earthquake far below
　Where the still forces sleep ?
Doth the volcano shriek and glow,
　Unseen beneath the deep ?
We know not; suddenly as death
Comes the great Wave with fatal breath

God works his ends for ever thus,
   And lets the great plan roll.
He wrought all things miraculous,
   The Sea, the Earth, the Soul ;
And nature from dark springs doth draw
Her fatal miracles of law.

O well may this Man wring his hands,
   And utter a wild prayer ;
He built above the shifting sands
   A Feast-house passing fair.
Long years it stood, a thing of shame :
At last the mighty moment came.

Crashing like glass into its grave,
   Fell down the fair abode ;
The despot struggled in the wave,
   And swimming screamed to God.
And lo, the waters with deep roar
Cast the black weed upon the shore.

Then with no warning, as they rose,
   Shrunk back to their old bounds :
Tho' still with deep volcanic throes
   And sad mysterious sounds

They quake.   The Man upon their brim
Sees wreck of Empire washed to him.

Vast Sea of life, that 'neath the arc
    Of yonder glistening sky,
Spreadest thy waters strange and dark
    While windy years blow by,
Creep closer, kiss his feet, O Sea,
Poor baffled worm of Destiny !

Fain would he read with those dull eyes
    What never man hath known,
The secret that within thee lies
    Seen by God's sight alone ;
Thou watchest Heaven all hours ; but he,
Praying to Heaven, watches thee.

So will he watch with weary breath
    Musing beside the deep,
Till on thy shore he sinks in death,
    And thy still tides upcreep,
Raise him with cold forgiving kiss,
And wash his dust to the Abyss.

NAPOLEON. *A* BISHOP.

NAPOLEON.

Speak out thy tidings quickly,
How fares it with the Empress and my son ?

BISHOP.

Well, Sire. They bid thee look thy fate in
    the face,
And be of cheer.

NAPOLEON.

Where didst thou part with them ?

BISHOP.

In England, Sire, where they have found a
    home
Among the frozen-blooded islanders,
Who yesterday called blessings on thy brow,
And now rejoice in thy calamity.
Thus much thy mighty lady bade me say,
If I should find thee private in thy woe :—

With thy great name the streets are garru-
    lous :
Mart, theatre, and church, palace and prison,
Down to the very commons by the road
Where Egypt's bastard children pitch their
    tents,
Murmur "Napoleon ; " but, alas ! the sound
Is as an echo that with no refrain,
No loving echo in a living voice,
Dies a cold death among the mountain
    snow.

NAPOLEON.

Old man, I never looked for friendship there,
I never loved that England in my heart ;
Tho' twas by such a sampler I believed
To weave our France's fortunes thriftily
With the gold tissues of prosperity.

BISHOP.

Ah, Sire, if I dare speak—

NAPOLEON.
          Speak on.

BISHOP.

Too much
Thine eyes to that cold isle of heretics
Turn'd from thy throne for use and precedent;
Too little did they look, and that too late,
On that strong rock whereon the Lord thy God
Hath built His Holy Church.

NAPOLEON.

Something of this
I have heard in happier seasons.

BISHOP.

Hear it now
In the dark day of thine adversity.
O Sire, by him who holds the blessed Keys,
Christ's Vicar on the earth for blinded men,
I do conjure thee, hearken—with my mouth,
Tho' I am weak and low, the Holy Church
Cries to her erring son!

NAPOLEON.

Well, well, he hears.

BISHOP.

Thou smilest, Sire. With such a smile, so
    grim,
So bitter, didst thou mock our blessed cause
In thy prosperity.

NAPOLEON.

      False, Bishop, false !
I made a bloody circle with my sword
Round the old Father's head, and so secured
    him
Safe on his tottering Seat against the world,
When all the world cried that his time was
    come.
What then ? He totter'd on. I could not
    prop
His Seat up with my sword, that Seat being
    built,
Not on a rock, but sand.

BISHOP.

      The world is sick
And old indeed, when lips like thine blas-
    pheme.

Whisper such words out on the common air,

And, as a child,

Blow thy last hopes away.

NAPOLEON.

Hopes, hopes !   What hopes ?

What knowest thou of hopes ?

BISHOP.

Thy throne was rear'd

(Nay hear me, Sire, in patience to the end)

Not on the vulgar unsubstantial air

Which men call Freedom, not on half consent

Of unbelievers—tho', alas ! thou hast stoop'd

To smile on unbelievers—not on lives

That saw in thee one of the good and wise,

Not wholly on the watchword of thy name ;

But first on this—the swords thy gold could

buy,

And most and last, upon the help of those

Who to remotest corners of our land

Watch o'er the souls of men, sit at their

hearths,

Lend their solemnity to birth and death,
Guide as they list the motions of the mind,
And as they list with darkness or with light
Appease the spiritual hunger. Where
Had France been, and thou, boasted Sun of
 France,
For nineteen harvests, save for those who
 crept
Thine agents into every cottage-door,
Slowly diffusing thro' each vein of France
The sleepy wine of empire? Like to slaves
These served thee, used thy glory for a charm,
Hung up thine image in a peasant's room
Beside our blessed Saints, and cunningly,
As shepherds drive their sheep unto the
 fold,
Gather'd thy crying people where thy hand
Might choose them out for very butchery.
Nay, more; as fearful men may stamp out
 fire,
They in the spirits of thy people killed
The sparks of peril left from those dark days,
When France being drunk with blood and
 mad with pain

Sprang on the burning pyre, and with her
    raiment
Burning and streaming crimson in the wind,
Curst and denied her God. They made men
    see,
Yea, in the very name of Liberty,
A net of Satan's set to snare the soul
From Christ and Christ's salvation: in their
    palms
They welded the soft clay of popular thought
To this wish'd semblance yet more cunningly;
Till not a peasant heir of his own fields,
And not a citizen that own'd a house,
And not a man or woman who had saved,
But when some wild voice shriek'd out
    "Liberty!"
Trembled as if the robber's foot were set
Already on his threshold, and in fear
Clutch'd at his little store. These things did
    they,
Christ's servants serving thee; they were as
    veins
Bearing the blood through France from thee
    its heart

Throbbing full glorious in the capital.

And thou, O Sire, in thine own secret mind

Knowest what meed thou hast accorded
them,

Who, thy sworn liegemen in thy triumph-
hour,

Are still thy props in thy calamity.

NAPOLEON.

Well ; have you done ?

BISHOP.

Not yet.

NAPOLEON.

What more ?

BISHOP.

Look round

This day on Europe, look upon the World,

Which like a dark tree o'er the river of Time

Hangeth with fruit of races, goodly some,

Some rotten to the core.   Out of the heart
Of what had seem'd the sunset of the west,
Rises the Teuton, silent, subtle, and sure,
Gathering his venom slowly like a snake,
Wrapping the sleepy lands in fold by fold ;
Then springing up to stab his prey with fangs
Numerous as spears of wheat in harvest time.
O, he is wise, the Teuton, he is deep
As Satan's self in perilous human lore,
Such as the purblind deem philosophy !
But, be he cunning as the Tempter was,
Christ yet shall bruise his head ; for in him-
    self
He bears, as serpents use,
A brood of lesser snakes, cunning things too
But lesser, and of these many prepare
Such peril as in his most glorious hour
May strike him feebler than the wretched
    worms
That crawl this day on the dead lambs of
    France.
Meantime, he to his purpose moves most slow,
And overcomes.   Note how, upon her rock,
The sea-beast Albion, swollen with idle years

Of basking in the prosperous sunshine, rolls
Her fearful eyes, and murmurs.   See how
   wildly
The merciless Russian paceth like a bear
His lonely steppes of snow, and with deep
   moan
Calling his hideous young, casts famished
   eyes
On that worn Paralytic in the East,
Whom thou of old didst save.   Call thou to
   these
For succour; shall they stir?   Will the sea-
   beast
Budge from her rock?   Will the bear leave
   his wilds?
Then mark how feebly in the wintry cold
Old Austria ruffles up her plumage, Sire,
Covering the half-heal'd wound upon her
   neck;
See how on Spain her home-bred vermin
   feed,
As did the worms on Herod; Italy
Is as a dove-cote by a battle-field,
Abandoned to the kites of infamy;

Belgium, Denmark, and Helvetia,
Like plovers watching while the wind-hover
Strikes down one of their miserable kind,
Wheeling upon the wind cry to each other;
And far away the Eagle of the West,
Poised in the lull of her own hurricane,
Sits watching thee with eyes as blank of love
As those grey seas that break beneath her
    feet.

NAPOLEON.

This is cold comfort, yet I am patient.   Well?
To the issue!   Dost thou keep behind the
    salve
Whose touch shall heal my wounds? or dost
    thou only,
As any raven on occasion can,
Croak out the stale truth, that the day is lost,
And that the world's slaves knee the con-
    queror?

BISHOP.

Look not on these, thy crownéd peers, for aid,
But inward.   Read thy heart.

NAPOLEON.

It is a book
I have studied somewhat deeply.

BISHOP.

In thine heart,
Tho' the cold lips might sneer, the dark brow
frown,
Wert thou not ever one believing God?

NAPOLEON.

I have believed, and do believe, in God.

BISHOP.

For that, give thanks to God.   He shall uplift thee.

NAPOLEON.

How?

BISHOP.

By the secret hands of His great Church.
Even now in darkness and in tilths remote

o

They labour in thy service; one by one
They gather up the fallen reins of power
And keep them for thy grasp; so be thou
    sure,
When thou hast woven round about thy
    soul
The robe of holiness, and from the hands
Of Holy Church demandest thy lost throne,
It shall be hers to give thee.

NAPOLEON.

                              In good truth,
I scarce conceive thee. What, degenerate
    Rome,
With scarce the power in this strong wind of
    war
To hold her ragged gauds about her limbs;
Rome, reft of the deep thunder in her voice,
The dark curse in her eye; Rome, old, dumb,
    blind,—
Shall Rome give Kingdoms?—Why, she hath
    already
Transferred her own to Heaven.

BISHOP.

Canst thou follow

The coming and the going of the wind,

Fathom the green abysses of the sea?

For such as these, is Rome:—the voice of God

Sounding in darkness and a silent place;

The morning dew scarce seen upon the
 flowers,

Yet drawn to heaven and grown the thunderbolt

That shakes the earth at noon. When man's
 wild soul

Clutches no more at the white feet of Christ;

When death is not, nor spiritual disease;

When atheists can on the black mountain
 tops

Walk solitary in the light of stars,

And cry, "God is not;" when no mothers
 kneel

Moaning on graves of children; when no
 flashes

Trouble the melancholy dark of dream;

When prayer is hush'd, when the Wise Book
 is shut—

Then Rome shall fall indeed : meantime she
    is based
Invulnerable on the soul. of man,
Its darkest needs and fears ; she doth dispense
What soon or late is better prized than gold,—
Comfort and intercession ; for all sin
She hath the swiftest shrift, wherefore her
    clients
Are those that have sinned deeply, and of such
Is half the dreadful world ; all these she holds
By that cold eyeball which hath read their
    souls,
So that they look upon her secretly
And tremble,—while in her dark book of Fate
E'en now she dooms the Teuton.

           [*Enter a* MESSENGER.

       NAPOLEON.

            Well, what news ?

      MESSENGER.

'Tis brief and sad.   The mighty Prussian
    chiefs,
Gathering their fiery van in silence, close

Toward the imperial City—in whose walls

Treason and Rage and Fear contend together

Like hunger-stricken wolves; and at their cry,

Echoed from Paris to the Vosges, France,

Calling her famish'd children round her
  knees,

Looks at the trembling nations. All is still,

Like to that silence which precedes the storm,

And shakes the forest leaves without a
  breath;

But surely as the vaporous storm is woven,

The German closes round the heart of France

His hurricane of lives.

NAPOLEON (*to* BISHOP).

　　　　　The Teuton thrives

Under the doom we spake of. (*To* MES-
SENGER.) Well, speak on!

MESSENGER.

Meantime, like kine that see the gathering
  clouds

And shelter 'neath the shade of rocks and
  trees,

Thy timorous people fly before the sound
Of the approaching footsteps, seeking woods
For shelter, snaring conies for their food,
And sleeping like the beasts; some fare in
    caves,
Fearing the wholesome air, hushing the
    cries
Of infants lest the murderous foe should
    hear;
Some scatter west and south, their frighted
    eyes
Cast backward, with their wretched house-
    hold goods;
And where these dwelt, most blest beneath
    thy rule,
The German legions thrive, let loose like
    swine
Amid the fields of harvest, in their track
Leaving the smoking ruin, and the church
Most desecrated to a sleeping-sty;—
So that the plenteous lands that rolled in
    gold
Round thy voluptuous City, lie full bare
To shame, to rapine, to calamity.

NAPOLEON.

O for one hour of empire, that with life
I might consume this sorrow! 'Tis a spell
By which we are subdued!

MESSENGER.

Strasbourg still stands,
Stubborn as granite, but the citadel
Is falling.   Within, Famine and Horror
    nest,
And rear their young on ruin.   [*Exit.*

[*Enter a* MESSENGER.

NAPOLEON.

How, peal on peal!
Like the agonizing clash of bells when
    flame
Hath seized on some fair city.   News, more
    news?
Dost thou too catch the common trick o' the
    time,
And ring a melancholy peal?

MESSENGER.

My liege,
Strasbourg still stands.

NAPOLEON.

And then ?

MESSENGER.

Pent up in Metz,
Encircled by a river of strong lives,
Bazaine is faithful to the cause and thee,
And from his prison doth proclaim himself,
And all the host of Frenchmen at his back,
Thy liegemen to the death.

NAPOLEON.

Why, that last peal
Sounds somewhat blither.　Well ?

MESSENGER.

From his lone isle,
The old Italian Red-shirt in his age
Hath crawl'd, tho' sickly and infirm, to France,

And slowly there his leonine features breed

Hope in the timid people, who——

NAPOLEON.

Enough! [*Exit* MESSENGER.

That tune is flat and tame.

[*Enter a* MESSENGER.

What man art thou,

On whose swart face the frenzied lightning

plays,

Prophetic of the thunder on the tongue?

Speak!

MESSENGER.

Better I had died at Weissenburg,

Where on the bloody field I lay for dead,

Than live to bring this woe. Ungenerous

France,

Forgetful of thy gracious years of reign,

Pitiless as a sated harlot is

When ruin overtaketh him whose hand

Hath loaded her with gems, shameless and

mad,

France, like Delilah, now betrays her lord.

The streets are drunken—from thy palace-
    gate

They pluck the imperial eagles, trampling
    them

Into the bloody mire ; thy flags and pennons,

Torn from their vantage in the wind, are
    wrapt

In mockery round the beggar's ragged limbs ;

And thine imperial images in stone,

Dash'd from their lofty places, strew the
    ground

In shameful ruin.   All the ragged shout,

While Trochu from the presidential seat

Proclaims the empire dead, and calleth up

A new Republic, in whose chairs of office

Thine enemies, scribblers and demagogues,

Simon, Gambetta, Favre, and link'd with
    these

The miserable Rochefort, trembling grasp

The reins of power, unconscious of the scorn

That doth already doom them.   To their feet

Come humming back, vain-drunken, all the
    wasps

Whom in thine hour of glory thou didst brush

With careless arm-sweep from thy festal cup:

Shoulder'd by mobs the pigmy Blanc de-
claims,

The hare-brain'd Hugo shrieks a maniac
song

In concert, and the scribblers, brandishing

Their pens like valiant lilliputians

Against the Teuton giant, frantically

Scream chorus. Coming with mock-humble
eyes

To the Republic, this sham shape of straw,

This stuff'd thing of a harlot's carnival,

The dilettante sons of Orleans, kneeling,

Proffer forsooth their swords, which being
disdain'd

They sheathe chapfallen and with bows
withdraw

Back to their pictures and perfumery.

NAPOLEON.

Why, thine is news indeed. Nor do I weep

For mine own wrong, but for the woes of
France,

Whose knell thou soundest.   With a tongue
   of fire
Our enemy shall like the ant-eater
Devour these insect rulers suddenly.
(*Aside*) Now, may the foul fiend blacken all
   the air
Above these Frenchmen, with revolt and
   fear
Darken alike the wits of friends and
   foes,
With swift confusion and with anarchy
Disturb their fretful councils, till at last,
Many-tongued, wild-hair'd, mad, and hor-
   rible
With fiery eyes and naked crimson limbs,
Upriseth the old Spectre of the Red,
And as of yore uplifts the shameful knife
To stab unhappy France; then, in her
   need,
Fearful and terror-stricken, France shall
   call
On him who gave her nineteen plenteous
   years—
And he may rise again.   [*Exeunt.*

CHORUS.

Who in the name of France curses French
 souls this day ?
How ! shall the tempter curse ? Silence ; and
 turn away ;
Turn we our faces hence white with a wild
 desire,
Westward we lift our gaze till the straining
 balls flash fire,
Westward we look to France, sadly we
 watch and mark :—
Far thro' the pitch-black air, like breaking
 foam in the dark,
Cometh and goeth a light across the stricken
 land,
And we hear a distant voice like the wash of
 waves on the sand.

VOICES.

Set the cannon on the heights, and under
 Let the black moat gape, the black graves
  grow !

Now let thunder

Answer back the thunder of the foe !

France has torn her cerements asunder,

France doth live to strike the oppressor
low.

CHORUS.

O hark ! O hark ! a voice arises wild and
strong,

Loud as a bell that rings alarm it lifts the
song.

See ! see ! the dark is lit, fire upon fire up-
springs,

Loudly from town to town the fiery tiding
rings.

Now the red smithies blaze and the blue steel
is sped,

They twist bright steel for guns, they cast the
fatal lead ;

Cannon is drawn to the gate,—and lo, the
bravest stand

Bare to the shoulder there, smoke-begrim'd,
fuse in hand,

Now to the winds of heaven the Flag of Stars
    they raise,
While those sing martial songs who are too
    frail for frays.
France is uprisen again! France the sworn
    slayer of Kings!
With bleeding breast and bitter heart at the
    Teuton's throat she springs.

VOICES.

Now like thunder
  Be our voice together while we cry;
Kings shall never hold our spirits under,
    Kings shall cast their crowns aside and
      fly:
Latin, Sclav, or Teuton, they shall wonder;
    The soul of man hath doom'd them—let
      them die.
We have slain Kings of old, they were our
    own to slay,
But now we doom all Kings until the Judg-
    ment day,

Raise ye the Flag of Stars! Tremble, O
    Kings, and behold!

Raise ye the Flag of Man, while the knell of
    anarchs is tolled.   .

This is a festal day for all the seed of Eve;

France shall redeem the world, and heal all
    hearts that grieve;

France with her sword this day shall free all
    human things,

With blood drain'd from her heart our France
    shall write the doom of Kings.

CHORUS.

Silence and hearken yet!   O but it is a cry

Heard under heaven of old, tho' the terrible
    day blew by.

The red fire flames to heaven, and in the
    crimson glow

Black shapes with prayers and cries are
    gliding to and fro.

VOICES.

Fill each loophole with a man! and finding
    Each a foe, aim slowly at the brain,

While the blinding

   Lightnings flash, and the great guns refrain.

To the roofs! and while beneath the foe are
winding,

   Dash ye stones and missiles down like
rain.

Watch for the grey-beard King : to drink his
blood were great.

Watch for the Cub thereto—aim at his brain
full straight.

Watch most for that foul Knave who crawls
behind the crown,

Who smiles befooling all with crafty eyes
cast down ;

Sweeter than wine indeed his wretched blood
would flow,

Curst juggler with our souls, he who hath
wrought this woe.

France hath uprisen again! Let the fierce
shaft be sped

Till all the foul satanic things that flatter
Kings be dead.

CHORUS.

Echo the dreadful prayer, let the fierce shaft
    be sped,
Till all the foul satanic things that flatter
    Kings be dead!

VOICES.

Send the light balloon aloft with singing,
    Let our hopes rise with it to the sky,
Let our voices like one fount upspringing
    Tell the mighty realm that hope is nigh!
See, in answer, from the distance winging
    Back unto our feet the swift doves fly!

CHORUS.

We see the City now, dark square and street
    and mart,
The muffled drum doth sound réveille in its
    heart,
The chain'd balloon doth swing, while men
    stand murmuring by,
Then with elastic bound upleaps into the sky.
We see the brightening dawn, the dimly
    dappled land,

The shapes with arms outstretch'd that on the
 housetops stand,

The eyes that turn to meet with one quick
 flash of fear

The birds that sad and slow wing nearer and
 more near.

O courage! all is well—yea, let your hearts
 be higher,

North, south, east, west, the souls of Frenchmen are as fire,

The reaper leaves the wheat, the workman
 leaves his loom,

Tho' the black priest may frown who heeds
 his look of gloom ?

Flash the wild tidings forth! ring them from
 town to town,

Till like a storm of scythes ye rise, and the
 foe like wheat go down.

VOICES.

See! how northward the wild heavens lighten,
 Red as blood the fierce aurora waves,
Let it bathe us strong in blood and brighten
 Sweet with resurrection on our graves,

Lighten, lighten,

Scroll of God!—unfold above and brighten,

  Light the doom of monarchs and their
     slaves.

This is a day indeed—be sure that God can
     see.

Raise the fierce cry again, "Liberty!
     Liberty!"

Courage! No man dies twice, and he shall
     live in death,

Who for the Flag of Stars strikes with his
     latest breath.

Nay, not a foe shall live to tell if France be
     slain:

If the wild cause be lost, only the grave shall
     gain.

Teuton and Frank in fierce embrace shall
     strew the fatal sod,

And they shall live indeed who died to save
     their souls for God.

CHORUS.

O Spirits turn and look no more and hark
     not to their cry,

A Hand is flashed before our eyes, a Shape
    goes sadly by.
And as it goes, it looks on us with eyes that
    swim in tears,
And bitter as the death-cry sounds the echo
    in our ears.
O look no more and seek no more to read the
    days unborn,
'Tis storm this night on the world's sea, and
    'twill be storm at morn.
The Lord hath sent his breath abroad, and all
    the waves are stirr'd :
Amid the tempest Liberty flies like a white
    sea-bird,
And, while the heavens are torn apart and
    the fierce waters gleam,
Doth up and down the furrow'd waves dart
    with a sea-bird's scream.
O bow the head, and close the eyes, and pray
    a quiet prayer,
But let the bitter curse of Man go by upon
    the air.

[NAPOLEON. *An* OFFICER.

NAPOLEON.

Is there no hope for France ?

OFFICER.

None.   Yet I know not!
A nation thus miraculously strengthen'd,
And acting in the fiercest wrath of love,
Hath risen ere this above calamity,
And out of anguish conjured victory.
If strength and numbers, if the mighty hands
Of the Briareus, shall decide the day,
Then surely as the sun sets France must fall ;
If love or prayer can make a miracle
And bring an angel down to strike for her,
Then France may rise again.

NAPOLEON.

Have we not proved
Her children cowards ?   Yea, by God!   Like
dogs
That rend the air with wrath upon the chain,

And being loosen'd slink before the thief,

They fail'd me—those who led and those who
follow'd ;

Scarce knowing friend from foe, while inch by
inch

The Germans ate their ranks as a slow fire

Devoureth wind-blown wheat. I cannot
trust

In France or Frenchmen.

OFFICER.

Sire——

NAPOLEON.

Why dost thou hang

Thy head, old friend, and look upon the
ground ?

Nay, if all Frenchmen had but hearts like
thine,

Then France were blest in sooth, and I, its
master,

Were safe against the swords of all the
world.

OFFICER.

Sire, 'twas not that I meant — my life is
   yours
To give or take, to blame or praise; I
   blush'd
Not for myself, but France.

NAPOLEON.

                    Then hadst thou cause
For crimson cheeks indeed.

OFFICER.   '
                    Sire, as I live,
Thou wrongest her! The breast whereon we
   grew
Suckled no cowards. For one dizzy hour
France totter'd, and look'd back; but now
   indeed
She hath arisen to the very height
Of her great peril.

NAPOLEON.

                    'Tis too late. She is lost.
She did betray her master, and shall die.

OFFICER.

Not France betrayed thee, Sire ; but rather
    those
Whom thy most noble nature, royally based
Above suspicion and perfidious fear,
Welcom'd unto thy council; not poor France,
Whose bleeding wounds speak for her loud
    as tongues,
Bit at the hand that raised her up so high ;
Not France, but bastard Frenchmen, doubly
    damn'd
Alike by her who bare them and by thee
Who fed them. These betrayed thee to thy
    doom,
And falling clutch'd at thine imperial crown,
Dragging it with them to the bloody dust ;
But these that held her arms like bands of
    lead
Being torn from off her, France, unchain'd
    and free,
Uplifts her pale front to the stars, and stands
Serene in doom and danger, and sublime
In resurrection.

NAPOLEON.

How the popular taint
Corrupts the wholesome matter of thy mind !
This would be treason, friend, if we were
  strong—
Now 'tis less perilous : the commonest wind
Can blow its scorn upon the fallen.

OFFICER.

Sire,

Behold me on my knees, tears in mine eyes,
And sorrow in my heart.   My life is thine,
My life, my heart, my soul are pledged to
  thine ;
And trebly now doth thy calamity
Hold me thy slave and servant.   If I pray,
'Tis that thou mayst arise, and thou shalt rise ;
And if I praise our common mother, France,
Who for the moment hath forgot her lord,
'Tis that my soul rejoices for thy sake,
That when thou comest to thine own again
Thy realm shall be a realm regenerate,
Baptized a fair thing worthy of thy love
In its own blood of direful victory.

NAPOLEON.

Sayest thou ?—Rise !—Friend, thou art little
  skilled
In reading that abstruse astrology
Whereby our cunning politicians cast
The fate of Kings.   France robed in victory
Is France for ever lost to our great house.
France fallen, is France that with my secret
  hand
I may uplift again.   But tell thy tale
Most freely : let thy soul beat its free wings
Before me as it lists.   Come ! as thou
  sayest,
France is no coward ;—she hath at last
  arisen ;
Nay, more—she is sublime.   Proceed.

OFFICER.
                                  My liege,
God, ere he made me thy most loving servant,
Made and baptized me, Frenchman ; and my
  heart,
A soldier's heart, yearns out this day in pride

To her who bare me, and both great and low
My brethren.   Courage is a virtue, Sire,
Even in a wretched cause.   In Strasbourg
    still
Old Uhrich with his weight of seventy years
Starves unsubdued, while the dull enemy
Look on in wonder at such strength in woe;
Bazaine still keeps the glittering hosts at
    bay,
And holds them with a watchful hand and
    eye;
The captain of the citadel at Laon,
Soon as the foeman gather'd on his walls,
Illumed the hidden mine, and Frank and
    Teuton,
With that they strove for, strew'd the path in
    death;
From Paris to the Vosges, loud and wild
The tocsin rings to arms, and on the fields
The fat ripe ear empties itself unreapt,
While every man whose hand can grasp a
    sword
Flocks to the petty standard of his town;
The many looms of the great factory

Stand silent, but the fiery moulds of clay

Are fashioning cannon, and the blinding
    wheels

Are sharpening steel. In every market-
    place

Peasant and prince are drilling side by side ;

Roused from their wine-fed torpor, changed
    from swine

To men, the very country burghers arm,

Nay, what is more to them than blood, bleed
    gold

Bounteously, freely. I have heard that
    priests,

Doffing the holy cossack secretly,

Shouting uplift the sword, and crying Christ

To aid them strike for France. Only the
    basest,

Only the scum, shrink now ; for even women,

Catching the noble fever of the time,

Buckle the war-belts round their lovers'
    waists,

And clapping hands, with mingled cries and
    sobs,

Urge young and old against the enemy.

NAPOLEON.

Of so much thunder may the lightning spring.

I know how France can thunder, and I have
felt

How women's tongues can urge. But what
of Paris?

What of the city of light? How doth it bear

The terror and the agony?

OFFICER.

Most bravely,

As doth become the glorious heart of France:

Strong, fearless, throbbing with a martial
might,

Dispensing from its core the vital heat

Which filleth all the members of the land;

Tho' even now the sharp steel pricks the
skin,

To stab it in its strength.

NAPOLEON.

Who holds the reins

Within the gates?

OFFICER.

Trochu.

NAPOLEON.

      Still? Why, how long
Have the poor fools been constant? Favre
    also?
Gambetta? Rochefort? All these gentlemen
Still flourish? And Thiers? Hath the arch-
    schemer
A seat among the gods, a place of rank
With the ephemera?

OFFICER.

      Not so, my liege.

NAPOLEON.

Well, being seated on Olympus' top,
What thunderbolts are France's puny Joves
Casting abroad? Or do they sit and quake
For awe of their own voices, which in France,
As in the shifting glaciers of the Alps,
May bring the avalanche upon their heads?

OFFICER.

The men, to do them justice, use their power
Calmly and soldierly, and for a time
Forget the bitter humours of the senate
In the great common cause. Paris is strong,
And full of noble souls.

NAPOLEON.

Paris must fall.

OFFICER.

Not soon, my liege—for she is belted round
And arm'd impregnable on every side.
Hunger and thirst may slay her, not the
    sword ;
And ere the foeman's foot is heard within,
Paris will spring upon her funeral pyre
And follow Hope to heaven. Last week I
    walk'd
Reading men's faces in the silent streets,
And, as I am a soldier, saw in none

Fear or capitulation : very harlots
Cried in their shame the name of Liberty,
And, hustled from the gates, shriek'd out a
    curse
Upon the coming Teuton : all was still
And dreadful ; but the citizens in silence
Drilled in the squares ; on the great boulevard
    groups
Whisper'd together, with their faces pale
At white heat ; in the silent theatre,
Dim lit by lamps, were women, wives and
    mothers,
Silently working for their wounded sons
And husbands ; in the churches too they sat
And wrought, while ever and anon a foot
Rung on the pavement, and with sad red eyes
They turn'd to see some armëd citizen
Kneel at his orisons or vespers.   Nightly,
Ere the moon rose, the City slept like death ;
Yet as a lion sleeps, with half-shut eyes,
Hearing each murmur on the weary wind,
Crouching and ready for the spring.   Each
    dawn
I saw the country carts come rumbling in,

Q

And the scared country-folk, with large wild
    eyes
And open mouths, who flock'd for shelter
    bringing
Horrible tidings of the enemy
Who had devoured their fields and happy
    homes.
Then suddenly like a low earthquake came
The rumour that the foe was at the gates;
And climbing a cathedral roof that night,
I saw the pitch-black distance sown with fire
Gleam phosphorescent like the midnight sea,
And heard at intervals mysterious sound,
Like far off thunder or the Atlantic waves
Clashing on some great headland in a storm,
Come smother'd from afar. But, lingering yet,
I haunted the great City in disguise,
While silently the fatal rings were wound
Around about it by the Teuton hosts:
Still, as I am a soldier, saw no face
That look'd capitulation: rather saw
The knitted eyebrow and the clenchëd teeth,
The stealthy hand that fingered with the
    sword,

The eye that glanced as swift as hunger's doth
Towards the battlements.   Then (for at last
A voice was raised against my life) I sought
Trochu, my schoolfellow and friend in arms,
And, though his brow darkened a moment's
    space,
He knew me faithful and reached out his hand
To save me.   By his secret help I found
A place in a balloon, that in the dusk
Ere daylight rose upon a moaning wind
And drifted southward with the drifting
    clouds ;
And as the white and frosty daylight grew,
And opening crimson as a rose's leaves
The clouds to eastward parted, I beheld
The imperial City, gables, roofs, and spires,
White and fantastic as a city of dream,
Gleam orient, while the muffled drums within
Sounded réveille ; then a red flash and wreath
Of vapour broke across the outer line,
Where the black fortifications frowning rose
Ring above ring around the imperial gates,
And flash on flash succeeded with a sound
Most faint and lagging wearily behind.

Still all without the City seemed as husht
As sleep or death. But as the reddening
   day
Scattered the mists, the tiny villages
Loomed dim; and there were distant glim-
   merings,
And far-off muffled sounds : yet scarce a sign
Showed the innumerable enemy,—
Who snugly housed and canopied with stone
Lay hidden in their strength ; only the watch-
   fire
Gleam'd here and there, only from place to
   place
Masses of shadow seem'd to move, and
   light
Was glittered dimly back from hidden steel ;
And, woefullest sight of all, miles to the
   west,
Along the dark line of the foe's advance,
On the straight rim where earth and heaven
   meet,
The forests blazed and to the driving clouds
Cast blood-red phantoms growing dim in
   day.

Meantime, like one whirl'd in a dizzy dream,
Onward we drove below the driving cloud,
And from the region of the burning fire
And smouldering hamlet rose still higher, and
    saw
The white stars like to tapers burning out
Above the region of the nether storm,
And the illimitable ether growing
Silent and dark in the deep wintry dawn.

[*Enter a* MESSENGER.

MESSENGER.

Most weighty news, my liege, from Italy.

NAPOLEON.

Yes?

MESSENGER.

Rome is taken.   The imperial walls
Yawn where the cannon smote; in the red
    streets
Romans embracing shout for Liberty;

From Florence to Messina bonfires blaze,
And rockets rise and wild shouts shake the
      air;
And with the thunder in his aged ears,
Surrounded by his cold-eyed Cardinals,
Clutching his spiritual crown more close,
Trembling with dotage, sits the grey-haired
      Pope
Anathematizing in the Vatican.   [*Exit.*

OFFICER.

Woe to the head on whom his curse shall
      fall,
For in the day of judgment it shall be
Better with Sodom and Gomorrah.   Wait!
This is the twilight; red will rise the dawn.

NAPOLEON.

Peace, friend; yet if it ease thy heart, speak
      on.
I would to God, I did believe in God
As thou dost.   Twilight surely—'tis indeed

A   twilight — and   therein   from   their   fair
    spheres
Kings shoot like stars.   How many nights of
    late
The heavens have troubled been with fiery
    signs,
With characters like monstrous hieroglyphs,
And the aurora, brighter than the day
And red as blood, has burnt from west to
    east.

OFFICER.

I do believe the melancholy air
Is full of pain and portent.

NAPOLEON.

                              Would to God
I had more faith in God, for in this work
I fail to trace His hand ; but rather feel
The nether-shock of earthquake everywhere
Shaking old thrones and new, those rear'd on
    rock
As well as those on sand.   All darkens yet,

And in that darkness, while with cheeks of
    snow
The affrighted people gaze at one another,
The Teuton still, mouthing of Deity,
Works steadfastly to some mysterious end.
My heart was never Rome's so much as
    now,
Now, when she shares my cup of agony.
Agony! Is this agony? then indeed
All life is agony.

OFFICER.

      Your Imperial Highness
Is suffering! Take comfort, Sire.

NAPOLEON.

          It is nought—
Only a passing spasm at the heart—
'Tis my disease, comrade; 'tis my disease!
So leave me: it is late; and I would rest.

OFFICER.

God in his gracious goodness give thee health.

NAPOLEON.

Pray that He may; for am I deeply
    sick—

Too sick for surgery—too sick for drugs—

Too sick for man to heal. 'Tis a com-
    plaint

Incident to our house; and of the same

Mine imperial uncle died.   [*Exit Officer.*

                 France in the dust,

With the dark Spectre of the Red above
    her!

Rome fallen! Aye me, well may the face of
    heaven

Burn like a fiery scroll. Had I but eyes

To read whose name is written next for
    doom!

The Teuton's? O the Serpent, that has
    bided

His time so long, and now has stabbed so
    deep!

Would I might bruise his head before I die!

                     [*Exit.*

Night. NAPOLEON *sleeping.* CHORUS *of*
SPIRITS.

A Voice.

What shapes are ye whose shades darken his
rest this night?

Chorus.

Cold from the grave we come, out of the dark
to the light.

A Voice.

Voices ye have that moan, and eyes ye have
that weep,
Ah! woe for him who feels such shadows
round his sleep!

Chorus.

Tho' thou wert buried and dead,
Still would we seek thee and find thee,
Ever there follows the tread
Of feet from the tomb behind thee;

Sleep, shall thy soul have sleep?
    Nay, but be broken and shaken.
Gather around him and weep,
    Trouble him till he awaken.

A VOICE.

Who, in imperial raiment, darkly frowning
    stand,
Laurel-leaves in their hair, sceptred yet
    sword in hand.

ANOTHER VOICE.

Who in their shadow looms, woman-eyed,
    woe-begone,
And bares his breast to show the piteous
    wounds thereon?

CHORUS.

Peace, they are Kings, they are crowned;
    Kings, tho' their realms have departed,
Realms of the grave they have found,
    And they walk in the same heavy-hearted.

Sleep? did their souls have sleep?
  Nay, for like his was their being.
Gather around him and weep,
  Awake him to hearing and seeing.

Spirit of Cæsar.

Greater than thou I fell.   Die; for thy day is
    o'er.
Thou reap the world with swords? thou wear
    the robe I wore?
Up like the bird of Jove, I rose from height to
    height,
Poised on the heavenly air, eyes to the blood-
    red light;
Swift came the flash of wrath, one long-
    avenging glare—
Down like a stone I fell, down thro' the
    dizzy air;
Dark burnt the heaven above, red ran the
    light of day,
In the great square of Rome, bloody I fell,
    and lay.

CHORUS.

Kings of the realms of fear,
　Each the sad ghost of the other,
One by one step near,
　Look in the eyes of a brother.
Hush! draw nearer and speak—
　And ere he waketh each morrow
Blow on his bloodless cheek
　With the chilly wind of your sorrow.

SPIRIT OF BUONAPARTE.

Greater than thou I fell. Die, Icarus, and
　give place.
Thou take from my cold grave the glory and
　the grace!
Out of the fire I came, onward thro' fire I
　strode;
Under my path earth burnt, o'er it the pale
　stars glow'd;
Sun of the earth, I leapt up thro' the wonder-
　ing sky,
Naming my name with God's, Kings knelt
　as I went by.

Aye; but my day declined;—to one glad cry
    of the free
My blood-red sunset died on the eternal Sea.

A VOICE.

What spirit art thou, with cold still smile and
    face like snow?

SPIRIT.

Orsini; and avenged.   Too soon I struck the
    blow.

A VOICE.

And thou, with bleeding breast and eyes that
    roll in pain?

SPIRIT.

I am that Maximilian, miserably slain.

A VOICE.

And ye, O shadowy things, featureless, wild,
    and stark?

VOICES.

We are the nameless ones whom he hath
    slain in the dark.

A VOICE.

Ye whom this man hath doom'd, Spirits, are
ye all there?

CHORUS.

Not yet; they come, they come—they darken
all the air.

A VOICE.

O latest come, and what are ye? Why do ye
moan and call?

CHORUS.

O hush! O hush! they come to speak the
bitterest curse of all.

SPIRITS.

With Sin and Death our mothers' milk was
sour,
The womb wherein we grew from hour to
hour
Gather'd pollution dark from the polluted
frame—
Beside our cradles naked Infamy
Caroused, and Lust sat smiling hideously—
We grew like evil weeds apace, and knew not
shame.

With incantations and with spells most
    rank,
The fount of Knowledge where we might
    have drank,
And learnt to love the taste, was hidden from
    our eyes;
And if we learn'd to spell out written
    speech,
Thy slaves were by, and we had books to
    teach
Falsehood and Filth and Sin, Blasphemies,
    Scoffs, and Lies.

We drank of poison, ev'n as flowers drink
    dew;
We ate and drank of poison till we grew
Noxious, polluted, black, like that whereon
    we fed;
We never felt the light and the free
    wind—
Sunless we grew, and deaf, and dumb, and
    blind—
How should we dream of God, souls that were
    slain and dead?

Love with her sister Reverence passed
  our way
As angels pass unseen, but did not
  stay—
We had no happy homes wherein to bid them
  dwell;
We turn'd from God's blue heaven with
  eyes of beast,
We heard alike the atheist and the priest,
And both these lied alike to smooth our
  hearts for Hell.

Of some, both Soul and Body died; of
  most,
The Body fatten'd on, while the poor
  ghost,
Prison'd from the sweet day, was withering in
  woe;
Some robed in purple quaff'd their fatal
  cup,
Some out of rubied goblets drank it up—
We did not know God was; but now, O God,
  we know.

R

Lambs of thy flock, but oh! not white and
    fair;
Beasts of the field, tamed to thy hand, we
    were;
Not men and women—nay, not heirs to light
    and truth:
Some fattening ate and fed; some lay at
    ease;
Some fell and linger'd of a long disease;
But all look'd on the ground—beasts of the
    field forsooth.

Ah woe, ah woe, for those thy sceptre
    swayed,
Woe most for those whose bodies, fair
    arrayed,
Insolent, sat at ease, smiled at thy feet of
    pride;
Woe for the harlots with their painted
    bliss!
Woe for the red wine-oozing lips they
    kiss!
Woe for the Bodies that lived, woe for the
    Souls that died!

SEMI-CHORUS I.

Tho thou wert buried and dead,
  Still would they seek thee and find thee,
Ever there follows the tread
  Of feet from the grave behind thee.

SPIRIT OF HORTENSE.

Woe! woe! woe!

SEMI-CHORUS II.

Ye who saw sad light fall,
  Thro' the chink of the dungeon gleaming,
And watch'd your shade on the wall
  Till it took a sad friend's seeming;
Ye who in speechless pain
  Fled from the doom and the danger,
And dragging a patriot's chain
  Died in the land of the stranger;
Men who stagger'd and died,
  Even as beasts in the traces,
Women he set aside
  For the trade of polluting embraces,

Say, shall his soul have sleep,
  Or shall it be troubled and shaken ?

CHORUS.

Gather around him and weep,
  Trouble him till he awaken.

NAPOLEON (*awakening*).

Who's there ?   Who speaks ?—All silent.   O
    how slowly
Moveth the dark and melancholy night !
I cannot rest—I am too sick at heart—
I have had ill dreams.   The inevitable
    Eyes
Are watching, and the weary void of sleep
Hath voices strangely sad.
            [*He rises, and paces the chamber.*
                O those dark years
Of Empire !   He who tames the tiger, and
    lies
Pillow'd upon its neck in a lone cave,
Is safer.   Who could sleep on such a bed ?

Mine eyes were ever dry of the pure dew
God scatters on the lids of happy men :
Watching with fascinated gaze the orbs,
Ring within ring of blank and bestial light,
Where the wild fury slept : seeking all arts
To soothe the savage instinct in its throes
Of passionate unrest. One cold hand
    held
Sweet morsels for the furious thing to lap,
And with the other, held behind my back,
I clutch'd the secret steel : oft, lest its
    teeth
Should fasten on its master, cunningly
Turning its wrath against the shapes that
    moved
Outside its splendid lair ; until at last,
Let forth to the mad light of War, it sprang
Shrieking and sought to rend me. O thou
    beast!
Art thou so wild this day? and dost thou
    thirst
To fix on thine imperial ruler's throat ?
Why, have I bidden thee " down," and thou
    hast crouch'd

Tamely as any hound! Thou shalt crouch
    yet.
And bleed with shamfuller stripes!

                   Let me be calm,
Not bitter. 'Tis too late for bitterness.
Yet I could gnaw my heart to think how
    France
Hath fail'd me! nay, not France, but rather
    those
Whom to high offices and noble seats
In France's name I raised. I bought their
    souls—
What soul can power not buy?—and, having
    lost
The blessed measure of all human truth,
Being soulless, these betrayed me; yea,
    became
A brood of lesser tigers hungering
With their large eyes on mine. I did not
    build
My throne on sand; no, no,—on Lies and
    Liars,
Weaker than sand a thousandfold!

                                    In this
I did not w rk for evil.   Though my means
Were dark and vile perchance, the end I
    sought
Was France's weal, and underneath my care
She grew as tame as any fatted calf.
I never did believe in that stale cry
Raised by the newsman and the demagogue,
Tho' for mine ends I could cry " Liberty ! "
As loud as any man.   The draff of men
Are as mere sheep and kine, with heads held
    down
Grazing, or resting blankly ruminant.
These must be tended, must be shepherded.
But Frenchmen are as wild things scarcely
    tamed,
Brute-like yet fierce, mad too with some few
    hours
Of rushing freely with an angry roar.
These must be awed and driven.   By a
    scourge
Dripping with sanguine drops of their own
    blood,
I awed them : then I drove them : then in time

I tamed them.   Fool! deeming them wholly
    mine,
I sought to snatch a little brief repose ;
But with a groan they found me, and I woke ;
And since they seem'd to suffer pain I said
" Loosen the yoke a little," and 'twas done,
And they could raise their heads and gaze at
    me ;
And the wild hunger deepen'd in their eyes,
While fascinated on my throne I sat
Forcing a melancholy smile of peace.
O had I held the scourge in my right hand,
Tighten'd the yoke instead of loosening,
It had not been so ill with me as now !
But Pity found me with her sister Fear,
And lured me.   He who sitteth on a throne
Should have no counsellers who come in
    tears ;
But rather that still voice within his brain,
Imperturbable as his own cold eyes
And viewless as his coldly flowing blood ;
Rather a heart as strong as the great heart
Driving the hot life through a lion's thews ;
Rather a will that moves to its desire

As steadfast as the silent-footed cloud.

What peevish humour did my mother mix

With that immortal ichor of our race

Which unpolluted fill'd mine uncle's veins?

He lash'd the world's Kings to his triumph-
car

And sat like marble while the fiery wheels

Dript blood beneath him : tho' the live earth
shriek'd

Below him, he was calm, and like a god

Cold to the eloquence of human tears,

Cold to the quick, cold as the light of stars,

Cold as the hand of Death on the damp
brow,

Cold as Death brooding on a battle-field

In the white after-dawn,—from west to east

Royal he moved as the red wintry sun.

He never flatter'd Folly at his feet ;

He never sought to syrup Infamy ;

He, when the martyrs curst him, drew around
him

The purple of his glory and passed on

Indifferently like Olympian Jove.

There was no weak place in the steel he wore,

Where woman's tongues might reach his
    mighty heart
As they have reach'd at mine.   O had I kept
A heart of steel, a heart of adamant ;
Had I been deaf to clamour and the peal
Of peevish fools ; had I for one strong hour
Conjured mine uncle's soul to mix with
    mine,
Sedan had never slain me!   I am lost   '
By the damn'd implements mine own hands
    wrought—
Things that were made as slavish tools of
    peace,
Never as glittering weapons meet for war.
He never stoop'd to use such peaceful
    tools ;
But, for all uses,
Made the sword serve him—yea, for sceptre
    and scythe ;
Nay more, for Scripture and for counsellor.

Yet he too fell.   Early or late, all fall.
No fruit can hang for ever on the tree.
Daily the tyrant and the martyr meet

Naked at Death's door, with the fatal mark
Both brows being branded.   Doth the world
    then slay
Only its anarchs?   Doth the lightning flash
Smite Cæsar and spare Brutus?   Nay, by
    heaven!
Rather the world keeps for its paracletes
Torture more subtle and more piteous doom
Than it dispenses to its torturers.
Tiberius, with his foot on the world's neck,
Smileth his cruel smile and groweth grey,
Half dead already with the weight of years
Drinketh the death he is too frail to feel,
While in his noon of life the Man Divine
Hath died in anguish at Jerusalem.
[*He opens a Life of Jesus and reads. A long pause.*

Here too the Teuton works, crafty and slow,
Anatomizing, gauging, questioning,
Till that fair Presence which redeem'd the
    world
Dwindles into a phantom and a name.
Shall he slay Kings, and spare the King of
    Kings?

In her fierce madness, France denied her
    God,
But the still Teuton doth destroy his God
Coldly as he outwits an enemy.
Yet doth he keep the Name upon his lips,
And coldly dedicating the dull deed
To the abstraction he hath christen'd God,
To the creation of his cogent brain,
Conjures against the blessed Nazarene,
That pallid apparition masculine,
That shining orb hem'd in with clouds of
    flesh ;
Till, darken'd with the woe of his own words,
The fool can turn to Wilhelm's wooden face
And Bismarck's crafty eyes, and see therein
Human regeneration, or at least
The Teuton's triumph mightier than Christ's.
Lie there, Iconoclast !   Thou art thrice a fool,
Who, having nought to set within its place
But civic doctrine and a naked sword,
Would tear from out its niche the piteous
    bust
Of Him whose face was Sorrow's morning
    star.   [*Takes up a second Book, and reads.*

Mark, now, how speciously Theology,
Leaving the broken fragments of the Life
Where the dull Teuton's hand hath scatter'd
    them,
Takes up the cause in her high fields of air.
"Darkness had lain upon the earth like blood,
And in the darkness human things had
    shriek'd
And felt for God's soft hand, and agonised.
But overhead the awful Spirit heard,
Yet stirred not on His throne. Then lastly,
    One
Dropt like a meteor stone from suns afar,
And stirred and stretch'd out hands, and
    lived, and knew
That He indeed had dropt from suns afar,
That He had fallen from the Father's breast
Where He had slumber'd for eternities.
Hither in likeness of a Man He came—
He, Jesus, wander'd forth from heaven and
    said,
' Lo, I, the deathless one, will live and die !
Evil must suffer—Good ordains to suffer—
Our point of contact shall be suffering,

There will we meet, and ye will hear my voice;
And my low tones shall echo on thro' time,
And one salvation proved in fatal tears
Be the salvation of Humanity.' "

Ah, old Theology, thou strikest home!
" Evil *must* suffer—Good *ordains* to suffer "—
Sayst thou? Did He then quaff His cup of
    tears
Freely, who might have dash'd it down, and
    ruled?
The world was ready with an earthly crown,
And yet He wore it not.   Ah, He was wise!
Had He but sat upon a human throne,
With all the kingdom's beggars at His feet,
And all its coffers open at His side,
He had died more shameful death, yea, He
    had fallen
Even as the Cæsars.   Rule the world with
    Love?
Tame savage human nature with a kiss?
Turn royal cheeks for the brute mob to smite?
He knew men better, and He drew aside,
Ordain'd to do and suffer, not to reign.

My good physician bade me search in
    books
For solace. Can I find it ? Verily,
From every page of all man's hand hath writ
A dark face frowns, a voice moans " Vanity !"
There is one Book—one only—that for ever
Passeth the understanding and appeaseth
The miserable hunger of the heart—
Behold it—written with the light of stars
By God in the beginning.

          [Looks forth. A starry night.

                I believe
God is, but more I know not, save but this—
He passeth not as men and systems pass,
For while all change the Law by which they
    change
Survives and is for ever, being God.
Our sin, our loss, our misery, our death,
Are but the shadows of a dream : the hum
Within our ears, the motes within our eyes ;
Death is to us a semblance and an end,
But is as nothing to that central Law
Whereby we cannot die.

Yonder blue dome,
Gleaming with meanings mystically wrought,
Hath been from the beginning, and shall be
Until the end.   How many awe-struck eyes
Have look'd and spelt one word—the name of
        God,
And call'd it as they listed, Law, Fate, Change,
And marvell'd for its meaning till they died,
And others came and stood upon their graves
And read in their turn, and marvelling gave
        place.
The Kings of Israel watch'd it with wild orbs,
Madden'd, and cried the Name, and drew the
        sword.
Above the tented plain of Troy it bent
After the sun of day had set in blood.
The superstitious Roman look'd by night
And trembled.   All these faded phantom-
        like,
And lo! where it remaineth, watch'd with
        eyes
As sad as any of those this autumn night,—
The Higher Law writ with the light of Stars
By God in the beginning . . .

Let me sleep!
Or I shall gaze and gaze till I grow wild
And never sleep again. Too much of God
Maketh the heart sick. Come then forth,
thou charm,
Thou silent spell wrung from the blood-red
flower,
With power to draw the curtains of the soul
And shut the inevitable Eyes away.

Dead mother, at thy knees I said a prayer—
Lead me not into temptation, and, O God,
Deliver me from evil. Is it too late
To murmur it this night? This night, O
God,
Whate'er Thou art and whereso'er Thou art,
This night at least, when I am sick and fallen,
Deliver me from evil!

CHORUS.

Under the Master's feet the generations
Like ants innumerably come and go:
He leans upon a Dial, and in patience
Watches the hours crawl slow.

S

In His bright hair the eternal stars are burn-
　　ing,
　　Around His face heaven's glories burn
　　　sublime:
He heeds them not, but follows with eyes
　　yearning
　　The shadow men call Time.

Some problem holds Him, and He follows
　　dreaming
　　The lessening and lengthening of the
　　　shade.—
Under His feet, ants from the dark earth
　　streaming,
　　Gather the men He made.

He heeds them not nor turns to them His
　　features—
　　They rise, they crawl, they strive, they run,
　　　they die;
How should He care to look upon such crea-
　　tures,
　　Who lets great worlds roll by?

He shall be nowise heard who calls unto Him,
  He shall be nowise seen who seeks His face;
The problem holds Him—no mere man may
    woo Him,
  He pauseth in His place.

'

So hath it been since all things were created,
  No change on the immortal Face may fall,
Having made all, God paused and fascinated
  Watch'd Time, the shade of all.

Call to the Maker in thine hour of trial,
  Call with a voice of thunder like the sea :
He watches living shadows on a Dial,
  And hath no ears for thee.

He watches on—He feels the still hours
    fleeing,
  He heeds thee not, but lets the days drift by ;
And yet we say to thee, O weary being,
  Blaspheme not, lest thou die.

Rather, if woe be deep and thy soul wander,
    Ant among ants that swarm upon a sod,
Watching thy shadow on the grass-blade,
        ponder
    The mystery with God.

So may some comfort reach thy soul way-
        faring,
    While the days run and the swift glories
        shine,
And something God-like shall that soul grow,
        sharing
    The attitude divine.

Silent, supreme, sad, wondering, quiescent,
    Seeking to fathom with the spirit-sight
The problem of the Shadow of the Present
    Born of eternal Light.

CHORIC INTERLUDE:

THE TWO VOICES.

CHORIC INTERLUDE:

THE TWO VOICES.

SEMI-CHORUS I.

SPIRIT of England, art thou sleeping?
  Soul of the Ocean, art thou fled?
Behold thy Sister is wailing and weeping;
The waves are leaping, the storm is creeping
  Hither to burst on thy helmless head.
England, awake! for the sword gleams over
      thee—
Awake, awake! or the tomb shall cover
      thee—
  England, awake!—if thou be not dead.
The waves are crying, the clouds are flying,
  Fair France is dying—her blood flows red,
Europe in thunder is rent asunder,
  But the mother of nations is lying dead.

SEMI-CHORUS II.

Weep; and pray that our tears may wake
    her;
  Pray;—tho' prayers have been vain of old;
Scream;—tho' the thunder is weak to shake
    her—
In the name of the Maker, awake her, awake
    her:
  The storm hath struck—let the bells be
    toll'd.
England, awake! they are weaving a shroud
    for thee;
Awake, awake, we are wailing aloud for
    thee:
  They will bury thee quick, for thy pulse is
    cold.
O God! to be sleeping, with thy children
    weeping,
  And the red death leaping round farm and
    fold:
Dark is the motion of heaven and ocean.
  Why is the mother of nations cold?

First Voice.

Fly to me, England! . . . Hie to me
   Now in mine hour of woe;
Haste o'er the sea, ere I die, to me;
Swiftly, my Sister; stand nigh to me,
   Help me to strike one blow!
Over the land and the water,
   Swifter than winds can go,
Up the red furrows of slaughter,
   Down on the lair of the foe :
Now, when my children scream madly and
   cling to me;
Now, when I droop o'er the dying they bring
   to me;
Come to me, England! O speak to me, spring
   to me!
   Hurl the invader low!

Second Voice.

Woe to thee! I would go to thee
   Faster than wind can flee,
   Doth not my fond heart flow to thee?

Would I might rise and show to thee
　　All that my love would be!
But behold, they bind me and blind me;
　　Cowards, yet born of me:
They fasten my hands behind me—
　　I am chain'd to a rock in the sea.
Alas! what availeth my grief while I sigh for
　　thee?
Traitors have trapt me—I struggle, I cry for
　　thee;
Come to thee, Sister?—yea, were it to die for
　　thee!
　　O that my hands were free!

FIRST VOICE.

Pray for me, Sister! say for me
　　Prayers until help is nigh;
Send thy loud voice each way for me,
Trouble the night and the day for me,
　　Waken the world and the sky;
Say that my heart is broken,
　　Say that my children die,
With blood and tears for thy token,

Plead till the nations reply ;
Plead to the sea and the earth and the air for
me—
Move the hard heart of the world till it care for
me—
Come to me, England !—at least, say a prayer
for me,
Startle the winds with a cry.

SECOND VOICE.

Doom on me, Hell's own gloom on me,
Blood and a lasting blame !
Already the dark days loom on me,
Cold as the shade of the tomb on me ;
I am call'd by the coward's name.
Shall I heark to a murder'd nation ?
Shall I sit unarm'd and tame ?
Then woe to this generation,
Tho' out of my womb they came.
Betrayed by my children, I wail and I call for
thee ;
Not tears, but my heart's blood, O Sister,
should fall for thee :

My children are slaves, or would strike one
　　and all for thee :
　　　Shame on them! shame! shame! shame!

First Voice.

Pain for thee! all things wane for thee
　　In truth, if this be so ;
Fatal will be the stain for thee :
Wild tears mine eyes shall rain for thee
　　Since thou art left so low ;
For death can come once only,
　　Tho' bitterly comes the blow ;
But shame abideth, and lonely
　　Feels a sick heart come and go.
Homeless and citiless, yet I can weep for
　　thee ;
Fast comes the morrow with anguish most
　　deep for thee ;
Dying, I mourn for the sorrow they heap for
　　thee.
　　　Thine is the bitterest woe.

SECOND VOICE.

Mourn me not, Sister, scorn me not!
　Pray yet for mine and me!
Tho' the old proud fame adorn me not,
The sore grief hath outworn me not—
　Wait; I will come to thee;
1 will rend my chains asunder,
　I will tear my red sword free,
I will come with mine ancient thunder,
　I will strike the foe to his knee.
Yea, tho' the knife of the butcher is nigh to
　thee ;
Yea, while thou screamest and echoes reply to
　thee ;
Comfort, O France!·for, in God's name, I fly
　to thee,
　　Sword in hand, over the sea.

SEMI-CHORUS I.

Spirit of England, false vows wrong her!
　Peace; she waiteth in vain for thee.

SEMI-CHORUS II.

Ah, that thy voice is a spell no longer,
  Ah, that the days of thy truth should flee.

CHORUS.

Sing a song, her heart to make stronger,
  Sing what the perfect State should be.

SEMI-CHORUS I.

Spirit of England, thou whose hoary
  Cliffs gleam bright to the gleaming sea—

SEMI-CHORUS II.

Shut thy coffers and think of glory,
  Nor pray beside them on bended knee.

CHORUS.

Read in sorrow thine own bright story,
  Queen of the States that were brave and free.

CHORIC EPODE.

Where is the perfect State
Early most blest and late,
 Perfect and bright?
'Tis where no Palace stands
Trembling on shifting sands
 Morning and night.
'Tis where the soil is free,
Where, far as eye may see,
Scatter'd o'er hill and lea,
 Homesteads abound ;
Where clean and broad and sweet
Market, square, lane, and street,
Belted by leagues of wheat,
 Cities are found.

Where is the perfect State
Early most blest and late
 Gentle and good?
'Tis where no lives are seen
Huddling in lanes unseen,
 Crying for food ;

'Tis where the home is pure,
'Tis where the bread is sure,
'Tis where the wants are fewer,
    And each want fed;
Where plenty and peace abide,
Where health dwells heavenly-eyed,
Where in nooks beautified
    Slumber the Dead.

Where is the perfect State
Unvexed by Wrath and Hate,
    Quiet and just?
Where to no form of creed
Fetter'd are thought and deed,
    Reason and trust?
'Tis where the great free mart
Broadens, while from its heart
Forth the great ships depart,
    Blown by the wind;
'Tis where the wise men's eyes,
Fixed on the earth and skies,
Seeking for signs, devise
    Good for mankind.

Where is the perfect State,
Holy and consecrate,
  Blessedly wrought ?
'Tis where all waft abroad
Wisdom and faith in God,
  Beautiful thought.
'Tis where the poet's sense
Deepens in reverence,
While to his truths intense
  Multitudes turn.
Where the bright sons of art,
Walking in street or mart,
Feel mankind's reverent heart
  Tremble and yearn.

Say, is the perfect State,
Strong and self-adequate,
  There where it stands,
Perfect in praise of God,
Casting no thoughts abroad
  Over the lands ?
Nay ; for by each man's side
Hangeth a weapon tried ;
Nay, for wise leaders guide

Under the Lord.
Nor, when a people cries,
Smiling with half-shut eyes
Waiteth this State,—but flies,
Lifting the Sword.

Where is the perfect State?
Not where men sit and wait,
Selfishly strong;
While some lost sister State
Crieth most desolate,
Ruin'd by wrong:
Not where men calmly sleep,
Tho' all the world should weep;
Not where they merely heap
Gold in the sun:
Not where in charity
Men with mere dust are free,
When o'er the weary sea
Murder is done.

Which is the perfect State?
Not the self-adequate

Coward and cold ;
Not the brute thing of health,
Swollen with gather'd wealth,
    Sleepy and old.
Nay, but the mighty land
Ever with helping hand,
Ever with flaming brand,
    Rising in power :
This is the fair and great,
This the evangel State,
Letting no wrong'd land wait
    In the dark hour.

This is the perfect State,
Early in arms and late ;
    Blessed at home ;—
Ready at Freedom's cry
Forward to fare and die,
    Over the foam.
Loving States great and small,
Loving home best of all,
Yet at the holy call
    Springing abroad :

This is the royal State,

Perfect and adequate,

Equal to any fate,

   Chosen of God !

THE DRAMA OF KINGS.

PART III

THE TEUTON AGAINST PARIS.

SPEAKERS.

The Kaiser.

Princes and Leaders of the German Host.

The Royal Chancellor.

A Bonapartist Officer.

Protestant Priests.

Choristers.

A French Deputy.

The Governor of Paris.

A Deserter.

Messengers.

Chorus of Sisters of the Red Cross.

Scene—*The German Camp before Paris.*
Time—*Winter,* 1871.

SCENE.—HEIGHTS BEFORE PARIS, AND
EXTERIOR OF A PALACE. *A Winter's
Night.*

Chorus of Sisters of the Red Cross.

CHORUS.

CITY of loveliness and light and splendour,
    City of Sorrows, hearken to our cry ;
        O Mother tender,
        O mother marvellously fair,
        And fairest now in thy despair,
    Look up ! O be of comfort ! Do not die !
        Let the black hour blow by.

Cold is the night, and colder thou art lying.
    Gnawing a stone sits Famine at thy feet
        Shivering and sighing ;
        Blacker than Famine, on thy breast,
        Like a sick child that will not rest,

Moans Pestilence; and hard by, with
    fingers fleet,
      Frost weaves his winding-sheet.

Snow, snow : the wold is white as one. cold
    lily.
    Snow : it is frozen round thee as hard as
      lead ;
        The wind blows chilly ;
    Thou liest white in the dim night,
    And in thine eyes there is no light,
And the Snow falleth, freezing on thy head
    And covering up thy dead.

Ah, woe! thy hands, no longer flower-bearing,
    Press stony on thy heart; and thy heart
      bleeds ;
        Thine eyes despairing
    Watch while the fierce Fire clings and
      crawls
    Through falling roofs and crumbling
      walls.
    Ah, woe! to see thee thus, the wild soul
      pleads,
        The wild tongue intercedes.

O, we will cry to God, and pray and plead for
    thee ;
We with a voice that troubles heaven and
    air
      Will intercede for thee:
    We will cry for thee in thy pain
    Louder than storm and wind and rain ;
What shape among the nations may com-
    pare
      With thee, most lost, most fair ?

Yea, thou hast sinned and fallen, O City
    splendid,
Yea, thou hast passed through days of
    shamefullest woe—
      And lo ! they are ended—
    Famine for famine, flame for flame,
    Sorrow for sorrow, shame for shame,
Verily thou hast found them all ;—and lo !
      Night and the falling snow.

Let Famine eat thy heart, let Fire and Sorrow
    Hold thee, but turn thy patient eyes and see
      The dim sweet morrow.

Better be thus than what thou wast,
Better be stricken and overcast,
Martyr'd once more, as when to all things
free
Thy lips cried "Liberty!"

Let the Snow fall! thou shalt be sweeter and
whiter;
Let the Fire burn! under the morning sky
Thou shalt look brighter.
Comfort thy sad soul through the night;
Turn to the east and pray for light;
Look up! O be of comfort! do not die!
Let the black hour blow by!

CHORUS.   *The* ROYAL CHANCELLOR.

CHORUS.

See where slow-footed, silent, and alone,
Cometh the grim gray soul of all this woe.
He climbs the knoll, and in the frosty moon-
light
Standing gigantic, looketh silently
On the imperial City that afar
Looms as a phantasm through the vitreous air.

CHANCELLOR.

Paris ! they did not lie who call'd thee fair ;
And never wert thou fairer than this night
When God and Man conspire to write thy
    doom.

CHORUS.

He speaks; and brightly on his glittering
    helm,
And on his frosty face and grizzled beard,
Glimmers the silver radiance of the moon.

CHANCELLOR.

What women are ye ?—who, clad like Hecaté,
Gather and turn your faces white one way,
Hither, like lilies wind-blown on a mere ?

CHORUS.

Poor sisters, bearing in our hands the Cross.

CHANCELLOR.

What do ye abroad, at midnight, and alone ?

CHORUS.

Searching the heaps of slain lest any live.

CHANCELLOR.

From what land are ye? Children of what
　　mother?

CHORUS.

Daughters of France, for whom we weep this
　　night.

CHANCELLOR.

Weep not for France.　She reapeth her own
　　seed.

CHORUS.

Yea—but we sicken, lest she wholly die.

CHANCELLOR.

Die?　Let France die; for she hath lived too
　　long,
The white-skin'd Leper of a wholesome
　　world,

Creeping from porch to porch of peaceful
    dwellings,
Clad in fine linen and with scented locks,
Leaving in her foul trail disease and doom,
Heart-eating ennui, and accurst desire
Bred of the marrow of corrupted bones.
Die? If a dagger-stroke could slay this
    France,
This unclean harlot, this infecting fraud,
Envenoming all lips that she doth kiss,
Cursing the lips that will not kiss at all,
I would strike home this night unto her heart,
And bury her to the deep and solemn sound
Of thanksgiving from a world purified.
But since I cannot slay her as I would,
Since she is many-lived and subtle and
    quick,
We will try Fire, and let it on her heel
Fasten like a red wolf and drag her down;
And in her snake's-eyes we will flash the
    sword
So that she screams remembering her sins;
And she shall see those Temples desolate
Wherein she sat with sick face altar-wards

Worshipping Thammuz and all gods ob-
    scene;

And while she moans, out of the earth shall
    steal

Famine, and like a toad slip down her throat,

And in the belly of her coil and spit;

Frost too shall fasten on her quivering
    limbs,

And slowly, with blunt teeth, bite to the
    bone;

And then, perchance in the eleventh hour,

This France may gaze upon the world she
    curst,

And pray to God to heal her long disease,

Or send swift lightning down, and let her
    die!

CHORUS.

Why art thou bitter?   Is thy wrong so great?

CHANCELLOR.

Mountainous, women; and revenge is sweet.

CHORUS.

Name not revenge, but give thy wrong a
    name.

CHANCELLOR.

I am a Teuton—see, my wrong is said.

CHORUS.

Teuton or Frank, utter thy wrong from France.

CHANCELLOR.

Then listen.   Ye are women, and ye weep
For France who bare ye; I am a man, and
    born   .
Out of a fruitful and a perfect womb;
And not with feverish fancies, peevish care,
Nor yet with easy tears, yet passing well,
In mine own fashion, more with deeds than
    words,
I cling to her that bare me—Germany,—
Yea, she who yonder sits beside the Rhine,

And with large eyes that measure heaven and
    earth
Looks hither.   Shall I tell an old wife's tale
Of how your France in her most drunken
    hour
Sprang to our vineyards, to our tranquil fields,
And struck, with all a furious harlot's hate
For what is purer than her own foul self,
At the great mother,—slew her shrieking
    children,—
Drove her from lair to lair across the dark
Hungry and naked, while the moaning babe
Drank from her wounded breast not milk but
    blood?
Shall I remind ye of that fiery scourge
France held with maniac-strength to lash
    the world,
Till the world rose, and tore it from her grasp,
And flung it far into the silent sea?
Or of that other meaner, gaudier whip,
A baby's rattle, a mere infant's toy,
Snatch'd from her trembling hand and flung
    despised
Into a corner only yesterday?

These things are stories for old men to
    tell,
Women to wonder at, and bards to rhyme.
How! shall a harlot threaten all earth's
    kings?
What! shall a painted reveller of the stews,
Full-teeth'd with all the spitefulness of lust,
Crawl with a dagger up and down the earth
So that no mortal man can sleep at night?
Shall France, this Messalina of the nations,
This thing of many lovers, luring all,
Constant to none, adulterous with all,
Constant to nothing but inconstancy,
Shall this crown'd strumpet break the peace-
    ful air
Now with red revel, now with the sharp
    sword,
Just as the whim comes, as the wine inspires,
As peevish passion and unnatural lust,
Impotent to allay their own foul fire,
Urge on and prompt the miserable will?
No, but an arm, a man's hand clad in mail,
Hath struck one blow, and there the scarecrow
    lies,

And I, and every man that walks the world,
May sleep more freely now this thing is done.

CHORUS.

If it be so, then leave her now to God—
Nor trample on a thing so wholly fallen.

CHANCELLOR.

Nay, God's avenging Furies first shall work.

CHORUS.

To what avail, since she is impotent ?

CHANCELLOR.

That she may taste the cup of ills she gave.

CHORUS.

She hath drunk deep; O let her drink no
    more !

CHANCELLOR.

'Tis but begun. She must be bound with
    cords,
And gagged, and stript of all her gauds and
    gold.

CHORUS.

Ah, woe! what shall she do thus bound and
    stript?

CHANCELLOR.

Her sons shall till the ground and fill her
    mouth,
Her daughters weave her homely homespun
    raiment,
And when she hath knelt and sworn a mighty
    oath,
And writ this oath upon a charter down,
Why we may loose her bonds and set her
    free.

CHORUS.

To wander out o'er the waste world in shame.

CHANCELLOR.

Peace, women; for these things shall come to
    pass,
Since it is written he who cares to sow
Shall reap the harvest, be it grain or
    weed.
Let France walk forth in sackcloth, let her
    wrists
Wear gyves; set, too, a fool's-cap on her
    head,
With " Glory " for a label writ in blood;
Then let a trumpeter before her go,
And let him sound, and between whiles
    aloud
Read the long record of enormities,
And ending each, strike sharply with the
    scourge
On the bare shoulders of the penitent;
And let the little children of the earth
Follow and point, while good wives raise their
    hands,
And honest burghers nodding pipe in mouth,

Standing at doors with broad good-humour'd
    stare,
Mutter aloud, "Thank God! the world is free!"

CHORUS.

Mother! faintly on thy dark towers beaming
    Yonder moon is sailing eastward slow;
All around thee silent hills are dreaming,
    Coldly sheeted in the wintry snow;
From thy husht heart stealing to the ocean,
Underneath the blue ice dimly gleaming,
Crawls the river with a serpent motion,
    Wafting the chill whisper of thy woe.

O for words to shine upon and cheer thee
    Where thou liest dark and desolate!
Mother! shapes not human gather near thee,
    Crouch'd beneath the night-shade of thy
        fate;
Spirits watch thee where thou liest stricken.
Pray, and while thou prayest they shall hear
    thee—

Comfort!—they who strike thee may be
  stricken,
 Gathering like storm-clouds at thy gate.

On thy crownless head are dust and ashes,
  On thy fair white throat are marks of
    flame—
Low thou liest, drooping proud eyelashes,
  Clenching hands and heaving breasts in
    shame;
Naked to the frost-wind art thou lying;
Snow-white is thy face, and yet it flashes,
Answering the last look of the dying,
  While they seek thine eyes and name thy
    name.

'Tis a name that shook the trembling
  nations
 Trumpeted upon the heights of old;
'Tis a name the earth with acclamations
 Murmured, dancing round thy Throne of
   Gold;

'Tis the name of earth's sublimest schemer;
'Tis the name that freed the generations :
Still the same, grown sadder and supremer,
    Blesseder, O Martyr, twenty-fold.

By the flag with thine own heart's-blood
    gory,
    Lifted up and waved in the world's eyes ;
By the strange and ne'er forgotten story
    Of the flight of Kings and death of Lies ;
By the light that never since hath dwin-
    dled,
Man again shall see thee in thy glory ;
By the fire upon the mountains kindled—
    Beautiful, a Queen, thou shalt arise.

Bitterer than gall have been the days for
    thee,
    Yet they shall be blessed days indeed,
For the very blood thereof shall raise for
    thee
    Men and women of diviner seed.

Weary of fulfilling what was written,
Even the Avenging Angel prays for thee!
Smiter of the nations, thou art smitten—
  Freer of the nations, be thou freed!

Meantime, sleep!—worn with thy weary
    yearning—
  Sleep a space beneath the stars this night;
With thy many watch-fires dimly burning,
  Scatter'd red upon the wold snow-white,
Slumber in the dark, O mother City!
O'er thee, dim and strange to our discerning,
Miraculously fair, a Shape of Pity
  Waiteth with a drawn Sword and a Light.

Blessed is the Light in his hand swinging,
  Waving bright white pinions like a dove;
Blessed is the Sword that he is bringing,
  Such as holy spirits wield above;
Such another brand arose in beauty
O'er the Gate of Paradise up-springing.
Mother, hearken—it is the Sword of Duty;
  Mother, hearken—it is the Light of Love!

Awakening, in one strong hand, O mother,
　　Take the shining weapon of the free,
And the sweet Lamp grasping in the other,
　　Lift it high that all the world may see.
Bought with bloody tears and bitterest sor-
　　　　row,
They are thine for ever, martyr-mother!
Thou shalt wear them on some golden mor-
　　　　row,
　　Dawn shall come, the storm of God shall
　　　　flee.

And because thy queenly robe is riven,
　　Thou shalt win a raiment star-enwrought—
Under the new dawn and the blue heaven
　　Thou shalt wear this raiment blood hath
　　　　bought;
Further, since thy heart hath cast off weak-
　　　　ness,
For thy forehead shall a crown be given.
Mother, hearken—it is the Robe of Meekness;
　　Mother, hearken — it is the Crown of
　　　　Thought!

O, but all the nations shall adore thee
　When thy days of bitterness are fled ;
With the Robe of Meekness shining o'er
　　thee,
　With the Lamp of Love to light thy tread,
Clad in lily raiment, O my mother,
Holding in one hand the light before thee,
Lifting up the bright Sword in the other,
　Smiling, with the Crown upon thy head !

Dream of it this night, O queen of nations,—
　Dream of it, tho' crusht and undertrod,—
Freer of the souls of generations,
　Raise that face of sorrow from the sod;
Casting off thy sins and thy disgraces,
Issuing from utter tribulations,
Struggling from the serpent's fierce embraces,
　Pass along the narrow path of God.

The ROYAL CHANCELLOR.

How long shall I to this sick world, this
　　mass
Of social sores, this framework of disease,

This most infected many-member'd earth,

Play the hard surgeon, dexterous in my
craft,

Impassive, smiling with a shrunken heart,

And hated by the very thing I cure?

Why now, this night a pen-stroke like a
knife

Falls, and at dawn the people corporate

May feel one limb the less; should the pen
fail,

A sword-stroke settles all, and the rich life

That oozed into the limb and wasted there,

Withdrawn into the body of the state

Deepens the blood to livelier crimson, strikes

Fresh thrills of fire through the electric brain.

Europe forsooth is piteously sick,

Polluted every fibre with old sores

And new diseases, and I shall not fail

In my cold healing mission, though it
yields

Its life up, agonizing 'neath my hand.

To stand this night alone with Destiny,

Alone in all the world beneath the stars,

And hold the string that makes the puppets
    dance,
Is something; but to feel the steadfast
    will
Deepen, the judgment clear itself, the gaze
Grow keener, all the purpose that was
    dim
Brighten distinct in the serene still light
Of conquest—that is more; more than all
    power,
More than lip-homage, more than crowns and
    thrones,
More than the world; for it is life indeed.
O how the dreams and hopes and plans
    cohere!
How the great phalanx broadens! Like a
    wave
It washes Europe, and before its sweep
The lying idols, based on quicksand, shift,
Totter, and fall: strewn with the wreck and
    dead,
It shrieks and gathers up a flashing crest
In act to drown the lingering life of France.
Wave of the Teuton, is it wonderful

The grand old King sees in thy victory
The strength and wrath of God?

                      Here then I pause
And let me whisper it to mine own heart,
I tremble. I have played with fire; behold,
It hath devour'd God's enemy and mine;
And tamely at my bidding croucheth now
With luminous eyes half closed. This fire is
    Truth,
And by it I shall rise or fall. This fire
Is very God's—I know it; and thus far
God to my keeping hath committed it.
What next? and next? There at my feet
    lies France,
Bound, stricken, screaming,—yonder, good as
    dead,
Pluckt of his fangs, the imperial adder crawls,
Tame as a mouse. I have struck down these
    twain,
The Liar, and the creature of the Liar;
I have slain these twain with an avenging
    flame,
And while I stand victorious comes a voice

Out of the black abysses of the earth
Whereat I pause and tremble.   'Tis so
    easy
To cast down Idols!   The tide so pitilessly
Washes each name from the waste sands of
    time!
'Twas yestermorn the Man of Mysteries fell—
Whose turn comes next?

           Not thine, not thine, at least,
O sovereign Lord and King! thou great grey
    head,
Simple and child-like in the aureole
Thou deemest holy,—no, thou shalt not fall;
But rather, like Empedocles of old,
I who have led thee on, thy loving slave,
Would plunge into the crater, and with life
Appease the awful hunger of the earth.
From Italy to the blue Baltic rolls
A voice, a wind, a murmur in the air,
A tone full of the sense of winds and waters
And the faint whispers from ethereal fields,
A cry of anguish and of mystery
Echoed by the volcano in whose depths

The monarchs one by one have disap-
peared.

And men who hear it answer back one
word,

"Liberty!"—Cities echo through their streets;

The word is wafted on from vale to vale:

Heart-drowsy Albion answers with a cheer,

Feeble yet clear; the great wild West refrains;

Italy thunders, and Helvetia

Blows the wild horn high up among her
hills;

France, wounded, dying, stretch'd beneath
my feet,

Gnaws at her bonds and shrieks in mad
accord

(For she indeed first gave the thing a name);

And even the wily Russian, with his yoke

Prest on innumerable groaning necks,

Sleek like the serpent, smooths his frosty
cheek

To listen, and half-smiling hisses back

The strange word "Liberty!" between his
teeth,

And shivers with a bitterer sense of cold

Than ever seized him in the lonely realm
O'er which he paceth hungry and alone.

CHORUS.

Light on the brow
    Of the hill of Time,
What light art thou,
Whither all men now
    Turn eyes and climb?
Still gleaming afar,
    While the wild days go,
Still shining a Star
    In the region of snow:
We crave thee, we cry for thee,
We faint and we sigh for thee,—
    Thou shinest above,—
Yea, we dare die for thee,
    Light that we love.

Not yet, O Light,
    Alas not yet,
May we reach the height
Where dim and bright
    Thy lamp is set,—

Like waves we whiten

   In the waste below,

We darken and brighten,

   We ebb and we flow :

Dim stretch the heights above

All days and nights above,—

   Past the storms stream,—

Light of all lights above

   Art thou a dream ?

No dream, O far

   Sweet Light and strange !

Not as dreams are,

But a thronëd Star

   That doth not change !

O'er the world thou hast gleamed

   Since the first dim day :

Dreams have been dream'd

   And have passed away ;

All dreams have burn'd to thee,

All days have turn'd to thee,

   O Liberty !

And as all have yearned to thee

   We yearn and see !

On the mountain's brow
Dimly discern'd,
What Light art thou,
Whither all turn now
As they ever turn'd ?—
The great earth flowers to thee,
The earth's tongues name thee,
All things, all hours, to thee
Upturn, and claim thee ;—
And the world's waves wail for thee,
And our cheeks flash pale for thee,
Yet art thou sure—
And though all hopes fail for thee,
Thou shalt endure !

The ROYAL CHANCELLOR.

What is this thing that men call " Liberty ? "
Not force, not tumult, not the wind and rain
And tempest, not the spirit of mere storm,
Not earthquake, not the lightning, not swift
Fire,
Not one of these, but mightier far than
these,—

The everlasting principle of things,
Out of whose silence issue all, the rock
Whereon the mountain and the crater stand,
The adamantine pillars of the earth,
Deep-based beneath the ever-varying air
And under the wild changes of the sea,
The inevitable, the unchangeable,
The secret law, the impulse, and the thought,
Whereby men live and grow.

                          Then I, this night
As ever, dare with a man's eyes and soul
Hold by this thing whereof the foolish rave,
And cry, " In God's name, peace, ye winds
        and waves,
Ye froths and bubbles on the sea, ye voices
Haunting the fitful region of the air!
God is above ye all, and next to God
The Son and Holy Spirit, and beneath
These twain the great anointed Kings of
        Earth,
And underneath the Kings the Wise and
        Good,
And underneath the Wise the merely Strong,

And least of all, clay in the hands of all,
The base, the miserable, and the weak.
What, then, is this that ye name " Liberty " ?
There is evermore a higher. Not like
    waves
Beating about in a waste sea are men,
But great, small, fair, foul, strong, weak,
    miserable ;—
And Liberty is law creating law
Wherein each corporal member of the world
Filleth his function in the place ordain'd.
Child at the knee, look in thy mother's
    face !
Boy-student, reverence the philosopher !
Clown, till the earth, and let the market
    thrive !
Citizen, doff to beauty and to grace,
To antique fame and holy ancestry !
Nobles, blood purified from running long,
Circle of sanctity, surround the King !
King, stand on the bare height and raise
    thine eyes,
For there sits God above thee, reverencing
The perfect mirror of the soul of things

Wherein He gazes calmly evermore,
And knows Himself divine !

Thus stands for ever
The eternal Order like a goodly tree,
The root of which is deep within the soil.
And lo! the wind and rain are beating
    on it,
And lightning rends its branches ; yet anon
It hangs in gorgeous blossom still-renewed,
And shoots its topmost twig up through the
    cloud
To touch the changeless stars.   Herr Demo-
    crat
Comes with his blunt rough axe, and at its
    root
Strikes shrieking; the earth's parrots echo
    him;
Blow follows blow ; the air reverberates ;
But the Tree stands.   Come winds and waves
    and lightnings,
Come axe-wielders, come ye iconoclasts,
And spend your strength in vain.   What!
    ye would stretch

This goodly tree, this very Iggdrasil,

Down to the dusty level of your lives,

Would strew the soil with the fair blooms
thereof,

Would tear away the succulent leaves and
make

A festal chaplet for Silenus' hair,

A drunken garland for the Feast of Fools.

See, yonder blow the branches where the
great

Tremble like ripen'd fruit; yonder the holy

Gleam in the silvern foliage, sweet and
fair;

There, just beneath the cloud, most dim in
height,

The flowers of monarchy open their buds

And turn their starry faces upward still.

Strike at the root, my little democrat,

Down with them! Down with the whole
goodly tree!

Down even with that fair shoot beyond the
cloud,

Down with the unseen bloom of perfect
height,

Down with the blossom on the topmost twig,
Down with the light of God !

                 I compare further
This Order to a Man, body and brain,
Heart, lungs, eyes, feet to stand on, hands to
     strike.
The King is to the realm what conscience is
To manhood; the true statesman is the
     brain;
And under these subsist, greater and less,
The members of the body politic.
Behold now, this alone is majesty :
The incarnate Conscience of the people, fixed
Beyond the body, higher than the brain,
Yet perfect fruit of both,—the higher sense
That flashes back through all the popular
     frame
The intuitions and the lights divine
Whereby the world is guided under God.
Nor are all Kings ancestral, though these
     same
Are highest. Yonder in the stormy West
The plain man Lincoln rose to majesty,

Incarnated the conscience and the will
Of the strong generation, moved to his end,
Struck, triumph'd in the name of conscience,
    fell,
And like a sun that sets in bloody light,
In dying darken'd half earth's continents.˝

. . . What, art thou there, old Phantom of the
    Red,
Gambetta? Urge thy legions, for in truth
There is no face in France this day with
    light
So troublous to the eyes of victory.
O brave one, wert *thou* France's will and
    soul,
Why we might tremble. Let there rise a
    land,
As strong in conscience and as stern in soul
As we have been to follow a living truth,
And it might slay us even as we have
    slain
Imperial France and the Republic. Now
Supreme we stand, our symbol being the
    sword,

Our King the hand that strikes ; in that one
    hand
I strike, all strike, yea every Teuton strikes.
Reason and conscience knitted in accord
Are deathless, and must overcome the world.
The higher law will shape them. I believe
There is evermore a higher.

CHORUS.

Blue arc of heaven whose lattices
    Are throng'd with starry eyes ;
Vast dome that over land and seas,
    Dost luminously rise,
With mystic characters enwrought
More strange than all poetic thought !

Hear, Heaven, if thou canst hear ! and see,
    O stars, if see ye can !
Mark, while your speechless mystery
    Flows to a voice in man :
He stands erect this solemn hour
In reverent insolence of power.

Order divine, whose awful show
    Dazzles all guess or dream;
Sequence unseen, whose mystic flow
    Fulfils the immortal scheme;
Thou law whereby all stand or stir,—
Here breathes your last interpreter!

Because one foolish King hath slain
    Another foolish King;
Because a half-born nation's brain
    With dizzy joy doth ring;
Because at the false shepherd's cry
The silly sheep still throng to die;

Because purblind philosophy
    Out of her cobweb'd cave
Croaks in a voice of senile glee
    While empty patriots rave;
Because humanity is still
The gull of any daring will;

Because the tinsel order stands
    A little longer yet;
Because in each crown'd puppet's hands
    A laurel-sprig is set,

While the old lame device controls
The draff of miserable souls;

Because man's blood again bathes bright
    The purple and the throne,
And gray fools gladden at the sight,
    And maiden choirs intone;
Because once more the puppet Kings
Dance, while Death's lean hand pulls the
    strings;

Because these things have been and are,
    And oft again may be,
Doth this man swear by sun and star,
    And oh our God by Thee,
Framing to cheat his own shrewd eyes
His fair cosmogony of lies.

O Lord our God whose praise we sing,
    Behold he deemeth Thee
A little nobler than the King,
    And greater in degree,
Set just above the monarch's mind,
Greater in sphere but like in kind!

O calm Intelligence divine,
    Transcending life and death,
He deems these bursting bubbles Thine,
    Blown earthward by Thy breath,—
He marks Thee sitting well content,
Like some old King at tournament.

The lists are set; upon the sod
    The gleaming columns range;
The sign is given by Thee, O God,
    From Thy pavilion strange:
The trumpets blow, the champions meet,
One screams—Thou smilest on Thy seat.

Behold, O God, the Order blest
    Of Thy great chivalry!
See tinsel crown and glittering crest,
    Cold heart and empty eye!
The living shout, the dying groan,
All reddens underneath Thy throne!

Accept Thy chosen! great and good,
    Vouchsafe them all they seek!
Deepen their purple in man's blood!
    Trumpet them with man's shriek!

Paint their escutcheons fresh, O Sire ;
With heart's blood bright and crimson fire !

And further, from the fire they light
    Protect them with Thy hand,
Beyond the bright hill of the fight
    Let them in safety stand ;
For 'twere not well a random blow
Should strike thy next-of-kin below.

O God! O Father! Lord of All !
    Spare us, for we blaspheme,
See,—for upon our knees we fall,
    And hush our mocking scream—
Let us pray low ; let us pray low ;
Thy will be done ; thy Kingdom grow !

Blue arc of heaven whose lattices
    Are throng'd with starry eyes,
Still dome that over earth and seas
    Doth luminously rise ;
Fair Order mystically wrought,
More strange than all poetic thought.

He fears ye all, this son of man,
　　To his own soul he lies,
Lo! trembling at his own dark plan
　　He contemplates the prize:
He has won all, and lo! he stands
Clutching the glory in his hands!

To one, to all, on life's dark way,
　　Sooner or late is brought
The silent solemnizing ray
　　Illuminating thought;
It shines, they stand on some lone spot,
Its light is strange, they know it not.

Sleeps like a mirror in the dark
　　The conscience of the soul,
Unknown, where never eye may mark,
　　While days and seasons roll;
But late or soon the walls of clay
Are loosening to admit the day.

Light comes—a touch—a streak—a beam—
　　Child of the unknown sky—

And lo ! the mirror with a gleam
   Flashes its first reply :
Light brighteneth ; and all things fair
Flow to the glass and tremble there.

O Lord our God, Thou art the Light,
   We shine by Thee alone ;
Tho' thou hast made us mirrors bright,
   The gleam is not our own ;
Until thy ray shines sweet and plain
All shall be dark as this man's brain.

Thro' human thought as thro' a cave
   Creep gently, Lord, this hour ;
Tho' now 'tis darker than the grave
   There lies the shining power ;
Come ! let the soul flash back to Thee
The million lights of Deity !

CHORUS. *A DESERTER.*

DESERTER.

O I am spent ! My heart fails, and my limbs
Are palsied. Would to God that I were dead !

Y

CHORUS.

Stand! What art thou, who like a guilty
    thing
Creepest along the shadow, stooping low?

DESERTER.

A man. Now stand aside and let me pass.

CHORUS.

Not yet. Whence fleest thou? Whither dost
    thou go?

DESERTER.

From Famine and Fire. From Horror. From
    Frost and Death.

CHORUS.

O coward! traitor to unhappy France!
Stand forward in the moon, that it may light
The blush of shame upon thy guilty cheek!
Lo, we are women, yet we shiver cold
To look upon so infamous a thing.

DESERTER.

Nay, look your fill—I care not—stand and see.

CHORUS.

O horror! horror! who hath done this deed?

DESERTER.

What say ye? am I fair to look upon?

CHORUS.

The dead are fairer.   O unhappy one!

DESERTER.

Why do ye shudder?   Am I then so foul?

CHORUS.

There is no living flesh upon thy bones.

DESERTER.

Famine hath fed upon my limbs too long.

CHORUS.

And thou art rent as by the teeth of hounds.

DESERTER.

Fire tore me, and what blood I have I bleed.

CHORUS.

Thine eyes stare like the blank eyes of a
corpse.

DESERTER.

They have look'd so close on horror and so
long
I cannot shut them from it till I die.

CHORUS.

Thou crawlest like a man whose sick limbs
fail.

DESERTER.

Ha, Frost is there, and numbs me like a
snake.

CHORUS.

God help thee, miserable one; and yet,
Better if thou hadst perish'd in thy place
Than live inglorious tainted with thy shame.

DESERTER.

Shame? I am long past shame. I know her
    not.

CHORUS.

Is there no sense of honour in thy soul?

DESERTER.

Honour? Why see, she hath me fast
    enough:
These are her other names, Fire, Famine, and
    Frost,—
Soon I shall hear her last and sweetest,—
    Death.

CHORUS.

Hast thou no care for France, thy martyr'd
    land?

DESERTER.

What hath she given me? Curses and blows.

CHORUS.

O miserable one, remember God!

DESERTER.

God? Who hath look'd on God? Where
    doth He dwell?
O fools, with what vain words and empty
    names
Ye sicken me. Honour, France, God! All
    these—
Hear me—I curse. Why, look you, there's
    the sky,
Here the white earth, there, with its bleeding
    heart,
The butcher'd City; here half dead stand I,
A murder'd man, grown grey before my
    time,
Forty years old—a husband, and a father—
An outcast flying out of Hell. Who talks

To me of "honour?"   The first tears I wept
When standing at my wretched mother's knee,
Because her face was white, and she wore
    black,
That day the bells rang out for victory.
Then, look you, after that my mother sat
Weeping and weary in an empty house,
And they who look'd upon her shrunken
    cheeks
Fed her with "honour."   'Twas too gentle
    fare,—
She died.   Nay, hearken!   Left to seek for
    bread,
I like a wild thing haunted human doors
Searching the ash for food.   I ate and
    lived.
I grew.   Then, wretched as I was, I felt
Strange stirs of manhood in my flesh and
    bones,
Dim yearnings, fierce desires, and one pale
    face
Could still them as the white moon charms
    the sea.
Oh, but I was a low and unclean thing,

And yet she loved me, and I stretch'd these
    hands

To God, and blest Him for His charity.

Mark that:—I blest Him, I. Even as I
    stood,

Bright in new manhood, the drums beat,—a
    hand

Fell on my shoulder, and, "in France's
    name,"

A voice cried, "Follow." To my heart they
    held

Cold steel:—I followed; following saw her
    face

Fade to a bitter cry—hurl'd on with blows,

Curs'd, jeer'd at, scorn'd, went forth as in a
    dream,

And, driven into the bloody flash of war,

Struck like a blinded beast I knew not whom

Blows for I knew not what. The fierce years
    came

Like ulcers on my heart, and heal'd, and went.

Then I crept back, a broken sickly man,

To seek her, and I found her—dead! She had
    died,

Poor worm, of hunger. She had ask'd for
 bread,
And "France" had given her stones. She
 had pray'd to " God ; "
He had given her a grave. The day she
 died,
The bells rang for another victory.

CHORUS.

O do not weep! Yet we are weeping too.

DESERTER.

Now mark, I was too poor a worm to grieve
Too long and deeply. The years passed. My
 heart
Heal'd, and as wounds heal, harden'd. Once
 again
I join'd the wolves that up and down the earth
Rush tearing at men's lives and women's
 hearts.
That passed, and I was free. One morn I saw
Another woman, and I hunger'd to her,

And we were wedded. Hard days follow'd
    that;
And children—she was fruitful—all your
    worms
Are fruitful, mark—that is God's blessing
    too!
Well, but we throve, and farm'd a bit of land
Out yonder by the City. I learn'd to love
The mother of my little ones. Time sped;
And then I heard a cry across the fields,
The old cry, "Honour," the old cry, "To
    Arms!"
And like a wolf caught in his lair I shrunk
And shudder'd. It grew louder, that curst
    cry!
Day follow'd day, no bells rung victory,
But there were funeral faces everywhere;
And then I heard the far feet of the foe
Trampling the fields of France and coming
    nearer
To that poor field I sow'd. I would have fled,
But that they thrust a weapon in mine hands
And bade me stand and strike "for France."
    I laugh'd!

But the wolves had me, and we screaming
    drew
Into the City. Shall I gorge your souls
With horror? Shall I croak into your ears
What I have suffer'd there, what I have
    seen?
I was a worm, ever a worm, and starved
While the plump coward cram'd. Look at
    me, women!
Fire, Famine, and Frost have got me; yet I
    crawl,
And shall crawl on; for hark you, yester-
    night,
Standing within the City, sick at heart,
I gazed up eastward, thinking of my home
And of the woman and children desolate,
And lo! out of the darkness where I knew
Our hamlet lay there shot up flames and
    cast
A bloody light along the arc of heaven;
And all my heart was sicken'd unaware
With hunger such as any wild thing feels
To crawl again in secret to the place
Whence the fierce hunter drove it, and to see

If its young live ; and thither indeed I fare ;
And yonder flame still flareth, and I crawl,
And I shall crawl unto it though I die ;
And I shall only smile if they be dead,
If I may merely see them once again,—
For come what may, my cup of life is full,
And I am broken from all use and will.

CHORUS.

Pass on, unhappy one ; God help thee now !

DESERTER.

If ye have any pity, give me bread.

CHORUS.

Lean on us ! O thou lost one, come this way.

DESERTER.

And whither do ye lead me, O ye women ?

CHORUS

Look yonder where the light gleams from a
    door,
There shalt thou eat thy fill and warm thy
    limbs.

DESERTER.

'Tis well ; there is some pity in your hearts.

CHORUS,

We pity thee and bless thee, praying God.

DESERTER.

Nay, let "God" be—In truth I know Him
    not.

CHORUS.

Stars in heaven with gentle faces,
Can ye see and keep your places ?
Flowers that on the old earth blossom,
Can ye hang on such a bosom ?
Canst thou wander on for ever
Through a world so sad, O River ?

O ye fair things 'neath the sun,
Can ye bear what Man hath done?

This is Earth.   Heaven glimmers yonder.
Pause a little space and ponder!

Day by day the fair world turneth
Dewy eyes to heaven and yearneth,
Day by day the mighty mother
Sees her children smite each other:
She moans, she pleads, they do not hear her—
She prays—the skies seem gathering near
    her—
Yearning down diviner, bluer,
Baring every star unto her,—
Each strange light with swinging censer
Sweeter seeming and intenser,—
Yet she ceaseth not her cry,
Seeing how her children die.

On her bosom they are lying,
Clinging to her, dead and dying—
Dead eyes frozen in imploring
Yonder heaven they died adoring,

Dying eyes that upward glimmer
Ever growing darker, dimmer ;
And her eyes, too, thither turning,
Asking, praying, weeping, yearning,
Search the blue abysses, whither
He who made her, brought her hither,
Gave her children, bade them grow,
Vanish'd from her long ago.

Ah, what children ! Father, see them !
Never word of hers may free them —
Never word of love may win them,
For there burneth fierce within them
Fire of thine ; soul-sick and sinning,
As they were in the beginning,
Here they wander. Father, see !
Generations born of thee !

Blest was Earth when on her bosom
First she saw the double blossom,
Double sweetness, man and woman,
One in twain divine and human,
Leaping, laughing, crying, clinging,
To the sound of her sweet singing—

Flesh like lily and rose together,
Eyes as blue as April weather,
Golden hair with golden shadows,
In the face the light of meadows,
In the eyes the dim soul peeping
Like the sky in water sleeping.
" Guard them well! " the Father said,
Set them in her arms,—and fled.

Countless worlds around Him yearning,
Vanish'd He from her discerning ;—
Then she drooped her fair face, seeing
On her breast each gentle being ;
And unto her heart she prest them,
Raised her look to heaven and blest them :
And the fountains leapt around her,
Leaves and flowers shot up and crown'd her,
Flowers bloom'd and streams ran gleaming,
Till with bliss she sank to dreaming ;—
And the darkness for a cover
Gently drew its veil above her,
And the new-born smiled reposing,
And a million eyes unclosing

Yearn'd through all the veil to see
That new fruit of mystery.

Father! come from the abysses;
Come, Thou light the mother misses;
Come, while hungry generations
Pass away, she sits in patience.
Of the children Thou didst leave her,
Millions have been born to grieve her.
See! they gather, living, dying,
Coming, going, multiplying;
And the mother for the Father,
Though like waves they rise and gather,
Though they blossom thick as grasses,
Misses every one that passes,
Flashes on them peace and light
Of a love grown infinite.

Father, see them! hath each creature
Something in him of Thy nature?
Born of Thee and of no other,
Born to Thee by a sweet mother,
Man strikes man, and brother brother.

z

Hearts of men from Thy heart fashioned
Bleed and anguish bloody-passion'd,
Beast-like roar the generations,
Tiger-nations spring on nations ;
Though the stars yearn downward nightly,
Though the days come ever brightly,
Though to gentle holy couches
Death in angel's guise approaches,
Though they name Thee, though they woo
    Thee,
Though they dream and yearn unto Thee,
Ill they guess the guise thou bearest,
Ill they picture Thee, Thou Fairest ;—
Come again, O Father wise,
Awe them with those loving eyes !

Stars in heaven with tender faces,
Can ye see and keep your places ?
Flowers that on the earth will blossom,
Can ye deck so sad a bosom ?
Canst thou singing flow for ever
Through a world so dark, O River ?
Father, canst Thou calmly scan
All that Man hath made of Man ?

The CHANCELLOR. *A* DEPUTY FROM THE
CITY.

CHANCELLOR.

Yield up again those stolen provinces!

Take council! be the prince of peacemakers!

For, let me say it in thy private ear,

As one who knows thee nobler than thy
cause,

There is no other hope for France than this

We proffer.   We have bought this thing with
blood—

Be wise and yield it—lest with bitterer
blood

We buy the dearest flesh and blood of
Gaul,

And welding it as clay unto our will

Pour into it a new and Teuton soul.

DEPUTY.

That threat is empty, for the soul is God's;

These souls are French, they have thriven on
French air;

Rather than swell your triumph with their
 lives
They would return to Him from whom they
 came.

CHANCELLOR.

Why, let them go!—The way to Him is
 short,
Nor very tedious—though it seems a way
Ye French love little, loving so much more
The windy breath with which ye flout your
 foe.—
Why, friend, we are no word-mongers, we
 twain:
Yet here, like market-women cheapening fish,
We wrangle at each other to no end.
I tell thee (shall I swear by anything?
I know thy nation loveth a round oath!)
I tell thee we are fixed as adamant,
Inexorable as the sea, and strong
To exact our wish as is the thunderbolt
That for a moment in the rain-cloud burns
Before it strikes the affrighted herdsman
 down.

Two powers have wrestled — one is over-
    thrown—
How should the thrown man with his broken
    back
Clutch to his heart the prize of victory ?
There is a victory in being vanquish'd
Ye little understand.   Did ever school-
    boy
Howl so when whipt ?   The world scream'd
    not as loud
When like a swarm of locusts, like a
    cloud
Of fiery pestilence, from the West to the
    East
Ye overran the bleeding continents,
And sowed in one Man's miserable name
The crop all living men are reaping now.

DEPUTY.

If I conceive thee, 'tis no sin of ours
That ye avenge on the fair head of France,
No crime of yesterday or yesteryear,
No deeds of live men walking in the sun,

But wrongs long buried with the scourge of
    God
In that forsaken island where he sleeps.

CHANCELLOR.

They would not lie, man!—from that lonely
    grave
They have arisen again and yet again,—
Até-like, not to be laid by any charm
But blood of sacrifice sent up to God
From France the altar in whose name he
    slew.

DEPUTY.

Yet Cæsar's triumphs were avenged on
    Cæsar;
Remember Katzbach! Leipsic! Waterloo!

CHANCELLOR.

O we remember! The Colossus fell,
And from the throne of every living King

A shadow passed; yet still with hungry eyes
The hordes he had led glared hate across the
    Rhine,
Till from the charnel-house of that great name
Uprose in his due time the wordy "Man
Of Silence;" round his feet the brute hosts
    leapt;
And smiling a smooth smile he glanced the
    way
They hunger'd. We were scattered, and we
    crouch'd
Under the Austrian eagle. Then, one day,
A plain man, a deep fellow with a will,
Rose saying, "Craft for craft! The bird of
    prey
Hovers too much above the German Rhine—
'Ware hawk! till he is trapt there is no sleep
For any of us poor creatures who love peace!"
When lo! the Vulture cried, "I am a Dove!"
And croak'd the hoarse cry of Democracy;
And as the soul of Italy arose,
The Vulture struck the Austrian Eagle down,
While all earth's kingdoms shook; then,
    stretching claws,

He hovered o'er the imperial walls of Rome
To warn the victor back. Now, that same
    man
I spake of, looking very humbly on,
Thought, " Craft for craft! The Frenchman
    wins by craft—
Not boldly, as the old French Eagle won.
What Marshall Vorwärts to Napoleon was,
Let me become to this the Man of Lies;
With his own weapons let me vanquish him ;
First in the secret chamber, then with steel
Out in the light of the world." So said, so
    done.
Close to the dotard Austrian for a time
We crouch'd; but we were gathering strength
    and ire ;
And one by one with the new Teuton soul
We fill'd the scattered people of the Rhine.
Then came the time to cast the Austrian off.
'Twas done, we struck; your foul bird scream'd
    in vain ;
And lo! with that one blow we felt our
    strength
Flow from the soul and grow invincible.

There was a pause. We saw the enemy

Hovering afar and ever gathering

And darkening the mighty River's bank;

And year by year we waited for the storm

We knew must break upon our heads at last.

It came—no bigger than the prophet's hand—

Then the tornado blowing from the West,—

So that the world cried, " God help Germany !"

And lo! God sent a wind out of the East;

And all the storm and wrack and thunder-
    rheum

Gathered in groaning tumult o'er the Rhine.

One from the East, the other from the West,

Tornado met tornado. One huge crash—

'Twas o'er! The West recoil'd in blood and
    fire,

Leaving the poor sing'd Vulture on the
    ground,

Struck by the lightning, screaming broken-
    wing'd,

Flapping to rise in vain. On goes the storm,

Driven less by sheer volition than the wind

God sent to drive it West; and still it sweeps—

Still the earth groans and darkens under it,

And still, as Canute cried unto the sea,

Thou criest " Pause ! " How, like a summer
    cloud

Recoil, and leave ye fresher for our rain !

True, we have slain the evil-omen'd Bird,

And in so far have blest not punish'd France,

Who followed his stale cry ;—but mark me,
    friend,

The sworn foe of the Teuton is the Celt,

Not the mere instrument your evil hands

Could find whene'er they itch'd for butchery ;—

For birds of prey abound,—and it is easy

To fashion leaders for such hosts as yours.

But this time we will place ye in a pen

High as the Vosges, deeper than the Rhine,

So that though all the birds of earth should
    call,

Though all the wild free beasts should roar
    their best,

France, pent within the prison of her own fields,

Shall like a tame thing only roar again.

DEPUTY.

Yet think of mercy.

CHANCELLOR.

We are merciful.

DEPUTY.

Take pity.

CHANCELLOR.

We are very pitiful.
Our women wail and weep in every house,
Our babes are fatherless, our maiden flowers
Wither unpluckt on every village way.
Who says we are not pitiful?

DEPUTY.
The head
That wrong'd ye is a serpent's head, and
bruised
Is writhing underneath your armèd heel.
The blood of both the Teuton and the Celt
Be on that head,—but we are innocent.
Uplift thy knife from the poor lambs of
France;

Spare them for Christ's sake; let me shepherd them
To some sad fold of peace !

CHANCELLOR.

How call ye them ?
Lambs ? Lambs man-tooth'd, and most om-
nivorous !
Lambs ? We shall draw the teeth of these
same lambs,
Lest in a little season they may find
Another wolf to lead them.

DEPUTY.

My tongue fails,
And my heart sickens.   Courtesy is rank,
When I must listen to such words as these,
And pick my feeble speech for France's sake.

CHANCELLOR.

Pick nothing ; speak thy thought as man to
man.
And criticise.   I adore criticism.

DEPUTY.

It is all in vain.   Ye are too fiercely bent
On blood and most unhallowëd revenge.

CHANCELLOR.

How now ?   Why, these are words for women.
     True,
I am a bugbear to the ancient dames
Of Europe, and the nations in their dread
Picture me cloven-footed ; but do not thou,
A wise man in thy generation, echo
The stale flat talk of fools.   Am I a vam-
     pire
That I should love this blood ?   I love mine
     ease—
My wine, my mistress—all earth's tasty things
In moderation—though I never suffer
The cup to cloud my reason and my soul,
Nor sell my manhood for a strumpet's kiss,
As ye have done in France.   Yet I believe
There are worse hues than that of blood, and
     Life

More pitiful than Death ; and I, indeed,

Am your physician, though ye know me not.

Sick, body and soul, ye have polluted earth,

Ye have sown abroad that beauteous leprosy

Whereof your artists and your poets die,

But now in one supremer nobler hour

Your revellers, from the lupanar called,

Instead of sickening of a long disease

And rotting in the arms of harlotry,

Have passed in bloody martyrdom to God.

In truth the bitterest tears your eyes can
weep

Will not too freely purge your heated orbs

Of their adulterous mist of lust and lies.

These are worse things than dying ! things I
deem

More pitiful than Death !   Instead of these

We give ye sudden Conscience flasht from
grief,

Fire for your Phrynes, and a naked Sword !

DEPUTY.

Then I, in France's name, for France's sake,

Reject the shallow puritanic lie,

And calling God to witness hurl ye back
The taunt and smile.   The stale flat talk of
    fools
Offends thy sense, yet how thou echoest it!—
While ye ride rough-shod through the beau-
    teous world,
Like Cromwell's English troopers singing
    hymns,
Not that your hearts are full of God at all,
But that it helps your feet to march in time,
While to the God of David ye intone,
Seeking the grimmest ever even in God,—
We, Frenchmen, subtly, delicately wrought,
Feel Him so keenly in the sense and soul,
Catch with so swift a sense of fragrancy
The divine truths of being, that our lives
Become too rich for your harsh utterance.
Fairer of spirit and more exquisite,
Subtler of sense, more sensual if thou wilt,
We tremble in the beautiful world God made;
Yea, loving Beauty for her own fair sake,
Perceiving her so marvellously fair,
In her we find an impulse and an end
Beyond your stale and flat morality.

Wherefore we seek to shape our very lives
To beauty and to music, which ye deem
The harlot's privilege and stock-in-trade;
We plant within our simplest daily needs
Spiritual sweetness and divine desire;
We stir to every wind of ecstasy;
We love no truth that is not beautiful,
Since Beauty is the highest truth of all,
The sum and end of human destiny.

CHANCELLOR.

The glory of a strong man is his strength;
But ye—why ye are triflers; though I own
I like your novels; they are pleasant reading,
Most toothsome to the after-dinner taste.

DEPUTY.

O hear me! if a sneer could kill a race,
Then had ye Teutons died of Europe's sneer!
As ye abide, so shall the Frank abide.
To ye no delicate line of law divides
Beauty from harlotry; for ye are dull,

And turn your hard-grain'd Gretchens to their
    use
As tamely as ye sow and reap your corn ;
And unto ye all rapturous sights and sounds,
All married interchange of sense and soul,
Are perilous, for ye dread the very Sun
May come upon your kitchen Danaës
And breed ye bastards in your own despite.
Nay, ye fear Beauty as some witch whose
    eyes
May hold ye like Tannhauser in the hills.
While ye have trumpeted God's wrath abroad,
While ye have driven His strength into men's
    hearts
As did the kings of ancient Israel,
We, we whom ye despised, have whispered
    low
God's secret ; we have made the hand of Art
More reverent, human voice and instrument
More delicate, all sense of sight and sound
More cunning ; one by one we have laid bare
The slender links that bind the soul of man
To all fair things whence it has grown and
    blown ;

A A

And we have gain'd ye in your own de-
    spite :

For if ye sing, ye sing more tenderly,

And if ye dream, ye dream more beauti-
    fully,

And if ye pray, perchance unconsciously

Ye blend into your prayer some beauteous
    sense

That till we Frenchmen cull'd it blew un-
    guess'd.

All this we have done and more for Beauty's
    sake,

And this forsooth ye christen "harlotry."

Ye are as Israël, and ye know no God

Unless He thunders; ye perceive no strength

Save when ye look upon a hurricane;

Your dry blood turns all beauty back to
    use,

By a coarse huswife's sampler fashioning

All gentle woofs of loveliness and youth,

Forgetting beauty blossoms out of use,

Not use from beauty, but from perfect use

The perfect flower of beauty crowning all.

Ye walk within a garden, and with care

Water your shrubs of hardy sentiment,

And train your creeping virtues; but ye
    frown

If the birds sing too loud, the blossoms
    scent

Too richly; ye speak, think, act, live, walk,
    fight

As if the beauteous world wherein ye dwell

Were leagued against ye and confederate

To seize ye as the woman in the Book

The man of strength and rob ye of your
    hair;

And in the very light of woman's eyes

Ye Werthers see no grade between the stare

Of lawful women sadly giving suck,

And what forsooth ye christen " harlotry."

CHANCELLOR.

A Jeremiad out of Babylon !

Let us return—yield the Rhine provinces.

DEPUTY.

What more ?

CHANCELLOR.

The rest is easy.   These come first.

DEPUTY.

And I have answer'd.   It can never be.

CHANCELLOR.

Never?   Why they are ours to have and
    hold.

DEPUTY.

To take is not to give.   We give them not.
We will appeal to Europe, to the world;
We will call out with one imploring voice,
Waking the sleeping Conscience of the earth!

CHANCELLOR.

Call.   Scream.   Have ye not call'd and
    screamed?   As loud
As underneath your sallow Corsican
We called of old.

DEPUTY.

Ye did not call in vain.

CHANCELLOR.

No; for our cause was righteous!—further-
more,
All backs like ours had felt that scourge of
God.
But now 'tis otherwise ; for ours indeed
Hath been a peaceful hand, and not a gauge,
A grim reminder and a daily threat,
A mailëd glove lying from day to day
Unlifted on the council-board of Kings ;
We play no tyrant, but iconoclast ;
And further, let me whisper in thine ear,
That were we thrice as bloody as ye deem,
The nations are too wise to risk the touch
Of that strong hand which like Belle-
rophon's
Hath slain the hugest Monster of the time.

DEPUTY.

They will not tamely see so foul a wrong.
We will call England.

CHANCELLOR.

Do not waste your breath :
England hath pined away into a voice.

DEPUTY.

Italy! Austria! Russia!   Shall not God
Conjure a soul in one or all of these?

CHANCELLOR.

Too late.   The days of chivalry are o'er.
On this side Time there is no hope for France
Save swift submission to her certain doom,—
Confinement in her mighty prison-house
West of the Vosges, o'er whose jagged walls
Let her glare thirsty at the flowing Rhine ;—
Thither indeed she comes not any more
In pomp of war or smile of amity.
Call?   Let her call till thunder echoes her !
But verily, friend, that thunder will be ours,
Such as now beats at yonder City's gates
Startling the timid eyelids of the dawn.

See! Fire and Death fill all the dreadful
    air.
Hearken!   Our guns are serenading now
Her who was late the Mistress of the world.
Speak; save her; save her miserable sons,
Fighting in vain against the hurricane.
No longer dally idly with your doom
As ye were wont to do with women's hair;
Speak, and speak quickly, lest ye wholly
    die!

CHORUS.

A DISTANT VOICE.

God! God! God!

CHORUS.

Hearken, O hearken!
The heavens darken,
The storm is growing,
The skies are snowing,
Whiter and whiter
Grows the ground, and brighter

The wild fires glisten,
As we moan and listen;
Wind-blown unto us
   A voice from the City
Thrills faintly through us.

VOICE.

Lord God, have pity !

CHORUS.

Gather in silence !
From mile on mile hence
Drearly is driven
Their cry to heaven ;
Like the faint intoning
Of the ocean moaning,
Like the murmur creeping
   Most faint and weak
From a dark cloud sleeping
   On a mountain peak.
'Tis the feeble crying
Of the sick and dying,

The famine-stricken ;
They sink and sicken,
They thirst, and creeping
Together moan,
In the damp dew sleeping
Pillow'd on stone—
And Sorrow above them
With her frozen cheek
Stoops—but to move them
Her breath is weak,—
Till with blank eyes glazing,
And their faint breath fled,
They sit there gazing,
Frozen and dead.

A VOICE.

Prepare !
.

CHORUS.

Like the opening of eyes
In a horrible dream,
Like the flash in the skies
When the thunder-cloud flies,

Comes the gleam.

It comes, and is gone;

The dark roars; and anon,

From fort to fort gleaming,

It burns in the night,

Till the long line is streaming

One glimmer of light—

Like the black swell that dashes

Round a headland and flashes

Foam-white!

A VOICE WITHIN THE CITY.

Woe! woe!

CHORUS.

'Tis begun, and they cry in the street,

As lambs rush together and bleat!

And the Horror above and around

Springs to a serpentine sound.

Lo! where the fiery spheres curve

Up through the air without swerve;

See how the bolts one by one

Speed to the flash of the gun!

Now, strain your eyes thro' the dark ;
Look on the City, and mark
How they strike on the roofs, and in thunder
Crash, and in flame rend asunder
To the groan of stone turret and column,
To the scream of the slain, to the solemn
Deep toll of the bell in the spire!

Voices Within.

Fire ! Fire !

Chorus.

See ! where it springs in the air,
With a scream and a rush and a glare,
Out of the roofs, while beneath
Blacker flames wrestle and seethe ;
Brighter and brighter! behold,
Wrapping the street in its fold,
Streaming and gleaming and burning,
Sinking, upspringing, returning,
Fierce, unappeasable, glowing
    Red-shadow'd on turret and vane—
While black shades are coming and going,
    Seeking to slake it in vain !

VOICE FROM WITHOUT.

Steady ! make ready ! aim higher—
Into the heart of the fire !

CHORUS.

See ! how the fiery guns gleam,
Flashing like eyes in a dream !
Hark—how the air and the skies
Groan, and the City replies—

VOICES WITHIN.

God ! God ! God !

CHORUS.

Where the flame is growing,
Leaping and blowing,
Where the people are calling,
See black rain falling,
Black rain, lead-rain,
Flashing to red rain,
Showering and flashing,
To the crumbling and crashing

Of column and steeple—
Striking and gleaming,
To the hollow screaming
   Of the stricken people,—
To the hollow thunder
   Of the cannon call,
To the rending asunder
   Of roof and wall !
And see !   O Pity !
   Answering,
Over the City
   Fires upspring :
First dim, then lighter,
Then lighter, brighter,
   Fire upon fire :
Till the air is glowing
And a red flame flowing
   On every spire—
And dome and column
Gleam,—to the solemn
   Incessant tolling
   From street to street,
And hark, far under,
   While we watch and wonder,

With a muffling rolling,
The deep drums beat!

[Day-break.

A Voice.

Forward for France!
Gather together!   Advance!

Chorus.

See! like a black snake there crawls,
Under the fire of the walls,
A dark mass, and over the snow
Speeds for the camp of the foe :
River-like, silent and still,
It rolleth under the hill,
And out on the plain white and bare
Spreads silent and strange.

A Sentinel.

Who goes there?

A Voice.

Forward, for France!

CHORUS.

Pray for France!

VOICE.

Gather together! Advance!

CHORUS.

Pray for them!

A VOICE.

Fire!

CHORUS.

God in heaven!

As a forest by lightning is riven,
As the rolls of the sea are plough'd white
By the wind, they are stricken; and bright
Blaze the manifold eyes of the fire
As they tremble and scream and expire;
Again and again and again,
Like the lightning-rent clouds of the rain,
Like the waves of the sea in the storm,
They gather together and form;
And again and again and again
They are scatter'd like hail, and the plain
Is black with the mounds of the slain.

O pray for them! Fire swift and fleet
Ploughs them as wind plougheth wheat!
O pray for them all! Pray for France!

A Voice.

Gather together! Advance!

Chorus.

Onward, still nearing
 The eyes that flash on them ;
Onward unfearing,
 Tho' the death-bolts crash on them,
Torn asunder
By lightning and thunder,
Though the black shells thicken
 And rain red death on them,
Rent and stricken,
 With Fire's fierce breath on them,
Still forward winning,
But ever thinning,
Onward they go,
 Over dying and dead,
Leaving the snow
 Not white but red.

And now like a torrent,
Furious, horrent,
From his lair in the dark
Springs the foe ; and hark !
Like waters meeting
They gather and scream,
While drums are beating
And the death's-eyes gleam !--
Like trees of the forest
When the storm-wind is sorest,
Like waves of the ocean,
They meet in wild motion,
They reel, they advance,
They gather—they stand;
Their wild weapons glance,
They are scattered like sand.

A VOICE.

Courage !—for France !

ANOTHER VOICE.

Fatherland ! fatherland !

B B

CHORUS.

The light is glowing
  Around blood-red,
The winds are blowing,
And the clouds are snowing
  On the heaps of dead.
The white snows cover them,
The swords flash over them,
Death waits each way for them,—
O bless them, pray for them!
They are mingled like water,
They are grappled in slaughter,
Face to face like wolves glaring,
With eyes fiercely staring,
Grappled and crying,
  Rank within rank,
Dead, living, and dying,
  Teuton and Frank;
Like a cloud struck by lightning
  And rent into rain,
Darkening and brightening
  They cover the plain.

VOICE.

Charge!

VOICES OF CAVALRY.

Fatherland!

A VOICE.

Gather together and stand!

VOICES.

Charge!

CHORUS.

Shaking the ground,
With a tramp and a roar,
  With a torrent's force,
With a sound like the sound
Of the sea on the shore,
  Come the Teuton horse.
How they ride! with their bare
Swords uplifted in air,
And each man bending low
O'er his steed's saddle-bow,

While his fiery eyes glow,

On they ride!   On they go!

Now, screaming aloud,

They have struck on the crowd,

Like the wind on a cloud,

    Like a knife at the heart;

It scatters, it rives

Into dark wreaths of lives

    That struggle apart.

VOICES.

Fly! fly! fly!

CHORUS.

Hark how they scatter and cry!

    Hark how a melody thin

    Sounds the retreat from within—

See how they linger and die!

VOICES.

Fly! fly! fly!

CHORUS.

O woe, O woe,

Like storms that blow

On a mount and shake it not,
Like waves that dash,
Crash after crash,
On a rock and break it not ;
Like wind against tide, only beating it whiter,
Like wind striking fire and but making it
brighter,
France striketh with passionate breath,
And closer and closer, and tighter and tighter,
The fiery Snake clings to her,
With glistening rings to her ;
She moans, she grows feeble in death.
O pray for her! plead for her!
Cry! intercede for her!

Voices Within.

Bread! give us bread!

Chorus.

We hearken and sicken—
'Tis the famine-stricken.
Ah, the deep moan in the air,
Blown from the depths of despair.
Hark, too, drums beat and feet tread.

A Voice.

Go forth and bury the dead.

Chorus.

Silent still falleth the snow,
Still the clouds drive, the winds blow—
Again, like fierce eyes in a dream,
The dreadful guns open and gleam
To a hollow reverberation,
And the shriek of a shatter'd nation :
Column and turret are riven,
Shrieking fire springeth to heaven.
Woe for the city of splendour!
Man hath no pity to lend her!
He calleth Hell's legions to rend her!—
Her sins were against her God—
　　May God forgive her them ;
She lieth opprest, under-trod,—
God striketh her hosts to the sod,
　　And His lightnings shiver them.

Voices Within.

Hear us, O God!

O God, deliver them!

The CHANCELLOR. *A* BONAPARTIST
OFFICER.

CHANCELLOR.

Bid him rest silent, watching from his prison
How the dice fall; for 'tis a game (he knows;
Where no man, let him reckon as he will,
Can quite sum up the chances.

OFFICER.

Is there hope?
He asks; and further, dost thou bid him
hope?

CHANCELLOR.

I know not. Why, hope comes of God, not
man.

OFFICER.

Should he return and grasp his scatter'd
crown,
Will ye oppose his path, or stand aside?

CHANCELLOR.

Now, softly ;—there upon the earth he lies,
A thing we never loved, an idol of gold
We vowed to shatter; but we sought forsooth
To break him not destroy him; and per-
    chance—
I say perchance—it might be well for Gaul
To take her ancient image for a space
In lieu of this red Spectre stalking now
Among the imperial shadows of the time.
Let him lie still, making no sign, and wait
For our uplifted finger.   Time will show.

OFFICER.

How fares it with the broken hosts of France ?

CHANCELLOR.

Ill.   Here come tidings.   Stand aside and
    hear.
                [*Enter a* MESSENGER.
Speak!
MESSENGER.

These despatches from the west.   Like chaff
Before the strong fan of the winnower,

The Breton host is flying.   Wild Misrule
And Superstition, in the gloomy camp
Stalking phantasmic, awe the ignorant ranks
And scatter them along the dark, like mists
Wind-broken into thin and wavering rain.
The priest-rid peasants in the act to advance
Linger to pray, and trembling count their
    beads;
And tho' the frantic leaders scream their best,
And conjure in the name of all the saints,
The squadrons melt between two strange
    extremes—
The brute-stare of inaction and the fire
Of sudden panic scattering at one flash
These—oxen.

        CHANCELLOR (*to* OFFICER.)

        Dost thou hear?

        MESSENGER.

          Even as a man
Lured by the dancing ignis fatuus,
The Greek Bourbaki step by step withdrew

To the east, and our two legions of the
    Loire,
No longer held asunder, struck Le Mans
At midnight. 'Twas a bloody blow and
    brief!
We did divide the host, from bourne to
    bourne
Drove them, devour'd their wavering lines
    with fire,
While staring frantic at the flame-lit dark
The Bretons saw in mingled lineaments
All horrible the looks of friend and foe,
Struck in the darkness at each other's
    hearts,
Clung to each other, drove like breaking
    waves
Hither and thither with no aim and will;
And now, torn thus into two broken hosts,
They for whom hungry eyes watch day by
    day
Out of the City yonder, drift to the south
Swift as the storm-wreck when the storm is
    spent.

                  [*Enter a* MESSENGER.

CHANCELLOR.

Whence comest thou?

MESSENGER.

From Belfort.   Thrice the sun

Arose and set above the bloody Luisne,

While   hour   by   hour,   ever   repulsed,   the
French

Struck   with   despairing   strength   upon   the
line

Of brave Von Werder, which like some great
rock

Stagger'd before the thunderbolt but stood;

And lo! even as a torrent spends itself

And scatters, the wild legions of the Greek

Fell   back   and   broke   with   their   own   furious
force.

And now, in bloody runlets, water-weak,

Southward they flow, a murmur in the fields,

A dark mass drifting to uncertain doom,

And with their impotent despairing cry,

Dies   the   last   hope   of   all   that   strike   for
France.

CHORUS.

Who passeth there
Naked and bare,
A bloody sword upraising?
Who with thin moan
Glides past alone,
At the black heaven gazing?
Limbs thin and stark,
Eyes sunken and dark,
The lightning round her leaping?
What shape floats past
Upon the blast,
Crouching in pain and creeping?
Behold! her eyes to heaven are cast,
And they are red with weeping.

Say a prayer thrice
With lips of ice:
'Tis she—yea, and no other;
Look not at me
So piteously,
O France—O martyr mother!
O whither now,
With branded brow

And bleeding heart, art flying?
 Whither away?
 O stand! O stay!
Tho' winds, waves, clouds are crying—
 Dawn cometh swift—'twill soon be day—
The Storm of God is dying.

  She will not speak,
  But, spent and weak,
Droops her proud head and goeth;
  See! she crawls past,
  Upon the blast,
Whither no mortal knoweth—
  O'er fields of fight,
  Where glimmer white
Death's steed and its gaunt rider—
  Thro' storm and snow,
  Behold her go,
With never a friend beside her—
  O Shepherd of all winds that blow,
To Quiet Waters guide her!

  There, for a space,
  Let her sad face

Fall in a tranquil mirror—
    There spirit-sore
    May she count o'er
Her sin, her shame, her error,—
    And read with eyes
    Made sweet and wise
What her strong God hath taught her,
    With face grown fair
    And bosom bare
And hands made clean from slaughter—
    O Shepherd, seek and find her there,
Beside some Quiet Water!

CHANCELLOR. BUONAPARTIST OFFICER.
A MESSENGER.

MESSENGER.

'Tis finished. In the south Gambetta screams,
Summoning all the winds to strike for France,
But the last breath is spent. The broken
    hosts
Have drifted wild into Helvetia,
And there, with faces sicker than the snow
That glimmers up above them silently,

Have twenty thousand men laid down their
    arms.

Nothing abides to conquer. 'Tis not war,

But mere sheep-chasing in the shambles
    now;

And our strong legions hold their hands and
    smile,

Having no hearts to strike like martial men

At things so little worthy of their steel. [*Exit.*

CHANCELLOR.

I know not what strange potion they have
    drunk,

What black magician holds them with his
    arts,

But struggling with these Frenchmen is to
    fight

With Circe's swine; they know no head, no
    hand,

But go like driftweed up and down the
    tide;

The land they dwell in is to them as strange

As Egypt's sand-hills or the Russian snows

To Buonaparté's thinning phalanxes;
They huddle and starve on their own hearths,
　　and find
The prospect foreign and barbarian;
They have no hearts, no stomachs, and they
　　fall
Before our bolts as the affrighted hordes
Before the prodigies whose flash foredoom'd
The Roman and the Goth.
As easy 'twere to animate the dead,
Or fill a flock of oxen with one soul,
As fashion those false Frenchmen to the form
Thy fathers wore to darken Christendom.

Officer.

They lack indeed a name to conjure with;
I know of one might animate them yet.

Chancellor.

Not *that*, which like a wind-bag at Sedan
Burst with a puff of lean and braggart speech.
The Man of Elba were himself too weak
To fill this thin and broken frame of France:

It lacks a soul indeed, and such a soul;
But it is broken in the body too.
I tell thee only he thou servest made
This body what it is.   Not such a soul
As filled it out of Buonaparté's breath,
But rather like a very Incubus,
Napoleon sat and fatten'd,—round the neck
Of France clung as a pamper'd slothful child
That drains the weary mother hour by hour:
A very Changeling, monstrous and unblest,
Ev'n such as thou hast heard thy grandam tell
Were dropt in peasants' cradles by the elves:
A crafty, strange, mysterious sort of birth,
Jealous, green-eyed, big-brain'd, and weak of
    feet,
Drawing not merely moisture from the breast
But blood and life itself.   Nay, hear me out !
These changeling babes had oftentimes the
    skill
To make the mother love them, as indeed
Poor France did love her monster for a time,
And she forgave him even Mexico,
Because he smiled her down ; and, day by day,
Fastened upon by her unnatural birth,

She like a mortal mother weakening
Crawled up and down the globe. For she
 was glad
Because the world was sunny, and the board
Well-stored, the fields most golden at her
 door,
Nor knew the fatal lips that drew her milk
Were subtly sucking at her strength and life.
Not till the thing fell from her, and the foe
Sprang at her, did she learn her feebleness,
Limbs, tongue, eyes, heart, all fail'd her as
 she strove,
Though with the fury of a thing that dies
She clings with weakening clutches to the
 end.

CHORUS.

STROPHE I.

Ay me, to dwell in some remote still valley,
 Far from the civil fret and martial pride,
To sit by some sweet river musically
 Singing for shepherds piping happy-eyed ;
 Ay me, to quit sad cities and abide

Where never name of king was ever
    known,

Where never sword is drawn or trumpet
    blown,

    Where the slow hours from morn to even-
      tide,

Sweet, silent, and alone,

    Move like a feeding flock on some green
      mountain-side.

ANTISTROPHE I.

For my heart bleeds, my soul with tears is
    swelling,

    To see mankind so tame to taunts and
      stings,

How, knowing not the might within them
    dwelling,

    They take the tyrant's yoke like soulless
      things ;

    Crouch, crawl beneath the lash of under-
      lings,

And even as silly sheep are bought and sold,

Driven from the pleasant pasture and the fold,

Drawn from the fresh fields and the crystal
   springs,
Slain for a little gold,
  Slaughter'd forsooth like beasts, to please
   the whim of Kings.

STROPHE II.

And even as silly seals in summer weather,
  With large eyes listening, from the deep
   below
Rise up, and gather hearkening together,
  Because some cunning fisher fluteth slow,
  And follow sleepily while the seamen row,
And so are led to doom and have no fear;—
Even such as these are foolish mortals here,
  With empty eyes that neither see nor
   know,
But blankly gaze and peer,
  And follow a vain sound wherever it doth go.

ANTISTROPHE II.

And, one by one, out of the wondrous portal,
  Whose backward darkness no man's eye
   may read,

Some monster comes, strong, subtle, and
    most mortal,
  And him the foolish people follow in-
    deed,
  Crying, " This is no man of mortal seed,
But more divine than any human thing ! "
And in his steps they follow clamouring ;
  Whither he listeth, though their sore feet
    bleed,
They follow him their King,—
  Until he sinks, and lo ! some other comes to
    lead.

STROPHE III.

O mortal men, awake, and gather, and go
    not ;
  Hear wise men speak, hear God's own
    prophets cry.
Be not as poor tame things that see not, know
    not,
  But smile, and let the unnatural birth go
    by ;
  Stop ye your ears against its human sigh,

And if it threatens, threaten ye again—
Yea, send it forth to sow and reap the
grain,
  As ye do, underneath the peaceful sky;
Or hold it with a chain;
  And if all chains are vain, strike it and let
    it die.

CHOIR WITHOUT.

Gloria Deo! Floreat Imperator!

ANTISTROPHE III.

O hearken, hearken! for I hear a crying
    Of many voices, and the clang of swords,
With what strange cry do voices multiply-
        ing
    Rend the day's darkness into thunderous
        words?
      " Glory to God!" cry these triumphant
        hordes,
Having made sacrifice most manifold;
And unto Him the armëd people hold,

With acclamations and most glad ac-
cords,
A foolish King and old;
 "Glory to God!" they cry;—yea, glory is
the Lord's.

CHOIR WITHOUT.

Glorea Deo! Floreat Patria!

EPODE.

Creep closer, hearkening. 'Tis a sound like
thunder,
 Deep as the roll of waves on some sad
shore,
And, listening, our hearts are torn asunder.
 Would we might die! would that the
world were o'er!
 For life is bitter, and mere breath is
sore,
Seeing how mortal men are slain and
slay
At will of each new creature of a day,

Crafty or foolish, him they will adore.

Oh might we pass away,

Die, cease, be done with earth; slumber, and

see no more.

CHORUS. *A* MESSENGER.

MESSENGER.

Why, women, do ye linger pale-faced here,

Hearkening, each with hand upon her

heart?

CHORUS.

We hear glad sounds, the tread of mailëd feet,

The playing of light music, and, moreover,

The organ's plagal cadence deep and low.

VOICES.

Gloria in excelsis Deo!

CHORUS.

Hark!

Yonder the City burns and moans; and here

There comes a ripple of music and glad

speech.

MESSENGER.

'Tis a blest day.   Within the triumph-hall
They hail our Wilhelm German Emperor.

VOICES.

Gloria Deo!   Plaudite, omnes gentes!

CHORUS.

O woe!—while France lies bleeding at his
    feet!

MESSENGER.

Hush; and stand back—why do ye wring
    your hands?
See; 'tis a sight to make an old man young.
    [*The Scene opens, revealing the interior of*
    the Hall of Mirrors. The KAISER,
    surrounded by the Princes and Leaders
    of the host. Priests pronouncing the
    Benediction, and Choristers intoning.
    Organ-music.
A Rainbow of the mighty of the Earth
Arching the great grey head; and mirror'd back,

Out of a thousand silver pools of glass,
A gleaming of rich robes, a flash of steel,
Waves of uplifted faces round the King,
All phosphorescent with their own wild light,
Like to the sea washing an ocean isle
Purpled with blooms and dim with orient
　　gold.'

CHOIR,

Gloria in excelsis Deo !

KAISER.

From Him the Highest, who alone can give,
This day I take the great imperial Crown
I sought not; at His bidding, at His hands,
I take the Crown and I uplift the Sword.

CHOIR.

Cantate Deo !　Jubilate, gentes !

PRIEST.

Hark to the Song of the Sword !
In the beginning, a Word

Came from the lips of the Lord ;

And He said, "The Earth shall be,

And around the Earth the Sea,

And over these twain the Skies ;

And out of the Earth shall rise

Man, the last and the first ;

And Man shall hunger and thirst,

And shall eat of the fruits in the sun,

And drink of the streamlets that run,

And shall find the wild yellow grains,

And, opening earth, in its veins

Sow the seeds of the same ; for of bread

I have written that he shall be fed."

Thus at the first said the Lord.

CHOIR.

Hark to the Song of the Sword !

THE PRIEST.

Then Man sowed the grain, and to bread

Kneaded the grain, and was fed,

He and his household indeed

To the last generation and seed :

Then the children of men, young and old,

Sat by the waters of gold,

And ate of the bread and the fruit,

And drank of the stream, but made suit

For blessing no more than the brute.

And God said, " 'Twere better to die

Than eat and drink merely, and lie

Beast-like and foul on the sod,

Lusting, forgetful of God ! "

And He whispered, " Dig deeper again,

Under the region of grain,

And bring forth the thing ye find there

Shapeless and dark ; and prepare

Fire,—and into the same

Cast what ye find—let it flame—

And when it is burning blood-bright,

Pluck it forth, and with hammers of sleight

Beat it out, beat it out, till ye mark

The thing that was shapeless and dark

Grown beautiful, azure, and keen,

Purged in the fire and made clean,

Beautiful, holy, and bright,

Gleaming aloft in the light ;—

Then lift it, and wield ! " said the Lord.

CHOIR.

Hark to the Song of the Sword!

PRIEST.

Then Man with a brighter desire
Saw the beautiful thing from the fire,
And the slothful arose, and the mean
Trembled to see it so keen,
And God, as they gather'd and cried,
Thunder'd a Word far and wide:
"This Sword is the Sword of the Strong!
It shall strike at the life's blood of wrong;
It shall kill the unclean, it shall wreak
My doom on the shameful and weak;
And the strong with this sign in their
    hands
Shall gather their hosts in the lands,
And strike at the mean and the base,
And strengthen from race on to race;
And the weak shall be wither'd at length,
For the glory of Man in his strength,
And the weak man must die," saith the Lord.

CHOIR.

Hark to the Song of the Sword!

PRIEST.

Sire, whom all men of thy race
Name as their hope and their grace;
King of the Rhine-water'd land,
Heart of the state and its hand,
Thou of the purple and crown,
Take, while thy servants bow down,
The Sword in thy grasp.

KAISER.
It is done.

PRIEST.

Uplift! let it gleam in the sun—
Uplift in the name of the Lord!

CHOIR.

Hail to the King and the Sword!

KAISER.

Lo! how it gleams in the light,
Beautiful, bloody, and bright—
Such in the dark days of yore
The monarchs of Israel bore ;
Such by the angels of heaven
To Charles the Mighty was given—
Yea, I uplift the Sword,
Thus in the name of the Lord!

THE CHIEFS.

Form ye a circle of fire
Around him, our King and our Sire—
While in the centre he stands,
Kneel with your swords in your hands,
Then with one voice deep and free
Echo like waves of the sea—
    " In the name of the Lord !"

CHANCELLOR.

Sire, while thou liftest the Sword,
Thus in the name of the Lord,

I too, thy slave, kneel and blend

My voice with the hosts that attend—

Yea, and while kneeling I hold

A scroll writ in letters of gold,

With the names of the monarchs who bow

Thy liegemen throned lower than thou ;

Moreover, in letters of red,

Their names who ere long must be led

To thy feet, while thou liftest the Sword,

Thus in the name of the Lord!

Voices Without.

Where is he ?—he fades from our sight !

Where the Sword ?—all is blacker than
      night.

Is it finish'd, that loudly ye cry ?

Doth he sheathe the great Sword while we die ?

O bury us deep, most deep;

Write o'er us, wherever we sleep,

" In the name of the Lord !"

Kaiser.

While I uplift the Sword,

Thus in the name of the Lord,

Why, with mine eyes full of tears,
Am I sick of the song in mine ears?
God of the Israelite, hear;
God of the Teuton, be near;
Strengthen my pulse lest I fail,
Shut out these slain while they wail—
For they come with the voice of the grave
On the glory they give me and gave.

CHORUS.

In the name of the Lord? Of what Lord?
Where is He, this God of the Sword?
Unfold Him; where hath He his throne?
Is he Lord of the Teuton alone?
Doth He walk on the earth? Doth he tread
On the limbs of the dying and dead?
Unfold him! We sicken, and long
To look on this God of the strong!

PRIEST.

Hush! In the name of the Lord,
Kneel ye, and bless ye the Sword!

D D

Bless it with soul and with brain,
Bless it for saved and for slain,
For the sake of the dead in the tomb,
For the sake of the child in the womb,
For the sake of these Kings on the knee,
For the sake of a world it shall free!
Bless it, the Sword! bless the Sword!
Yea, in the name of the Lord!

.

CHIEFS.

Deepen the circle of Fire
Around him, our King and our Sire!
While in our centre he towers,
Kneeling, ye spirits, ye powers,
Bless it and bless it again,
Bless it for saved and for slain,
Bless ye the beautiful Sword,
Aloud in the name of the Lord!

KAISER.

In the name of the Lord!

ALL.

In the name of the Lord!

THE CHOIR.

By the Light adored,

By Father, and Son, and Spirit,

By the Name and the Word,

By the blood of Christ we inherit—

Lord of the Rhenish land,

Heart of the state and its hand,

Take the Sword of the Lord,

Uplift and bear it!

Where the Rhine is pour'd

Round the German lands that are one

with it,

Where in sweet accord

Fair streams fall into and run with it,

Rise with the Sword in thy hand,

Glory and strength of the land;

Take the Sword from the Lord,

Stand up in the sun with it!

In the name of the Lord,
    'Tis done; and His hand hath deckt thee:
By the Light Adored,
    None may henceforth reject thee—
Heart of the Fatherland,
Heart and spirit and hand,
The Lord and the Word and the Sword,
    Keep and protect thee!

THE KAISER.

Princes, and powers, and principalities,
Kings, brethren, round whose lands the Rhine
        rolls waves
Blue as the German heaven that bends above,
Ye who henceforth shall shine around our
        throne
Like glorious constellations, in your places
Set by God's hand as light for human eyes,
Friends, brethren, Kings and kinsmen, words
        are weak,
All oratory dumb, music too faint,
All art too feeble and inadequate,
To measure the large issue of this day.

There is a God that cuts the path of Kings,
Leading them whither He listeth ; and that
    God—
Albeit at first I trembled at His hand,
Albeit the path seem'd dark before my feet,
And my heart fail'd me since the path was
    strange—
That God hath led me hither, safe, supreme,
Chief of a living people, arm and heart,
A King, the seed of Kings, and chosen head
Of Kings anointed. Him, the King of Kings,
Before whose feet I am as dust, I praise ;
And though the embers of my life grow cold,
And snow is on my hair, and in mine eyes
Doubt and a gathering darkness, Him I bless
That He hath led me just before the end
As to a mountain-summit, whence I see,
Not darkly, but with most ineffable light,
A fair long prospect of regenerate days ;
And even as one upon a lofty height
I hear afar-off very faint and sweet
The murmur of glad cities, the deep hum
Of happy millions moving to and fro
In gentle interchange of life and love.

I do believe that land God gave to us,

That land which robbers pillaged in the night,

That land we have redeem'd with precious
    blood,

Is blest henceforth, and the bright sword I
    hold

May in the strong hands of my son become

No firebrand but a symbol; not a thing

Left like the steel of some old warrior

To rust upon the wall, but ever bright

And beauteous; not a firebrand, not a threat,

But part of pomp and peaceful pageantry,

Flashing with memorable light and fire

Into the hungry eyes of those who prowl

Like wolves around the pastures and the
    pens

Where the Great Shepherd in the beginning
    set

The nations of the earth. Yea, may it rise,

Beautiful, terrible, and fiery fair,

Like to the living sword that trembled o'er

The golden Gates of Eden; and beneath

May very Eden blossom: light and flowers,

Rich vineyards, yellow harvests, hamlets glad

Bosom'd in greenness, churches whose fair
    spires
Gleaming in sunlight point the path to
    peace,—
The Land of the great River, yours and
    mine,
Our birthright, given back at last by God
To be the heirloom of our latest seed!

THE CHIEFS.

Flash the sword!—and even as thunder
    Utter ye one living voice,—
While the watching nations wonder,
    Hills of Fatherland, rejoice:
Echo!—echo back our prayers and accla-
    mations!

CHORUS.

France, O Mother! lie and hearken,
    Make no bitterer sign of woe,
Here within thee all things darken,
    All things brighten with thy foe:
Hush thy weeping; still thy bitter lamenta-
    tions.

The Chiefs.

Flash the sword !—A voice is flowing
From the Baltic bound in white,
Though 'tis blowing chill and snowing,
Blue-eyed Teutons see the light.
And the far white hills of Norway hear the
crying.

Chorus.

Thou too hearkenest, Mother dearest,
Thou too hearkenest through thy tears,
And thou tremblest as thou hearest,
For 'tis thunder in thine ears;
And thou gazest on the dead and on the
dying.

The Chiefs.

Lübeck answers and rejoices,
Though her dead are brought to her;
Potsdam thunders; there are voices
In the fields of Hanover;
And the spirits of the lonely Hartz awaken.

CHORUS.

And in France's vales and mountains
    Hands are wrung and tears are shed;
Women sit by village fountains,
    And the water bubbles red.
O comfort, O be of comfort—ye forsaken!

THE CHIEFS.

O'er Bavarian woods and rivers,—
    Where the Brunswick heather waves,—
On the glory goes and quivers
    Through the Erzgebirge caves;
And the swords of Styria gleam like moonlit
    water.

CHORUS.

There is silence, there is weeping
    On the bloody banks of Seine,
And the unburied dead are sleeping
    In the fields of trampled grain;
While the roadside Christs stare down on
    fields of slaughter.

The Chiefs.

Flash the Sword!   Where need is sorest,
　　Sitting in the lonely night,
While the wind in the Black Forest
　　Moans, the woodman sees the light;
And the hunters wind the horn and hail each
　　other.

Chorus.

Strasbourg sits among her ashes
　　With a last despairing cry,
East and west red ruin flashes
　　With a red light on the sky.
Not a word! Sit yet and hearken, O my
　　mother!

The Chiefs.

Flash the sword!   The glades of Baden
　　Echo; Jena laughs anon;
Dresden old and Stuttgart gladden,
　　There is mirth in Ratisbon :—
And underneath the Linden there is leaping.

Chorus.

In thine arms the horror tarries,
  And the sword-flash gleams on thee,
Hide thy funeral face, O Paris,
  Do not hearken; do not see;
Electra, clasp thine urn—and hush thy weep-
  ing.

The Chiefs.

Hamburg kindles, and her women
  Sadly smile remembering all ;
There are bitter smiles in Bremen,
  Where Vandamme's fierce feet did fall;
But the Katzbach, O the Katzbach laugheth
  loudly !

Chorus.

Comfort, mother! hear not, heed not;
  Let the dead bury the dead !
Fold thy powerless hands and plead not,
  They remember sorrows fled,
And their dead go by them, silently and
  proudly.

The Chiefs.

O that Fritz's soul could hear it
　　In the walks of Sans Souci!
O to waken Lützow's spirit,
　　Blucher's too, the grim and free;
And the Jäger, the wild Jäger, would they
　　listen'd!

Chorus.

Comfort, mother! O cease weeping!
　　Let the past bury the past:
Faces of the slain and sleeping
　　Gleam along upon the blast.
Yea, 'twas " Leipsic " that they murmur'd as
　　they glisten'd.

The Chiefs.

All the land of the great River
　　Slowly brightens near and far;
Lost for once, and saved for ever,
　　Körner's spirit like a star
Shooteth past, and all remember the begin-
　　ning.

CHORUS.

They are rising, they are winging,
  Spirits of her singers dead,
'Tis an old song they are singing—
  Fold thy hands and bow thy head—
But they sing for thee too, gentle to thy sin-
  ning.

THE CHIEFS.

And the River to the ocean
  Rolls ; and all its castles dim
Gleam ; and with a shadowy motion,
  Like a mist upon its brim,
Rise the Dead,—and look this way with shin-
  ing faces.

CHORUS.

Thine, too, rise !—and darkly cluster,
  Moaning sad around thee now,
In their eyes there is no lustre,
  They are cold as thy cold brow—
Let them vanish ; let them sleep in their dark
  places.

The Chiefs.

Flash the sword!   In the fair valleys
　Where the scented Neckar flows,
Fair-hair'd Teutons lift the chalice,
　And the winter vineyard grows,
And the almond forests tremble into blossom.

Chorus.

On thy vineyards the cold daylight
　Gleams, and they are deathly chill—
Women wander in the grey light,
　And the lean trees whistle shrill;
Hold thine urn, O martyr mother, to thy
　bosom.

The Chiefs.

Flash the sword!—Sweet notes of pleasure
　O'er the Rhenish upland swell,
And the overhanging azure
　Sees itself in the Moselle.
All the land of the great River gleams and
　hearkens!

CHORUS.

Dost thou hear them? dost thou see them?
　　There 'tis gladness, here 'tis pain;
One great spirit comes to free them
　　But he holds thee with a chain.
All the land of the great City weeps and
　　darkens!

THE CHIEFS.

River of the mighty people,
　　Broaden to the sea and flow—
Mirror tilth and farm and steeple,
　　Darken with boats that come and go.
Flow gently, like a babe that smiles and
　　prattles.

CHORUS.

Yea! and though thou flow for ever,
　　Bright and bloodless as to-day,
Scarcely wilt thou wash, O River,
　　Thy dark load of dead away,
O bloody River! O field of many battles!

THE CHIEFS.

On with great immortal waters
　　Brightening to a day divine,
Through the fields of many slaughters
　　Freely roll, O German Rhine.
Let the Teuton drink thy wine and wax the
　stronger.

CHORUS.

On and on, O mighty River,
　　Flow through lands of corn and vine—
Turn away, O France, for ever,
　　Look no more upon the Rhine ;
On the River of many sorrows look no
　longer.

THE CHIEFS.

Lo ! the white Alps for a token
　　With the wild aurora gleam,
And the Spectre of the Brocken
　　Stands aloft with locks that stream,—
All the land of the great River can behold it !

CHORUS.

Hide thine eyes and look not thither!

For in answer to their cries,

Fierce the Phantasm gazeth hither

With an Avenging Angel's eyes;

It is fading, and the mists of storm enfold it!

The KAISER. *The* CHIEFS. *The* IMPERIAL
CHANCELLOR. *The* GOVERNOR OF PARIS.

CHANCELLOR.

Behold! where even in our triumph-hour

Comes one with feet that linger, head that
    droops,

And eyes that pour their fire upon the ground.

CHORUS.

Woe to thee, Paris; then thy cup is full.

GOVERNOR.

O Sire and Princes, leaders of the host,

Kings, soldiers, strangers, hither have I come

E E

Reluctant as a captive led to death,

Woe in mine heart and on mine eyelids tears,

To offer up my sword, and on my knees,

Not used to bend their joints to mortal men,

To hold your skirts imploring in the name

Of the Imperial City overthrown,

Paris, the fallen Regent of the world.

There Fire hath cast our fairest temples down,

And now in the black embers flickers faint

Ready to spring once more; and Frost is
    there,

Most silent, with the paralysing touch

Of skeleton fingers, feeling for the heart

Under the thin rags blown apart by wind;

And, worst and direst, in the open square,

Witless upon a pile of fleshless bones

Sits Famine, smiling with a hungry eye

At Pestilence, who at her dark feet heaps

The blotch'd and swollen faces of the dead

In silence; and these four full well have done

Your dreadful bidding, serving as they do

The strong man ever against the weak.   But
    now,

I bid ye, I beseech ye, call them off,

And in the name of God and Christ His son,

Uplift your hands, and leave us, and depart.

I do not think your eyes may contemplate

More closely what ye have done; but silently,

Seeing we lay our arms down at your feet

And seeing we are broken as a reed,

Turn ye your conquering faces otherwhere

And leave this City once named "Beautiful"

To cleanse herself and feed her hungry brood

And wear her sackcloth, praying all alone

With open gates for food, and warmth, and
    light,

The homeward flying swallow and green
    shoots

Heralding harvest. For the sad red sun

Must come and go for many a dreadful day,

Ere these things ye have sent against her life

Perish forgotten ; and for many a day

Earth must be open'd for the countless dead

And dying; and indeed the City sad

Needeth the darkness of her own deep shame,

That she may hide herself from all men's
    sight,

Until she is clothëd, and the piteous wounds

Upon her gentle flesh are wholly heal'd.

Wherefore, O leaders of the Teuton host,

Accept our swords, our lives, but turn aside

Your faces, seeking not to look upon

More sorrow, nor to pass the dreadful gates;

For should ye gaze on our poor Paris now,

The scorn of your proud eyes, as sharp as
    steel,

Would stab her to the heart and she would
    die :

Or madden'd, anguish'd, with her dying
    breath,

Gather the last strength of supreme despair,

And seek to drag ye with her unto doom.

KAISER.

Yield up thy sword, and waste no further
    breath ;

Turn thine appeal to God, and go thy way.

THE CHIEFS.

Glory to God.   Long live the Emperor!

CHANCELLOR.

'Tis finished; at our feet great France lies
    dead.

CHORUS.

O God who leadest on the mortal race,
    Whither they know not, through the won-
        drous years,
Thou mystery whose sad meaning none may
        trace,
    Light on our eyes and Music in our ears,
Spirit that punishest and scatterest grace,
    Lord of all losses and all doubts and fears,
Shedding upon the self-same hour and place
The doubt that maddens and the faith that
        cheers,—
Is there ever a smile upon a living face
    That doth not mean some living face's
        tears?

END OF THE TRILOGY.

EPILOGUE.

EPILOGUE.

Enter TIME.

O SPIRITS seated in your just degrees,
Greater and lesser, wiser and most wise,
All beautiful and some most beautiful,
Thus far have ye beheld our Tragedy
Rise to its crest of meaning like a wave,
And break to the low murmur of mere foam
Call'd glory. Ye have seen the Star of France
Rise bloody; ye have seen it wax and burn,
Suffusing and consuming other lights
Around it; ye have watch'd it wane and
 fade;
Ye have beheld it rise i' the west again
With sicklier and yet less baleful light—
Less bloody, yet more like those leprous-
 spheres
Which follow and proclaim a pestilence;

And lastly, ye have seen it die once more

Frail as a taper in the wind of war,

While rising suddenly as the round moon

In harvest storms, Germania brighteneth

Above the wild eyes of the wondering world.

Is this the end? I hear ye smiling ask.

Why, God forbid.   Tho' for a time we pause,

We shall continue our strange Tragedy

To-morrow and to-morrow, for indeed

The end is dark even to all us who play;

For mark you, much must yet be said and
    done,

Many strange Leaders go and come, ere
    Heaven

Sees the last scene and awful spectacle

Concluding the strange Drama of the Soul.

Thus far of evil there hath issued forth

This good—a lesser evil; and the air

Is clearer for the thunders ye have heard

Shaking the thrones of Europe and appalling

The foolish-hearted people.   Ye have seen,

How Buonaparte swept away with fire   ·

The living lies and blots of monarchy;

How, when at last the Man became a pest,

The lesser evil fair as present good

Rose and destroyed him; how by slow
 degrees

That lie of lies, the sandstone Church of
 Rome,

Was slowly decomposing with the wash

Of the great tide of years; how Germany,

Grown subtle to the conscience and the will,

Sat like an eagle breeding in a cave,

Nursing her strength and teaching her fierce
 young

Dark secret flights to try their fledgeling
 wings;

How in these memorable later days

Cæsar's last Ghost rose up and walk'd abroad,

So hideous in the open common day

That Cæsarism, second lie of lies,

Perish'd for ever from the face of things;

How, in his turn, above the wandering world,

Stands up the Kaiser, with the living lie

Of Right Divine upon his lips, yet blest

For the time being as a feeble good,

Because the base of his imperial throne

Is set upon the conscience and the will
Of a great people now awakening
From torpor to a living hope and aim.

Wherefore, I say, these Kings whom ye have
    seen
Were God's unwilling servants, but for whom
The Titan Soul of Man were still asleep,
Trancëd to sorrow and forgetfulness;
And now that Soul is waken'd, now, O friends,
Begins the serious matter of our play,
For scene by scene we purpose to set forth,
To the same audience and on other nights,
The mighty spiritual brightening,
And the last laying of these ghosts of Kings.

"O foolish mortal race," I hear ye cry,
"Who will, yet will not learn, and live, and
    take
Their birthright, and be free!" Ay, friends,
    indeed,
Man is a scholar eager indeed to learn,
But most forgetful having learn'd. His wits
Go wandering, his vacant eyes are caught
By foolish pictures and by idle gleams,

Glibly he learns and instantly forgets.

Again, again, and o'er and o'er again,

He tries the same old lesson, utters it

So loud and well that out of every star

Angels look out with gleaming eyes and
    hope ;—

But in a moment his bewildered brain

Shuts like a lantern, and is dark as night.

O spirits seated in your just degrees,

O lights, O lamps, O principles divine,

Be patient.   Of each failure, of each loss,

Of each sad repetition, in his soul

Something remains—a word—a gleam—a
    thought—

A dim sensation—a faint memory—

And these perchance are working under God

More strangely and more surely than ye know.

Ay, but I weary.   O I weary.   Sleep

Were better.   Would the mighty play were
    o'er !

Again and yet again the same old scenes,

The same set speeches, the same blind de-
    spairs

And miserable hopes, the same sick fear
Of quitting the poor stage; so that I lose
All count of act and scene and speech, con-
    fuse
Scenes present and scenes past, actors long
    still
With actors flaunting now their little hour.
How like each other all the players speak
Who play the tyrants! how the kings and
    queens
Each follow each like bees from out a hive!
Still the old speeches, the old scenes, despite
The surface-change of costume and the trick
Of posture. Ay, I weary! O to see
The great black Curtain fall, the music cease,
All darken, the House empty of its host
Of strange intelligences who behold
Our Drama, till the great Hand, creeping
    forth
In silence, one by one puts out the lights.

EPILUDE

BEFORE THE CURTAIN.

EPILUDE.

Enter, on the stage, the CHANCELLOR, *followed
by a dark throng of Actors. They kneel.*

THE LORD.

Now what are ye who hither come and kneel?

CHANCELLOR.

The poor spent players of the Tragedy.

THE LORD.

First, ye who played the lowliest parts of all,
Fulfilling them with your best courtesy,
Ye who were slain and made the sport of
    Kings,
Come hither to my side; for thro' your masks
I see the fairest of my host.

SPIRITS.

We come!

THE LORD.

And ye who spake a little speech and went,
And stalk'd upon the stage in rich attire,
Go by, sit lower.   Where is Lucifer?

CHANCELLOR (*unmasking*).

Here.

THE LORD.

Thy dark part was excellently played—
A trifle dull, and modell'd after him
Who played the part of Man of Destiny.

LUCIFER

Master of souls—that part I also played.

THE LORD.

And Buonaparté.

LUCIFER.

My pet character!—
Sire, I prepared the play at thy command,
And being thy liege servant plotted out
The parts to each soul as stage-manager;
Nor willingly would have myself essayed
The mighty monologues and leading parts,
But that the other actors, one and all,
Were slow of study and too scrupulous
In the great text they spake.
To all the staff I offer'd Buonaparte—
None would essay it of our company;
Wherefore I made it mine, and for like
     reasons
Kept to myself the other leading parts.

THE LORD.

None could have played them better, or so
     well:
And never since the earthly Play began
Hast thou, mine evil Angel wrought for good,
Spoke the dark speech Divine more willingly.

LUCIFER.

Since we have played the drama to Thy
    liking,
Deign, King of Heaven,
To hear our Chorus sing the Final Song
Or Epode.   A poor actor on the scene,
Who in the crowded background stood and
    gaped,
A mortal poet, is the author, Sire!
It is a mere cantata—one of those
Wild songs which the obscure upon the stage
(Nobodies who would fain be somebodies,
Starving king-haters who would fain play
    kings)
Have ever made to while away the time;
And Thou, whose calm eyes measure all to
    come,
Will smile to see how oft this poet tries
To peer into the future and to sound
The advent of thy Kingdom; yet, indeed,
The thing is pleasant to the ear when sung—
Small service is true service—and we know
God is not critical.

The Lord

'Tis well.   Sing on.

Chorus.

The Soul shall arise.
Power and its vanity,
Pride's black insanity,
Lust and its revelry
Shall with war's devilry
Pass from humanity.
The Soul shall arise.

Semi-Chorus I.

As from night springs golden-wingëd morrow,
As a bloom on the grey bough in the May.

Semi-Chorus II.

From darkness, and from coldness, and from
sorrow
He shall issue living to the day.

SEMI-CHORUS I.

As a wild, wild rose-tree when 'tis snowing
  Feels the unborn roses and is bright,
Pants the Earth, and, though the storm be
      blowing,
  Knows the birth within her day and night.

SEMI-CHORUS II.

Like a fount by spring's warm breath unfrozen,
  Like a song-bird waking in the nest,
On the breast of Earth awakes the chosen,
  First and last, the brightest and the best.

CHORUS OF THE DEAD.

Where we sleeping lie, where we sleeping lie,
We hear the sound and our spirits cry;
As we sleeping lie in the Lord's own Breast,
Calm, so calm, for the place is blest,
We, who died that this might be,
Souls of the great, and wise, and free;

Souls that sung, and souls that sighed,

Souls that pointed to God and died;

Souls of martyrs, souls of the wise;

Souls of women with weeping eyes;

Souls whose graves like waves of the sea

    Cover the world from west to east;

Souls whose bodies ached painfully,

    Till they broke to prophetic moan and
        ceased;

Souls that sleep in the gentle night,

We hear the cry and we see the light.

Did we die in vain? did we die in vain?

Ah! that indeed were the bitterest pain!

But we see the light and we bless the cry,

Where we sleeping lie, where we sleeping lie.

CHORUS OF CITIZENS.

He cometh late, this greatest under God,

Promised for countless years, he cometh
    late—

Where shall he dwell? The cities of our
    state

        Are level with the sod.

Shall he upbuild them then? Meantime, we
    wait
And see black footsteps where our martyrs
    trod.
He cometh late, forsooth, he cometh late,
      This greatest under God!
Nor do we see the earth that he will
    claim
  Is riper yet than on the natal day.
All lands are bloody, and a crimson flame
  Eats Hope's poor heart away.
Where shall he turn for peace? whom shall
    he trust for stay?
The anarchs of the world still sit and
    sway
The hearts of men to evil;—Hunger and
    Thirst
Moan at the palace door; and birds of
    prey
Still scream above the harvest as at first.
      Should he then come at all,
      This Soul on whom ye call,
How should he dwell on earth? would he not
    find it curst?

SEMI-CHORUS I.

As the young lamb by its dam runs leaping,
　As the young bird to the old bough clings,
Born to Earth in darkness and in weeping,
　He shall cherish her from whom he springs.

SEMI-CHORUS II.

He shall guide her blind feet very slowly,
　He shall guide her as none other can,
He shall crown her brows and hail her holy,
　Mother of the mighty Soul of man.

CHORUS.

　The Soul shall arise.
Sweetness and sanity,
Slaying all vanity,
Shall to love's holiness,
Meekness and lowliness,
Shepherd humanity.
　The Soul shall arise.

SEMI-CHORUS I.

He shall rise a creature and a spirit,
  Guiding Earth, yet guided as they go.
If her low voice speaketh he shall hear it:
  Secrets of her bygone he shall know.

SEMI-CHORUS II.

He shall hear her voice and answer brightly;
  They shall wander on by ways untrod;
He shall rest upon her bosom nightly,
  Nestling there and looking up to God.

SEMI-CHORUS I.

Shall they dwell for evermore together,
  Earth and the fair creature of her breast?
Nay; but on some day of golden weather
  They shall find a pleasant spot and rest.

SEMI-CHORUS II.

Peace! ye souls who make sad acclamation,
  Wringing hands o'er broken towns of stone,
Soon the Soul shall build a habitation
  Fairer than the fairest overthrown.

EPODE.

Comfort, O true and free,
Soon shall there rise for ye
A City fairer far than all ye plan ;
Built on a rock of strength,
It shall arise at length,
Stately and fair and vast, the City meet for
man !

Towering to yonder skies
Shall the fair City rise
In the sweet dawning of a day more pure :
House, mart, and street, and square,
Yea, and a fane for prayer—
Fair, and yet built by hands, strong, for it
shall endure.

In the fair City then
Shall walk white-robëd men,
Wash'd in the river of peace that watereth it :
Woman with man shall meet
Freely in mart and street—
At the great council-board woman with man
shall sit.

Hunger and Thirst and Sin
Shall never pass therein.
Fed with pure dews of love, children shall
grow.
Fearless and fair and free,
Honour'd by all that see,
Virgins in golden zones shall walk as white
as snow.

There, on the fields around,
All men shall till the ground,
Corn shall wave yellow, and bright rivers
stream ;
Daily, at set of sun,
All, when their work is done,
Shall watch the heavens yearn down and the
strange starlight gleam.

In the fair City of men
All shall be silent then,
While, on a reverent lute, gentle and low,
Some holy Bard shall play
Ditties divine, and say
Whence those that hear have come, whither
in time they go.

No man of blood shall dare
Wear the white mantle there ;
No man of lust shall walk in street or mart ;
Yet shall the Magdalen
Walk with the citizen ;
Yet shall the sinner stand gracious and pure
of heart.

Now, while days come and go,
Doth the fair City grow,
Surely its stones are laid in sun and moon.
Wise men and pure prepare
Ever this City fair.
Comfort, O ye that weep; it shall arise full
soon.

When, stately, fair, and vast,
It doth uprise at last,
Who shall be King thereof, say, O ye wise ?—
When the last blood is spilt,
When the fair City is built,
Unto the throne thereof the Monarch shall
arise.

Flower of blessedness,
Wrought out of heart's distress,
Light of all dreams of saintly men who died,
He shall arise some morn
One Soul of many born,
Lord of the realms of peace, heir of the
Crucified.

O but he lingereth,
Drawing mysterious breath
In the dark womb where he was cast as seed.
Strange was the seed to sow,
Dark is the growth and slow;
Still hath he lain for long—now he grows
quick indeed.

Quicken, O Soul of Man!
Perfect the mystic plan—
Come from the womb where thou art darkly
wrought;
Wise men and pure prepare
Ever thy City fair—
Come when the City is built, sit on the Throne
of Thought.

Earth and all things that be

Wait, watch, and yearn for thee,

To thee all living things stretch hands be-
reaven ;—

Perfect and sweet and bright,

Lord of the City of Light,

Last of the fruits of Earth, first of the fruits of
Heaven.

THE END.

NOTES.

G G

NOTES.

Page 3.

Close round it snowing
Are the Seraphs white,
And next more dim
The Cherubim ;
And from rings to rings, &c.

un cerchio d'igne. . . .
E questo era d'un altro circuncinto,
E quel dal terzo, e'l terzo poi dal quarto, &c,
*   *   *   *   *   *   *
E quello avea la fiamma piu sincera,
   Cui men distava la favilla pura,
   Credo, perocchè più di lei s'invera.

Dante, Par., Cant. xxviii.

Page 8.

Have ye forgot the sin of Phrynichos ?

This sin was the celebration of the miseries of the Ionians, in a tragedy called the *Capture of Miletos.* When, however, two years after the Battle of Salamis, Phrynichos chronicled the defeat of Xerxes, he met with an enthusiastic reception, and his success encouraged Æschylos to write the *Persæ,*—in some respects the very finest of the extant Greek tragedies, for the very reasons which make it inferior in ghastly tremendousness to the Orestean Trilogy.

Page 23.

Enter STEIN.

Of Stein's character as a patriot and a statesman, it is unnecessary to say one word. How cruelly Prussia rewarded him
for his services is well known; but the day of his apotheosis is
at hand. We all know Arndt's songs, and his soul through
them. Jahn is less familiar to all but historical students; he
was, however, a great creature—a source of constant inspiration
to German patriots, and particularly the Gymnasiarchs. For
particulars concerning these men, and many others as great in
soul, who, rising in the moment of peril to save their country,
were first welcomed, and after victory treated as lunatics and
criminals, see Richter ("Geschichte des Deutschen Freiheit-
skrieges) and the volume called "Geschichte des Lützowschen
Frei-corps," published in 1826, at Berlin.

Page 28.

O spirits dreaming, &c.

Omnes enim per se divum natura necesse est, &c.
Luc., I. 45.

Page 40.

But yestermorn the old man Wieland stood
Enlarging his weak vision for an hour
Upon the demigod, who of Greece and Rome
Talked like a petulant schoolboy.

Menzel (Geschichte des Deutschens), while justly inveighing
against the literary heroes of Weimar, who were incapable of a
patriotic sentiment, alleges that Wieland was kept standing an
hour in Napoleon's presence, and when, unable from his old
age to continue on his feet, he asked permission to retire, Napoleon is said to have considered it an unwarrantable liberty.
This is manifestly unjust to Buonaparte, who reserved all his
brutality for queens and political opponents. Wieland himself,
in his letters, gives an excellent account of the interview: it is
more interesting and less familiar than the interview with Goethe.

"I had not been many minutes there before Napoleon came across the room towards us: the duchess then formally presented me to him; and he addressed me affably with some words of compliment, looking me steadily in the face. Few persons have appeared to me to see through a man so rapidly. He instantly perceived that, notwithstanding my celebrity, I was a plain unassuming old person, and, as he seemed desirous of making a good impression on me, he at once assumed the manner best adapted to attain his end. I never saw a man in appearance calmer, plainer, milder, or more unpretending. No trace was visible about him of the consciousness that he was a great monarch. He talked to me like an old acquaintance with his equal, and, which was very rare with him, chatted with me exclusively an entire hour and a half, to the great surprise of all who were present. At length, about midnight, I began to feel inconvenience from standing so long, and took the liberty of requesting his majesty's permission to withdraw. '*Allez donc,*' said he, in a very friendly tone; '*bon soir!*' The more remarkable traits of our interview were as follows:—The previous play having made Cæsar the subject of our conversation, Napoleon observed that he was one of the greatest characters in all history; and that indeed he would have have been without exception the greatest but for one blunder. I was about to inquire to what blunder he alluded, when he seemed to read the question in my eye, and continued, 'Cæsar knew the men who wanted to get rid of him, and he ought to have been rid of them first.' If Napoleon could have read all that passed in my mind, he would have perceived me saying, 'Such a blunder will never be laid to your charge.' From Cæsar our conversation turned to the Roman people; and he praised warmly their military and their political system; while the Greeks, on the contrary, seemed to stand low in his opinion. The eternal contest between their little republics was not formed, he said, to produce anything great; but the Romans were always intent on grand purposes, and thus created the mighty colossus which bestrode the world. I pleaded for the arts and literature of the Greeks; but he treated both with contempt, and said that they only served to make objects of dispute.

"He preferred Ossian to Homer. In poetry he professed to

value only the sublime, the energetic, and the pathetic writers, especially the tragic poets. Of Ariosto he spoke in some such terms as those which had been used by Cardinal Hippolito, of Este; not aware, however, I think, that in doing this he was giving me a box on the ear. For anything humorous he seemed to have no liking; and, notwithstanding the flattering friendliness of his apparent manner, he repeatedly gave me the idea of his being cast from bronze.

"At length, however, he had put me so much at my ease, that I asked him how it happened that the public worship, which he had in some degree reformed in France, had not been rendered more philosophic, and more on a par with the spirit of the times. 'My dear Wieland,' he replied, 'worship is not made for philosophers; they believe neither in me nor in my priesthood. As for those who do believe, you cannot give them or leave them wonders enough. If I had to make a religion for philosophers, it should be just the reverse.' In this tone the conversation went on for some time; and Buonaparte professed so much scepticism, as to question whether Jesus Christ had ever existed. This is very common every-day scepticism; so that in his free thinking I saw nothing to admire, but the openness with which he exposed it."

Page 57.

Enter LOUISA OF PRUSSIA.

I have here taken a slight liberty with history. The high-minded queen's famous interviews with Buonaparte took place at Tilsit, a year previous to the Congress at Erfurt in 1808, and two years after Buonaparte, standing at the tomb of Frederick Sanspareil, had publicly aspersed Louisa's fame.

Page 69.

Compound of Scapin and Olympian Jove.

So the Abbé de Pradt, in his savage character of Napoleon, against whom he felt all the bitterness of a slighted tool:—
"L'homme qui, unissant dan ses bizarreries tout ce qu'il y a de

plus élevé et de plus vil parmi les mortels, de plus majestueux dans l'éclat de la souveraineté, de plus peremptoire dans le commandment, avec ce qu'il y a d'ignoble et de plus lâche jusque dans ses plus grands attentats, joignant les guet-apens aux détrônements, présente *une espèce de Jupiter-Scapin* qui n'avait pas encore paru sur la scène du monde."

Page 73.

On Jena Prussia's feeble body died, &c.

Everbody has followed the miserable campaign of 1806. "Les Prussiens sont encore plus stupides que les Autrichiens," cried Buonaparte, amazed at the wretched pottering of the Duke of Brunswick, adding afterwards, on hearing that the enemy expected him from Erfurt when he was already at Nuremberg, "Ils se tromperont furieusement, ces perruques !"

Page 87.

Why, how now, hath Pope Pius lost his wits ? &c.

There can be no doubt that Napoleon's sharp dispute with, and subsequent savage treatment of, the aged Pope made the French supremacy trebly odious to the Catholic population. Pius VII. showed a spirit worthy of a grander cause. Of course, he was contending against the avalanche; but even such opposition hastened its rush into the gulf that awaited it.

Page 117.

O Spirit of Man !
A foolish Titan !

This picture of the Spirit of Man must not be read with any reference to the shallow and barbarous myth of Prometheus, which represents the demigod-like spirit of Humanity contending against a Deity of unutterable malevolence.

Page 128.

Light of the Lotus and all mortal eyes,
Whose orbit nations like to heliotropes
Shall follow with lesser circle and sweet sound!

Proclus, in his "Discourse on Magic," preserved in the Latin translation of Ficinus, has the following exquisitely-beautiful passage :—

" In the same manner as lovers gradually advance from that beauty which is apparent in sensible forms to that which is divine, so the ancient priests, when they considered that there is a certain alliance and sympathy in natural things to each other, and of things manifest to occult powers, and discovered that all things subsist in all, fabricated a sacred science from this mutual sympathy and similarity. Thus they recognised things supreme in such as are subordinate, and the subordinate in the supreme; in the celestial regions, terrene properties subsisting in a casual and celestial manner, and in earth celestial properties, but according to a terrene condition. For how shall we account for those plants called heliotropes— that is, attendants on the sun, moving in correspondence with the revolution of its orb; or for selenitropes, attendants on the moon, turning in exact conformity to her motion ? It is because all things pray and hymn the leaders of their respective orders ; but some intellectually, and others rationally; some in a natural and others after a sensible manner. Hence the sun-flower, as far as it is able, moves in a circular dance towards the sun, so that if any one could hear the pulsation made by its circuit in the air, he would perceive something composed by a sound of this kind, in honour of its being such as a plant is capable of framing. Hence, too, we may behold the sun and moon in the earth, although according to a terrene quality ; but in the celestial regions, all plants, and stones, and animals possessing an intellectual life according to a celestial nature. Now the ancients, having contemplated this mutual sympathy of things, applied for occult purposes both celestial and terrene natures, by means of which, through a certain similitude, they deduce divine virtues into this inferior abode. For, indeed, similitude itself is a sufficient cause of binding things together in union and content.

Thus, if a piece of paper is heated, and afterwards placed near a lamp, though it does not touch the fire, the paper will be suddenly inflamed, and the flame will descend from the superior to the inferior parts. This heated paper we may compare to a certain relation of inferiors to superiors, and its approximation to the lamp, to the opportune use of things according to time, place, and matter. But the procession of fire into the paper aptly represents the movement of divine light, to that nature which is capable of its reception. Lastly, the inflammation of the paper may be compared to the deification of mortals, and to the illumination of material natures, which are afterwards carried upwards like the enkindled paper, from a certain participation of divine seed.

"Again, the lotus, before the rising of the sun, folds its leaves into itself, but gradually expands them on its rising, unfolding them in proportion to the sun's ascent to the zenith; but as gradually contracting them, as that luminary descends to the west. Hence this plant, by the expansion and contraction of its leaves, appears no less to honour the sun, than men by the gestures of their eyelids and the motion of their lips."

Page 161.

Strange are the bitter things
God wreaks on cruel Kings;
Sad is the cup drunk up
By Kings accurst, &c.

A portion of this chorus is versified from Dio Chrysostom's "Treatise on Arbitrary Government." "Napoleon Fallen," when published in its first rough shape, opened with a chorus of German citizens, somewhat too colloquial in manner to suit the mystic quality of the scenes which followed, and therefore now suppressed. Most of the other choruses are new, and those retained are entirely altered and remodelled.

Page 239.

With Sin and Death our mothers' milk was sour,
The womb wherein we grew from hour to hour
Gather'd pollution dark from the polluted frame.

This measure is used once or twice by Shelley.

Page 250.

Yet he, too, fell. Early or late, all fall.
No fruit can hang for ever on the tree, &c.

An eminent friend "admits" that I do full justice to Napoleon on the intellectual side, but "is inclined to dispute" his title to a "moral consciousness," and to question whether he is "capable" of any such "remorse" as I portray. This is another illustration of how many meanings men may find in a poem according to their different lights. So far from attempting to represent the speaker as feeling mere "remorse," I was portraying, in his final soliloquy, a mood of unutterable perversity —a line of thought only possible to a fourth-rate intellect in which the moral consciousness was virtually inert and dead. From my own point of view, so utter was the wicked hopelessness of this soliloquy, that I should certainly have altered it, had my conscience not told me that every word was dramatically true.

Page 288.

Worshipping Thammuz and all gods obscene.

See the superb passage in "Paradise Lost," Book I., line 446.

> Thammuz came next behind,
> Whose annual wound in Lebanon allured
> The Syrian damsels to lament his fate
> In amorous ditties all a summer's day,
> While smooth Adonis, &c.

Page 300.

How long shall I to this sick world, this mass
Of social sores, this framework of disease,
This most infected many-member'd earth,
Play the hard surgeon ?

To the reader who may question the moral truth of my representation of Count Bismarck, I recommend a careful study of his speeches now collected and published at Berlin. Once

more, however, let me warn the student that the great statesman is approached from the divine side, during the highest
mood of which, from the dramatic point of view, he is capable.
That mood, unhappily, is a low enough one.

Page 412.

O to waken Lützow's spirit !

Richter writes thus of the corps organized by Lützow during
the German War of Liberation :—

" With the utmost truth we may say that in Lützow's volunteer corps lived the *idea* of the war. The universal enthusiasm
elevated itself here to a noble self-consciousness. In the other
corps this and that individual might attain the same high
intellectual position that was the property here of the whole
body; the soldier entered with full sympathy into the dignity
of his personal mission, and fought from clear conviction, not
from blind impulse. Those loose and roving adventurers that
to a certain extent will always mix themselves up with a volunteer corps, were kept in check here by the number of high and
noble spirits with whom they found themselves in daily communion. Here, whatsoever glowed with holy revenge against
the recklessness of a foreign tyranny ; whatsoever, in other parts
of Europe, had manifested itself to be animated by a spirit of
unyielding animosity to Napoleon's despotism ; whosoever had
learned, under long-conquering banners, to curse the conquests,
and to despise the conqueror, were gathered together in one
knot of many-coloured but one-hearted fellowship. These men
were all penetrated by the conviction that, in the nature of
things, no power merely military, no cunning of the most refined
despotism, can in the long-run triumph over native freedom of
thought and tried force of will. They looked upon themselves
as chosen instruments in the hand of the divine Nemesis,
and bound themselves by a solemn oath to do or to die. They
were, in fact, virtually free when Germany yet lay in chains ;
and for them the name of ' Free Corps ' (*Frei Schaar*) had a
deeper signifiance than that of free (volunteer) soldiers. Here
the deed of the individual was heralded by the thought that
measured inwardly, and rejoiced in the perception of its own
capability. Here the triumphant spirit of patriotism broke

forth in song, in poetry, which is the outspread wing of enthusiasm. The prince, the philosopher, the bard served under
Lützow, as volunteers, in the humblest capacity. The Prince
of Karolath, Steffens, Jahn, Theodore Körner, and many other
consecrated names belonged to this noble body; nay, even
females, under well-concealed disguises, came boldly forward to
share with this brave band all the toils and hardships of the
sterner sex. The enemies of France, from Spain and the Tyrol,
joined themselves to this corps, trusting to find here, at length,
that revenge of their righteous cause which a mysterious Provi-
dence had hitherto delayed. Riedl and Ennemoser commanded
a body of Tyrolese sharpshooters, and among them was the son
of Andrew Hofer. From the French armies, Dutchmen and
Saxons, Westphalians and Altmarkers, rejoiced to belong to the
" Black Corps " (*Die Schwarze Schaar*), as these troops, from
their uniform, were familiarly named. In the whole body there
was scarcely an individual who, on the plea of personal history
or qualities, might not claim peculiar distinction. And so free
were they from all prejudices of class, so jealous in a high self-
respect, that no person was admitted into their number who
refused to serve as a common Jäger. Their fame has remained
among the printed records of the war; a separate volume eter-
nizes the exploits of a small body of not more than 3,400
warriors '"

Page 436.

Deign, King of Heaven,
To hear our Chorus sing the Final Song
Or Epode . . . .
Thou, whose calm eyes measure all to come,
Will smile to see how oft this poet tries
To peer into the future and to sound
The advent of Thy Kingdom.

A crude early version of this " final song " was printed as a
sequel to "Napoleon Fallen;" but " Christ " appeared there
instead of "the Soul " in the final passages. I found that the
words, "Christ shall arise and reign," were too literally inter-
preted as a statement that Jesus Christ was to come in the flesh

and rule the world ; and as I meant nothing of the sort, but only that the spiritual part of Christ should be present during the reign of the perfect Spirit of Humanity, I have taken good care this time to avoid misconstruction. There is another misconstruction which I fear—that of a mere pantheistic reading of my "Cantata." Surely, however, no reader who has followed my representation of divine agencies throughout the Drama will do me the injustice of supposing that I consider man by any means the highest of beings. There are times, indeed, when I doubt if he is the highest of animals. We find on examination that those gentlemen who insist most on the superiority of man in the scale of nature, insist quite as much on the adjective "white," and coming a little nearer home, on the adjective "British." The formula that man is highest of beings, when uttered here in Britain, then generally resolves itself into this other formula—" the British white man is the highest of beings." Conceive a chain of development culminating in Mr. Carlyle at one point, at another in Mr. Disraeli, and at another in ex-Governor Eyre.

ON MYSTIC REALISM:

A NOTE FOR THE ADEPT.

ON MYSTIC REALISM.

"Poesie ist das absolut Reelle. Dies ist der Kern meiner Philosophie.
Je poetischer, je wahrer."—NOVALIS (Schriften, vol. iii. p. 171).

IN the present work, and in the works which have pre-
ceded it from the same pen, an attempt is made to com-
bine two qualities which the modern mind is accustomed to
regard apart—reality and mystery, earthliness and spiri-
tuality ; and this combination, whether a merit or a fault,
is a consequence of natural temperament, and perfectly
incurable. The writer dropped into a world a few years
ago like a being fallen from another planet. His first
impression was one of surprise and awe ;—he stood and
wondered—and here, on the same spot, he stands and
wonders still. What is nearest to him seems so sublime,
unaccountable, and inexhaustible, and occasionally, indeed,
so droll and odd, that he has never ceased to regard it
with all the eyes of his soul from that day to this.
Others may go to the mountain-tops and interrogate the
spheres. Wiser men may peruse the Past, and see there,
afar away, the dreamy poetry for which the spirit eternally
yearns. More acquiescent men may look heavenward,
slowly and strangely losing the habit of earthly perception
altogether. With all these, with all who love beauty near
or afar away, in any shape or form, abides the twofold
blessing of reverence and love. But the Mystic is
occupied hopelessly with what immediately surrounds
him. Minuter examination leads only to extremer joy

and wonder. To him this ever-present reality is the only mystery, and in its mystery lies its sublime fascination and beauty. Only what is most real and visible and certain is marvellous, and only that which is marvellous has the least fascination. What he sees may be seen by every soul under the sun, for it is the soul's own reflection in the river of life glassed to a mirror by its own speed.

This close examination of human nature from the mystic side is not so common that men will tolerate it calmly. "What is the dullard looking at?" cries the passer-by; "what are these wretched beings who surround him?—costermongers, thieves, magdalen-women, village schoolmasters, nomads,—what is the sentimentalist trying to find among these? He floods them with the light of his own vacant mind, and calls that light their *souls!*" So the speaker passes on—to the heights of the Alps, perhaps, where he finds communion; God communicating with all men somewhere. A more elaborate person pauses next before the Mystic. "The man is in error," is his criticism; "he would fain prove himself an artist, but art deals only with things beautiful,—with remote forms of nature, with the dreamy past, with antique turns of thought, with what is essentially exquisite in itself—and it has, moreover, a terminology quite at variance with ordinary speech. Man yearns to the unknown and illimitable, and demands *distance* in the subjects of his art." And this other goes his way, grateful to God for Greece and Italy, and for Lessing and Winkelman. Meantime the poor criticised barbarian has not budged. He looks on into the eyes nearest to him, and ah! what distance does he not find there? Approaching each creature as ever from the mystic side, he becomes, in spite of himself, an optimist. The moment he seizes or examination is the divine moment, when the creature under examination—be it Buonaparte or a street-walker, Bismarck or "Barbara Gray"—is at its highest and best, whether that "best" be intellectual beatification or the simple vicarious instinct which merges in the identity of another. He sees the nature spiritualised, in the dim strange light of whatever soul the creature possesses. This light is often very dim indeed, very doubtful—so doubtful that its very existence is denied by non-mystic men whose musings assume the purely spiritual and unimaginative form. But be the teaching true or false, be the light born in the subject examined or in the human sentiment that broods over it, this mystic approach to the creature at his highest point of spiritualisation, this mode of approach which seems unnatural to many because it involves the most minute enumeration of details and the most careful display of the very facts of life which artists try most to conceal, is the only procedure possible to the present writer. The personal key-note to all his work— poor enough, God knows, is all that work from his own point of view—is to be found in the " Book of Orm," and most of all in the poem entitled " The Man Accurst."

Imagination is not, as some seem to imply, the power of conjuring up the remote and unknowable, but the gift of realising correctly in correct images the truths of things as they are and ever have been. He who can see no poetry in his own time is a very unimaginative person. The truly imaginative being is he who carries his own artistic distance with him, and sees the mighty myths of life vivid yet afar off, glorified by the truth which is Eternal. How many people can walk out on a starry night, or sit by the side of the sea, unmoved ? But let a comet appear, or a star shoot, and they exclaim, " How beautiful !" Let a whale rise up in the water and roar, and they think, " How wonderful are the works of God !" These are the people, and their name is legion, who lack as yet the consecrating gleam of the imagination. As for the Mystic, he needs neither a comet nor a whale to fill his soul with a sense of the wonderful ; he needs still less the dark vistas of tradition or the archaic scenery of

obscure periods. He comes into the world, as has been
said, like a man dropped from the moon, and he walks all
his life as among wonderful beings in a strange clime.
How far has he not wandered, how far has he not yet to
wander ?—and every face he sees is turned in the same
direction. Faces ! how they haunt them with their weird
beauty and divine significance ! Go where he may, his
path swarms with poetic forms. All is glorified and
awful. What is nearest seems of all the most sublime
and unaccountable. It is with difficulty that he can bear
any book or contemplate any painted picture, seeing
what books and pictures present themselves in the
strangely-coloured lives of his fellow-beings. He turns
to history—not in disdain of what exists, but in search of
explanation and corroboration, and in order to discover
what part of the strange show there is perishable, what part
is durable and eternal. Having as he thinks discovered
that, he may become a poet, and put on record his own
idea or autobiography, written in reference to his own
time, but to be used in all after-times as explanatory and
corroborative. Homer, the Greek tragedians, Aristo-
phanes, Plato, David and the prophets, the authors of
the Sagas and Lieds, Dante, Boccaccio, Rabelais, William Langdale, Chaucer, the ballad-singers of Scotland
and England, Ben Jonson, Shakspere, La Fontaine, Burns,
Wordsworth, Jean Paul, Balsac, Shelley, Tennyson, Whit-
man,—do we find any of these men, poets all of them,
turning away from his own time because it is too unin-
teresting ? or, on the contrary, do we find them penetrat-
ing to the very soul of it, stirring to every breath of it,
uttering every dream and aspiration of it ? Does Dante
try to write like Virgil, though he sits at Virgil's feet ?
Does Chaucer ape Boccaccio, though he wears the Deca-
meron next his heart ? Does Ben Jonson reproduce Plautus
or La Fontaine Rabelais ? Does Burns, having drunk
Scotch ballads into his soul, sing as the ballad-writers
sang ? Do we find Wordsworth seeking for subjects far

back in the dark ages ? Has Shelley so little imagination
as to reproduce Greek tragedy as it was, or so much
imagination as to make of his " Prometheus " a veritable
modern poem [in spite of the falsehood and shallowness
of the myth it preserves] with a distinctly modern purpose
and scope ?

"But," some one again interposes, "this is such an
unpoetic age, and the surroundings of modern life are so
vulgar." The writer understands this objection, and
there is reason in it. The majority of people find their
ordinary associations vulgar and unpoetic, and like to be
lured away from them and interested. So much the
worse, alas ! for the majority. But let it be at once
admitted that the poet fails altogether if he fails to lure
readers and interest them as they desire. He is no mere
moral teacher, but a singer of the beautiful, and his real
business in this world is not to join in a chorus raised by
any group of people, but to explain some point of beauty
which has rested altogether hidden until his advent. If
people are unimaginative, he comes to teach them imagination : if people dislike modern subjects, he comes to
make them like modern subjects. If ordinary people
perceived the sublime mysteries of contemporary life, if
ordinary people understood the faces and souls they
behold daily, it would be a waste of time to sing to them.
If men in general understood the higher historical issues
and perceived the higher poetry of the siege of Paris,
what good would it be to celebrate it in song? And this
poem, for example, fails altogether—is veritably less than
nothing—is a futility, a mere wind-bag—if it does not
make the reader feel the events it describes as he never,
by any possibility, felt them before.

In the " Drama of Kings," as in " London Poems,"
" Inverburn," and " Meg Blane," in the presentment of
the characters of Buonaparte, Louis Napoleon, and Prince
Bismarck,—as in the characters of " Nell," " Liz," " Meg
Blane," and the rest,—one point of view is adopted ; not

the point of view of the satirist, nor that of the politician, nor that of the historian ; but that of the realistic Mystic, who, seeking to penetrate deepest of all into the soul, and to represent the soul's best and finest mood, seizes that moment when the spiritual or emotional nature is most quickened by sorrow or by self-sacrifice, by victory or by defeat.   In good honest truth, the writer has had far greater difficulty in detecting the spiritual point in these great leaders than in the poor worms at their feet.   The utterly personal moods of arbitrary power, the impossibility of self-abnegation for the sake of any other living creature, the frightful indifference to all ties, the diabolic supremacy of the intellect, make the first Emperor a figure more despairing to the Mystic than the coster girl dying in childbed in a garret, or the defiant woman declaiming over the corpse of her deformed seducer.   It is this sense of the superlatively diabolic that has made the author, in the Epilogue, attribute the performance of the three lead-ing characters to Lucifer himself ;—only let it be under-stood not to the irreclaimable and Mephistophelian type of utter evil, but to the Mystic's Devil, a spirit difficult to fathom individually, but clearly in the divine service working for good.   Perhaps, by the way, the supernatural machinery of Prelude and Epilude is a defect, like all allegory ; and if the consensus of wise criticism inclines to its condemnation as a defect, it will be obliterated, no author having a right to resist the wish of his readers where their dislike corresponds with a doubt of his own.   But if it serves to keep before the reader the fact that the whole action of the drama is seen from the spiritual or divine auditorium, he will not regret its intro-duction ; and in using it without perfect faith, he may plead the example of the greatest poetic sceptic of modern times.   No one did fuller justice to mystic truths than the great positivist who wrote the first and second "Fausts."

Concerning the mere form of the poem and its resemblances to the Greek, little need be said. It is the first serious attempt ever made to treat great contemporary events in a dramatic form and very realistically, yet with something of the massive grandeur of style characteristic of the great dramatists of Greece. In minor points of detail the author is sanguine that it is not at all Greek, nor in any sense of the word archaic. The interest is epic rather than tragic ; but what the leading character is to a tragedy France is to the "Drama of Kings,"—a wonderful genius guilty of many sins, terribly overtaken by misfortune, and attaining in the end perhaps to purification. It is unnecessary to add any more by way of explanation, save to say that most of the metrical combinations used in the choruses are quite new to English poetry, and that where a measure is employed which has been used successfully by any previous poet, the fact is chronicled in the notes.

One word in conclusion. For this new experiment in poetic realism, the writer asks no favour but one—a quiet hearing. He has a faint hope that if readers will do him the honour to peruse the work as a whole, and then patiently contemplate the impression left in their own minds, the first feeling of repulsion at an innovation may give place in the end to a pleasanter feeling. Perhaps, however, this is too much to ask from any member of so busy a generation, and he should be grateful to any one who will condescend to read the "Drama" in fragments.

> Die Masse könnt ihr nur durch Masse zwingen ;
> Ein Jeder sucht sich endlich selbst was aus.
> Wer vieles bringt, wird manchem etwas bringen,
> Und Jeder geht zufrieden aus dem Haus. . . .
> Was hilft's, wenn ihr ein Ganzes dargebracht!
> Das Publicum wird es euch doch zerpflücken.

ROBERT BUCHANAN.

VIRTUE AND CO., PRINTERS, CITY ROAD, LONDON.

WORKS BY ROBERT BUCHANAN.

I. UNDERTONES. By ROBERT BUCHANAN. Price
6s.

II. INVERBURN. By ROBERT BUCHANAN. Price 6s.

III. LONDON POEMS. By .ROBERT BUCHANAN.
Price 6s.

IV. THE BOOK OF ORM. By ROBERT BUCHANAN.
Price 6s.

LONDON: STRAHAN & CO., 56, LUDGATE HILL.

THE THOROUGH BUSINESS MAN. Memoirs of Walter Powell, Merchant, of Melbourne and London. By BENJAMIN GREGORY. Crown 8vo., 6s.

WHEN I WAS YOUNG. A Book for Boys. By CHARLES CAMDEN, Author of "The Boys of Axleford." With Illustrations. Crown 8vo., cloth gilt extra.

MRS. TAPPY'S CHICKS: Links between Nature and Human Nature. By Mrs GEORGE CUPPLES. With Illustrations. Crown 8vo., cloth gilt extra.

PEEPS AT FOREIGN COUNTRIES. By the Editor and Contributors to "Good Words," &c. With Illustrations. Crown 8vo., cloth gilt extra.

THE OLD MAID'S STORY. By E. MARLITT. Translated by H. J. G. Crown 8vo.

FAMILY PRAYERS. By C. J. VAUGHAN, D.D., Master of the Temple. Crown 8vo., 3s. 6d.

LORD BANTAM. The New Story. By the Author of "Ginx's Baby."

PASSAGES FROM THE FRENCH AND ITALIAN NOTE-BOOKS OF NATHANIEL HAWTHORNE. 2 vols., post 8vo.

THE PRINCESS AND THE GOBLIN. By GEORGE MACDONALD. With 30 Illustrations by ARTHUR HUGHES. Crown 8vo., cloth gilt extra.

PEASANT LIFE IN THE NORTH. Second Series. Post 8vo.

LILLIPUT REVELS. By the Author of
"Lilliput Levée." With Illustrations by ARTHUR HUGHES.
Square 8vo., cloth gilt extra.

LINNET'S TRIAL. By M. B. SMEDLEY,
Author of "Twice Lost," &c. Crown 8vo., cloth gilt extra. 5s.

HYMNS FOR THE YOUNG. With Music
by JOHN HULLAH.

HOW IT ALL HAPPENED, and other Stories.
By Mrs. PARR, Author of "Dorothy Fox." 2 vols, post 8vo.

THOUGHTS ON THE TEMPTATION OF
OUR LORD. By NORMAN MACLEOD, D.D.

THE CHILDREN'S JOURNEY, &c. By the
Author of "Voyage en Zigzag." Beautifully Illustrated.
Square 8vo.

BLIGHT AND BLOOM. By EDWARD GAR-
RETT, Author of "Occupations of a Retired Life." 2 vols.,
post 8vo.

COLLOQUIA CRUCIS. By DORA GREENWELL.
Crown 8vo.

THE CHARACTER OF ST. PAUL. By J. S.
HOWSON, D.D., Dean of Chester. Crown 8vo.

THE CHRISTIAN DOCTRINE OF PRAYER
FOR THE DEPARTED. With copious Notes and Ap-
pendices. By the Rev. FREDERICK GEORGE LEE, D.C.L.,
F.S.A., Vicar of All Saints, Lambeth.

SUNDAYS ON THE CONTINENT. By
Thomas Guthrie, D.D. Crown 8vo.

·

THE WINDOW; or, The Songs of the Wrens.
By Alfred Tennyson, D.C.L., Poet-Laureate. With
Music by Arthur Sullivan. 4to, cloth gilt extra, 21s.

DOROTHY FOX. By Mrs. Parr. Popular
Edition. Crown 8vo., 6s.

FRIENDS AND ACQUAINTANCES. By
the Author of "Episodes in an Obscure Life." 3 vols.,
post 8vo.

HEROES OF HEBREW HISTORY. By
Samuel Wilberforce, D.D. Bishop of Winchester.
Popular Edition. Crown 8vo., 5s.

GINX'S BABY: His Birth and other Mis-
fortunes. People's Edition. Crown 8vo., 2s.

SERMONS FOR MY CURATES. By the
Rev. T. T. Lynch. Edited by the Rev. Samuel Cox.
Crown 8vo., 9s.

EPISODES IN AN OBSCURE LIFE: A
Curate's Experiences in the Tower Hamlets. Popular Edition.
Crown 8vo., 6s.

FAUST. A Tragedy by Johann Wolfgang
von Goethe. Translated in the Original Metres by Bayard
Taylor. 2 vols. post 8vo., 28s.

THE COOLIE: His Rights and Wrongs.
Notes of a Journey to British Guiana, with a Review of the
System and of the Recent Commission of Inquiry. By the
Author of "Ginx's Baby." Post 8vo., 16s.

SHIRLEY HALL ASYLUM. By WILLIAM
GILBERT. New Edition. Crown 8vo., 10s. 6d.

FERNYHURST COURT. An Every-day
Story. By the Author of "Stone Edge." Crown 8vo., 6s.

BENONI BLAKE, M.D. By the Author of
"Peasant Life in the North." 2 vols., crown 8vo., 21s.

SHOEMAKERS' VILLAGE. By HENRY
HOLBEACH. 2 vols., post 8vo., 16s.

PEEPS AT THE FAR EAST. A Familiar
Account of a Visit to India. By NORMAN MACLEOD, D.D.
With numerous Illustrations. Small 4to., cloth extra, 21s.

THE RIVULET. A contribution to Sacred
Song. By the late T. T. LYNCH. New Edition. Small
8vo., 3s. 6d.

THE REIGN OF LAW. By the DUKE OF
ARGYLL. People's Edition. Crown 8vo., limp cloth, 2s. 6d.

MEMORIALS OF AGNES ELIZABETH
JONES. By her Sister. New Edition. With Portrait.
Crown 8vo., 6s.

ESSAYS, THEOLOGICAL AND LITERARY.
By R. H. HUTTON. 2 vols., post 8vo., 24s.

THE ECCLESIASTICAL POLITY of the NEW
TESTAMENT. A Study for the present Crisis in the Church of England. By the Rev. G. A. JACOB, D.D., late Head Master of Christ's Hospital. Post 8vo., 16s.

THE COMPANIONS OF ST. PAUL. By J.
S. HOWSON, D.D., Dean of Chester. Crown 8vo., 5s.

WALKS IN ROME. By AUGUSTUS J. C.
HARE. 2 vols., crown 8vo., 21s.

REASONS FOR RETURNING TO THE
CHURCH OF ENGLAND. By the Rev. J. M. CAPES. Second Edition. Crown 8vo., 5s.

THE NEW TESTAMENT. Authorised Ver-
sion revised by HENRY ALFORD, late Dean of Canterbury. Long Primer Edition, crown 8vo., 6s. Brevier Edition, fcap., 8vo., 3s. 6d. ; Nonpariel Edition, small 8vo., 1s. 6d.

THE SONGSTRESSES OF SCOTLAND. By
SARAH TYTLER and J. L. WATSON. 2 vols., post 8vo., 16s.

MEMORIALS OF CHARLES PARRY, Com-
mander, Royal Navy. By his Brother, the Right Rev. ED-WARD PARRY, D.D., Bishop Suffragan of Dover. Small 8vo., 5s.